SUMMER WISH

JILL SANDERS

GRAYTON
PRESS

Published by Grayton Press

ISBN-13: 978-1-945100-31-4

Paperback: 978-1-945100-38-3

SUMMARY

Dr. Lea Val has no time for cocky cops who continuously put themselves in harm's way. She's been trying to open her own practice and still find time to help her friends out at the swanky adult summer camp. Everything was going great until tall, tan, and sexy turned her life upside down.

Brett Jewel is a man of his word. After getting injured in the line of duty, he promised his friends he'd slow down and take over a new position as head of security at River Camps. After all, he's not going to let a silly gunshot slow him down. No, the only thing making him pause is the sexy doctor who is constantly yelling at him to get off his feet.

PROLOGUE

Ten-year-old Lea wasn't going to let some booger-picking Miami Dolphin's–loving bully win. Not this time.

Timmy Crawford had been calling her names since the moment she'd walked into her new school over a year ago.

So what if she was the only student of Southeast Asian descent in the entire two-hundred-student school district. Actually, she and her older sister were the only non-Caucasian students in the entire school system. Which of course put targets on them for bullies to home in on.

It didn't matter that she was a fifth-generation United States citizens. She was probably more American than Timmy himself, since he'd once boasted that his grandmother had lived in Germany when she'd been a child.

Lea's great-great-great-grandparents had come to the States on a ship from Thailand. Not from China, like Timmy and the other bullies in her class teased her about. Not that it would have mattered to them, since they assumed anyone who looked like her was a "Chinaman."

Some of the kids taunted that she should wash their clothes or do their nails or that she belonged in a dry cleaner rather than in school. They made fun of the way she talked, even though she spoke perfect English, better than most of them did. She pronounced her words clearly, whereas most of the kids in her class spoke with a southern drawl and dropped the last syllables in certain words. Lea was far too refined for that. After all, she'd been raised in New York, up until her family had decided to move to the Florida Panhandle.

Timmy wore the same faded Miami Dolphin's shirt almost every day, which had instantly made Lea hate the sports team. Not that she was really into sports in the first place. Nonetheless, she hated them now. She chose to make a point to cheer for any team that the Dolphins were playing against. If the other team won, she would mention it several times in the proximity of Timmy and his friends.

She didn't have many friends herself. Only a few kids braved the masses to speak to her or even just be nice to her.

Elle Saunders, a girl one class below Lea's, had arrived at the school at roughly the same time as she had. Then there was Aiden Stark, Lea's first crush. The boy was dreamy. Lea's older sister, Raya, who was in junior high, had used that slang to describe Matt Cooper, a boy in her class.

Matt Cooper was a sweaty, zit-faced boy that wore jeans that were too tight and always had large headphones on as he played basketball with his friends. His shoes were always untied, causing him to trip constantly. Aiden Stark was nothing like Matt Cooper.

Aiden had soft dark hair. Well, it looked soft, at any rate. Lea had never had the courage to reach out and touch it, but she knew that it would be soft, like her own hair. It had a slight curl to it, whereas hers was flat and boring, like the hair of everyone else in her family. She seriously doubted that anyone in her bloodline dating back to the dawn of time had ever had even a slight curl to their hair.

Aiden also had blue eyes, something else she dreamed of having. He was the kindest boy she'd ever met and one of the best-looking eleven-year-olds she'd ever seen.

The only problem with Aiden was his best friend, Brett Jewel.

Brett was completely the opposite of Aiden in the looks department, with his straight blond hair, which he wore longer in a classic surfer style. Like he ever surfed. There weren't big enough waves on the Gulf of Mexico to surf. Not like the ones she had seen in California the last time her family had vacationed out west. Brett was also always wearing baggy board shorts. He got in trouble a lot and teased her constantly.

But to be clear, the way Brett teased her was nothing like the way Timmy and his friends did. Brett had never thrown a racial slur at her or teased her about how she looked. Instead, he made light of how smart she was. He'd say things such as "Lea's so smart, she's going to be the first woman on Mars. Which is a good thing, because that's where all girls belong."

One of his other constant teases was "Wow! I can see your face. What? No books to hide behind?" That one always made her roll her eyes. He'd say it anytime he saw her without her nose buried in a book, which wasn't often, mainly only when she was thinking deeply or watching Aiden play basketball.

She was ten and by far the smartest person in the entire school system in the small town of Pelican Point. That wasn't saying much. Not really. That included her older sister, who was more determined to spend her time flirting with boys and singing along to and watching music videos.

Still, since her parents had moved their family there from New York a little over a year ago, she was stuck attending the small backwoods school.

Thankfully, her mother had agreed to let Lea take extra classes online, which kept her up to date in all her studies. At the rate she was going, she would graduate high school by the age of thirteen, which meant she could start taking her core college classes shortly after.

She knew exactly what she wanted to go to school for. Ever since she had gotten her tonsils out at the age of five, she'd dreamed of being a doctor.

Doctor Lea Val.

It had a nice ring to it. While most girls of ten had diaries or notebooks full of sketches, Lea had sketches of the human anatomy. Well, what she understood of it so far.

Her parents wouldn't let her check out any of the books that had real information in them. Not until she was sixteen. Or so they'd said. Still, she'd gotten information online, so she at least knew most of the basics.

Which was why Timmy was currently teasing her. He'd yanked her notebook from her hands after school. She'd been waiting for her parents to pick her up in the usual spot, and now Timmy was making fun of her attempt to sketch Leonardo da Vinci's Vitruvian Man.

"Lea's drawing porn," Timmy teased. "You sicko." He held up the page to any student nearby. Then he turned it around and looked at it before bursting into laughter. "You think boys look like this?" He laughed again.

"Lea doesn't know what boys look like," one of his friends teased.

"Haven't you ever seen a naked boy before?" someone else teased.

No. She hadn't. She had a sister, and she was ten, for Christ's sake. Where had they supposed she would see a naked boy?

"Give it back." She'd jumped up to her feet and stretched as far as she could to reach for her notebook. There were far more embarrassing things in there that she did not want Timmy or anyone else to see.

Timmy held it far above his head, making her jump to try and reach it while his friends continued to tease her. She was easily the shortest person in her grade. Not that that mattered to her.

Her face was heated, and she was growing breathless and desperate at this point. All the commotion had caused the game to stop and now everyone on the outside courts was looking in their direction.

If Lea didn't do something drastic, Aiden would come over and possibly even see some of the things in her notebook that she wanted to keep secret. Especially from him.

In a last-ditch effort, she swung her foot out and caught Timmy directly on his knee, causing him to fall towards her.

She cried out, since the kid was almost a foot taller than her and at least thirty pounds heavier.

She braced for the impact. Just as Timmy was about to take her down, she was quickly pulled out of harm's way. She blinked and focused and looked up into Brett's very angry face.

"Leave her alone," Brett said, his blue eyes focused on a point behind her.

Lea turned around and noticed that Timmy had not fallen, as she'd expected. Instead, he was being held back by Aiden, who had yanked Timmy away from her.

"Give it back," Aiden added, trying to reach for her notepad.

"Why?" Timmy laughed "You got a thing for the Chi—" He didn't get any further, since Brett moved forward and quickly plowed his fist into Timmy's gut.

"Say it again," Brett said in a low tone. "I dare you."

Timmy was hunched over, gasping, and holding his stomach. Her notepad fell onto the pavement, opened to a page that she'd feared Aiden would see.

Closing her eyes, she wished herself to another place. *Please, let me be in my bed, fast asleep. Let this be a nightmare,* she said over and over in her head.

"Here," Brett said.

She opened her eyes. He stood in front of her, holding out her notebook towards her. He'd closed it, and the shiny yellow sunshine cover was now facing her.

She took it and gripped it to her chest, avoiding looking towards Aiden, who was standing a few feet away, looking down at the ground where her notepad had been moments ago.

"Are you okay?" Brett asked in a concerned tone.

Instead of answering, she turned around and bolted. She ran as fast as she could towards her house. She wasn't supposed to walk home after school. It was more than two miles and took her past a major road, and her parents feared for her safety, but none of that mattered at this point.

The boy she'd had her first crush on had seen the stupid heart she'd drawn with their initials in the middle.

She stopped and wiped the tears from her eyes, then she yanked the page out of her notebook and tore it into tiny pieces. She scattered them in the tall grass that lined the road near the school.

Never again, she vowed on the side of the road. From now on, she was going to keep her emotions and dreams to herself. She would never again allow anyone the chance to see any sign of weakness.

CHAPTER 1

*D*r. Lea Val knelt on the gurney and counted out the chest compressions while they rushed down the hallway of the ER. The middle-aged man was easily two hundred pounds overweight. The fact that he was shirtless, shoeless, and wearing board shorts didn't affect her as much as it would most doctors.

This was the norm when you worked near a popular tourist spot along what had been called one of the best beaches on the Gulf of Mexico.

She'd ridden in the ambulance with the man all the way from her side job as a physician at River Camps, the swanky adult summer resort that she'd started working at almost three years ago.

She'd gotten the man's heart to start back up before the ambulance had arrived, but he was in bad shape. Halfway to the hospital, his vitals had taken a dive and she'd had to start CPR once more.

When the gurney finally stopped, her hands were replaced by the ER doctors, and she was helped off the gurney as she relayed vital information to the waiting nurses, people she worked side by side with at the other job she'd had over the past few years.

Her parents had been slightly shocked when she'd returned home to do her residency at Santa Rosa Beach hospital, the large hospital closest to her hometown. They had always believed that she'd want to head back up north, towards New York, after she graduated with her medical degree at the tender age of twenty-one and eight months, making her the second youngest person to do so in the States.

She'd spent a few weeks being photographed, interviewed, and praised by the media before being dropped for the next story. She'd been thankful for the reprieve, since she'd hated being in the spotlight.

It wasn't the first time she'd been made the center of attention, and she knew it wouldn't be the last. When she'd attended Harvard, it had all been good attention. She'd returned home and started working at the local hospital and the attention had turned negative. Not by her peers, but by those who she was trying to help.

For the first year, it had affected her more than she wanted to admit to anyone, including her parents. After a while, she grew accustomed to it, and it stopped mattering so much.

Now, at twenty-seven years old, she melted into the background for the most part, which she was thankful for.

When she had started work at River Camps, she instantly knew that it was one of the best decisions she'd made in her adult life. When Elle had approached her after talking to her at Elle's grandfather's funeral, she'd jumped at the chance to work with the only girl in school who had been friendly to her.

The way Elle and her other friends, the Wildflowers, had changed the run-down summer camp into the gorgeous adult resort was nothing short of a miracle.

The fact that Elle had hired Aiden, Elle's second cousin and Lea's long-ago school crush to work on the place, hadn't really been a factor in her decision. Sure, the man was still hot as hell, but over the years, their relationship had changed and moved into the friend zone.

Then Aiden had started dating Aubrey Smith, one of the Wildflowers, and she couldn't have been happier for the couple, especially when they had announced their engagement a few months later.

Out of all the Wildflowers, Aubrey was one of her favorites. Lea had made a point to attend some of the self-defense classes that Aubrey offered at the resort. Elle and the other Wildflowers, who all owned equal shares of the resort, had agreed to allow employees to access some of the amenities.

Lea took them up on the offer as often as she could. Since she worked thirty hours a week at the hospital and another thirty at the resort, what little time she had to enjoy herself she wanted to enjoy to the max.

Plus, she really did enjoy being around the resort more than any other place in town. There hadn't been a day since she'd started working there that she hadn't absolutely loved it. It wasn't a high-demand job like working at the hospital was. More often than not, she was allowed to roam the grounds or sit by the pool and catch up on some reading while enjoying the outdoors.

She worked out of a small cabin and saw any guests who needed medical advice or help. It was just a two-room twenty-by-twenty cabin, but it was all hers.

She carried a walkie-talkie with her whenever she was on site. When off-site, they had her cell number for camp emergencies, which had happened more than a few times.

When the opportunity had come up almost a year earlier for her to purchase her very own home in the new subdivision

Aiden was building along with Owen Costa, Hannah's husband, she'd jumped at it. After all, the house payments were far cheaper than the rent she'd been paying in her small Destin apartment.

She'd moved into the three-bedroom, twenty-one hundred square foot place in Hammock Cove less than eight months before. She loved decorating every square foot of the place. She'd never owned her own place before, so she might have gone a little overboard with picking items to put in it. At first, it was hard to pick a color or theme she wanted. She'd settled on soft gray and white and a somewhat watery or beachy theme since there was an abundance of those pictures and home decorations in the area.

For the past year, she'd been thinking of cutting her hours back at the hospital, as she was making a little more money working at the resort. But she hoped to someday open her very own practice in Pelican Point, and she needed the extra money. It was past time the one local doctor had a little competition.

She had her eye on a new commercial building on the edge of town. The land was just being cleared and if she was going to jump on the idea, she only had a few more weeks to make up her mind.

Her sister Raya had moved to Orlando shortly after graduating high school and had gotten a job at Disney, portraying Mulan, her sister's dream job.

She was proud of Raya, even though she believed that their parents wished she'd attended college. But Lea knew that it wasn't in her sister's cards. Raya had never been one for school. She'd barely gotten her diploma, and she doubted Raya would work any harder in college. Her sister was a social butterfly and had more friends than Lea would know what to do with.

This was why she loved the Wildflowers. The five friends made it easy to be around them. They laughed, joked, and included her in everything, and Lea never felt awkward or out of place. Even if Lea spent most of the time just listening to the friends talk, she always felt part of the group.

In truth, they were her only friends. She had acquaintances at her other job, a handful of people she'd known over the past few years that she liked, but she'd never spent any of her free time with them.

There were several people that worked at the resort besides the five friends and their husbands or fiancés that had invited her to hang out. The surprising part was that she had agreed to do so and had always had a good time.

"Burning the midnight oil?" Dr. Sanjay Rufkin asked her when she stepped out into the hallway after handing off her patient to the ER nurses and the doctor.

"You could say that," she answered, trying not to roll her eyes at the man who, for the six months since his divorce had been finalized, had been hitting on her nonstop.

"Still working for the swinger camp?" he asked, trying to tease her about River Camps.

It wasn't a swinger's camp. Sure, some of the guests liked to party, and there had been a few parties that had gotten out of hand at first. But for the most part, guests came there to relax and have fun. Something she hadn't allowed herself to have until recently. Fun, not sex. As far as sex went, Lea was... well, picky.

Okay, maybe it wasn't necessarily her that was picky. She'd tried dating in school. In college that was, not high school. She'd finished high school at the tender age of thirteen and a half.

Still, since the high school she'd gone to was small, most of her classmates were in all of her core classes.

Instead of listening to the teachers, she'd been taking online college classes. Being a teenager old at Harvard left her with a huge "Do not enter" sign on her forehead.

By the time she'd wanted to date, she'd been surrounded by men too old or too engrossed in women who looked like models to do anything about it.

"You know it," she answered Sanjay. She walked down the hallway towards the lady's restroom, the only way she knew, outside of having another emergency come in, to get away from the man.

Sanjay was your typical male doctor. He believed he knew more than anyone else in the building. He was nice enough and most of the staff liked working with him. But most of the staff didn't have medical degrees either.

Whenever Lea worked at the hospital, Sanjay questioned every decision she made. He was one of her main reasons for wanting to cut back her hours at the hospital.

Without looking back, she ducked down the outside hallway and slipped out of the building. It wasn't until she stood in the muggy late spring heat in the parking lot that she remembered she had ridden in the back of the ambulance from the resort. It wasn't normally this hot mid-March, but they'd been having a heat wave the past few days. The spring grass was still brown. The pollen in the air didn't help either.

Still, the tourists didn't mind. They just enjoyed the warmth, as always.

She pulled out her phone and had just opened the app to get a ride when a police car pulled up and stopped in front of her.

Without looking in, she knew instantly who it was.

Watching Brett Jewel step out of the car in his uniform had her mouthwatering. How had the guy fallen under her radar in school? Sure, she'd considered him annoying at first, then he'd shifted to being a friend, and now...

Just seeing him in his tight black uniform shirt, which stretched over those impressive muscles, had her temperature spiking. She'd never really had a thing for men in uniform. Not until she'd gotten a look at Brett shortly after she'd moved back into town.

She'd heard at college through the online grapevine that he'd become a cop. Even though he'd always been getting into trouble; she knew it had been a dream of his. But in the past few years, she'd bumped into him enough times at the hospital to see how well he fit into his new role.

"Afternoon," he said, moving around the hood of his patrol car. "Need a lift?"

Lea narrowed her eyes. "Who called you?" she asked.

The smile he flashed her confirmed that someone had indeed called him and informed him that she'd ridden in the back of the ambulance with the patient.

"Can't I just be driving by and decide to come to see you?" he said, leaning against the front of the car.

She crossed her arms over her chest and looked up at him. "Do you know what my IQ is?" she asked smoothly.

His smile widened. "Probably a great deal higher than mine."

"Then you know trying to lie to me is a waste of time," she replied. "Yours and mine."

He laughed and moved over to open the door. "I'm heading out to the resort anyway. You might as well ride along. Unless you want to wait an hour for an Uber. It is spring break, remember?" He cocked his head to the side and waited for her answer.

She narrowed her eyes towards the back seat, where he stood holding the door open.

"Do I really have to ride in the back?" she asked.

His blond eyebrow arched up. "I suppose you'd fit in the trunk."

She rolled her eyes and moved towards the back seat. She caught her breath when she passed him. Brett Jewel. Greek God.

No, scratch that. Nordic God. He was Thor and Hercules wrapped up in the same package.

His blond hair had darkened slightly over the years and was cut a great deal shorter than it had been in school. The day's growth of stubble on his chiseled chin held a slight hint of red to it. His dark blue eyes held humor in them and, if she thought about it, always had.

He was as comfortable to be around as any of her school friends. Yet a new awareness had her body reacting to him as it never had before.

"Thanks," she said as she slid into the back of the patrol car.

"Why are you heading out to the resort?" she asked when he climbed into the car and started driving out of the parking lot.

"Aiden asked me to take a look at their new security system." Brett glanced in the rearview mirror. "He mentioned that you'd had an emergency?"

"One of the guests had heart failure," she replied quickly. She didn't like giving out too many details. "He had a pacemaker."

"How's he doing?" Brett asked.

"When I left, he was stable." She looked down at her phone at the update from Karen, one of the nurses that had taken over for her. "They're moving him to a private room." She updated him then shot off a text to Elle, giving everyone there an update.

"Good to know," Brett said. "I guess it was a lucky thing that they had you there."

She thought about what would have happened to the older man if she hadn't been reading by the pool when he'd collapsed a few feet away from her.

"Yeah," she said, looking out the window. It was March and already hitting three-digit temperatures. "He'd had three River Camps specialty drinks in half an hour. Not to mention he'd plowed down one of Isaacs's specialty burger plates."

"Everything in moderation. Right?" Brett threw over his

shoulder.

"Right," she agreed.

"I'm sure I'd never catch you cutting loose like that"—his eyes met hers in the mirror— "again." He smiled and she felt her face heat with the memory of the night a few months back. Well, partial memory. She'd cut a little too loose that night since Brett had tagged along and had made a point of giving her extra attention. She'd needed the alcohol to relax around him that night.

He had just been injured by a bunch of out-of-control jocks on a golf cart and was limping around that night. She'd been reminding him—again—that he should be taking it easy when he'd cornered her in the club booth and kissed her.

She'd been several drinks in and had kissed him back before she'd realized what she was doing.

"I can cut loose when I want to," she countered, feeling foolish suddenly.

"Yeah." His smile grew. "I remember."

She wanted to change the subject. Quickly. But she heard herself saying instead, "It's not about cutting loose. I can have fun."

"Sure you can. When was the last time you had fun?" he teased her, another steady Brett fact that she could always count on.

"Liam and Elle's wedding," she threw out.

She saw Brett's eyebrows rise slightly in the rearview mirror. "What'd you have? A glass of wine? Danced a couple of songs?"

"Two glasses of wine and I danced until I had blisters on my feet," she countered again, making her feel even more foolish. It was times like this she was thankful that her cheeks didn't turn pink when she became flustered or embarrassed, like her sister's did. Still, she glanced down at her phone and avoided his eyes.

"You had blisters because of those sexy red spiky heels you

were wearing."

She held her breath, trying not to let the fact that he remembered the shoes she'd worn to a party over six months ago affect her. Or the fact that he'd just called them sexy.

"Is that why you sat alone for most of the party? Your feet hurt?" he asked.

"I... didn't." She frowned. Had she? She remembered hanging out with Aubrey and Aiden, who had just started officially dating. Or had just started letting people know that they were an item, at any rate. But then they had hit the dance floor and, sure enough, she'd sat there alone for most of the night, when she hadn't been dancing. Hannah and Owen's wedding was less than a month away, which meant that, in a year's span, she would have attended five weddings.

"What happened to the girl you were with? Crissy?" she asked, changing the subject. She remembered being hurt when he'd walked in with the pretty blonde on his arm. Part of her had hoped that he'd ask her to go to the event.

"Crystal. Her parents are friends with mine," he corrected with a shrug. "She's back in DC."

She smiled. "Wow, she had to leave the state after just one date with you?"

The stab had the opposite effect on him than she'd intended. Instead of frowning or getting hurt, he smiled.

"There wasn't really much there," he replied dryly.

"Oh, if I remember correctly, there was plenty there." She held her hands up to her chest, signaling just how large Crystal's assets had been.

Brett's smile grew. "Physically, sure, but up here." He tapped the side of his head. "She actually believed that this part of Florida was part of Mexico because we're next to the Gulf of..."

"Mexico," she finished with a chuckle. "Yeah, I can totally see that. I found her taking selfies in the bathroom."

"Don't most women do that?"

She laughed. "She had a selfie stick and easily took more than a hundred pictures."

He shrugged. "How many selfies do you take?"

She thought about it. In the last year, she'd taken maybe one? Two? Feeling embarrassed about that fact, she changed the subject.

"It was a nice wedding. I'm looking forward to the next three." She saw a look of calculation cross Brett's eyes. It reminded her of when he used to try and come up with an answer in class when he had been called on but hadn't been paying attention.

"Who are we talking about?" he asked.

She chuckled. "Hannah and Owen in less than a month." She counted on her fingers. "Scarlett and Levi this fall. And Aiden and Aubrey. They've scheduled their wedding for this winter. Rumors have it just around Christmas." She shrugged.

"Aiden and Aubrey? So soon?" he asked, causing her to smile.

"They've been seeing one another on and off for the past three years. I personally got the hint that they were an item long before anyone else did," she admitted.

"You did?" He frowned back at her as he turned into the resort.

"I saw them… one evening at the pool."

"Why didn't you say anything?" he asked as he parked.

"It wasn't my place," she said simply.

He turned off the car and turned around to look at her. When she reached over to open the door, she heard him chuckle again.

"Can't get out from inside." He wiggled his eyebrows. "You're stuck with me until I decide to let you out."

She narrowed her eyes. "Which is now," she said firmly.

His smile grew. "You're always so serious. Where do you

have to run off to? Do you honestly think there's going to be more than one emergency in a day?"

"Yes," she answered quickly. "There's usually a few."

"Seriously?" He frowned and glanced around the empty parking lot. "What kinds of emergencies?"

"Besides heart attacks? Sickness, sprained appendages, bug or snake bites, sunburns, cuts or other wounds. Not to mention how many times someone has been shot at or knifed around here." She thought about several incidents in the past that included not only a kidnapping but a stabbing. "Not to mention keeping Zoey from working too hard and watching out for baby to arrive any day now."

"Okay, so you've got job security," he said with a sigh. "Who would have thought that an old-people's camp could be so dangerous."

"Snowbirds, not old people," she corrected. "Calling anyone over the age of forty old is just plain rude. It's not a retirement home. Most of the guests that visit here are in their forties and fifties."

"Right," he said, sounding unconvinced.

"Actually, I'm surprised Elle hasn't hit you up to run security around here. With all the... recent incidents, they've been talking about hiring someone full time."

"Oh, she's mentioned it," he answered with a shrug.

"Too busy?" she asked.

He glanced back at her and, instead of answering, climbed out and opened the back door for her.

Once again, she realized just how nice it felt to be so close to Brett. He was leaning casually on the door as she passed by him. She could smell his scent and was shocked at how familiar it was. How it did funny things to her insides as she soaked it and the sight of his blue eyes in.

He stopped her from moving behind him by laying a hand

on her arm.

"I've thought about it. Working here," he said softly. "But I'm needed elsewhere." His eyes ran down to her lips.

Her heart jumped in her chest at the thought of him kissing her again. What was going on? Did that look mean that he was interested in her? They'd never been anything but friends. After all, he'd spent the first few years teasing her.

"Lea." Her walkie-talkie jolted her out of her thoughts. She pulled it from her pocket and answered.

"Yes?"

"Are you back on site?" Elle asked.

"Yes, just got here."

"Good. Mr. Ridges fell in a bushel of poison oak. He's waiting in your waiting room," Elle answered. "Oh, and Mrs. Lipton took a volleyball to the face. She has a black eye. She's there too."

"I'll be there in five." She tucked her walkie-talkie back into her pants.

"Duty calls," Brett said, his face void of any of the interest that had been there moments earlier.

"Yes." She sighed and turned to go.

"Is it everything you thought it would be?" he asked, stopping her.

"What?" she asked.

"Working here."

She smiled. "It's far better." She took off down the pathway that led to her small medical building, which sat off to the side of the main building.

It was a new building. New to her, anyway. Aiden and his crew had transformed it from an old supply cabin shortly after the hurricane had ripped its roof off. Her old rooms had been in the main building, but she liked the cabin space more. It was… all hers. Another reason she loved her job.

CHAPTER 2

*B*rett felt the sweat rolling down his back. He endured the ache of his muscles screaming at him as he pushed on through the deep white powdery sand. Running in full uniform in one-hundred-degree heat wasn't his idea of fun, even on one of the most beautiful beaches in the States. Neither was the fact that he was chasing a kid easily ten years younger than him, who was wearing nothing more than a sock over his junk. Hell, Brett's badge weighed more than that thing did.

He'd been chasing the guy for almost five minutes and was actually gaining ground when he passed the sock on the ground and cursed under his breath. Now he had to tackle a fully nude man on the beach. And it wasn't even noon yet.

Spring break was always like this. Well, maybe not the naked guy, but there was always a group that partied too hard and caused problems.

Flying through the air, he finally took down the kid and landed in the soft sand with a thud, making a point to keep his hands far away from the kid's junk.

Families gasped in shock as they watched the scene unfold.

He cuffed the kid, thankful someone had left a towel nearby. He tossed it over the kid's waist and stood up.

"Nothing to see here," he said, dusting the sand from his uniform. While he read the kid his rights, the guy's friends finally caught up with them and started harassing him.

"Leave him alone, man," one of the other drunk guys said.

"He wasn't doing nothin'," another one yelled at him.

"Indecent exposure isn't nothing," he replied dryly.

"If you hadn't chased him, he wouldn't be indecent," a girl shouted at him.

"Your friend is also under arrest for having an open container on the beach," he added.

"What?" all three of the other people shouted.

"Alcoholic beverages are not allowed on this stretch of beach during the month of March. There are signs everywhere clearly stating this." He motioned to the signs posted on the trash cans no less than fifteen feet away.

"That's bullshit," the kid he'd tackled said.

Brett was thankful he was at least holding the towel over his waist.

"Evading an officer, indecent exposure, and public intoxication are additional charges," he added. "I haven't even looked up your record yet. There might be more to add to that." He watched the kid pale even further under his bright red sunburn and knew instantly there would be more charges, maybe even a warrant. "Do you have some shorts for him?" He turned to his friends.

"Here, Robby." The girl moved forward and held out a pair of swim trunks and flip-flops.

He helped the cuffed guy into the shorts and shoes all while trying to hold the towel up to shield the bystanders from any more nudity.

It was a long walk back to his patrol car and by the time he set the kid in the back seat and gave him a drink of water, he figured he'd deserve the large burger he planned on having for lunch.

Taking a sip of his own bottled water as he drove to the station, he thought about what Lea had said the other day. How much she enjoyed working at the camp.

Whenever he visited the place himself, it felt like a vacation. He was more jealous than he wanted to admit.

How long had his best friend, Aiden, been begging him to work at the resort? Since before it had opened. Still, he liked his job, even if half the time was spent wrangling tourists.

But he had to admit it, given the opportunity, he'd cut back his hours and work both jobs like Lea was currently doing.

He'd felt lucky when he'd heard she'd returned from Harvard. He'd secretly had a crush on her since... well... forever. He'd fallen for her hard the moment he'd seen her walking across the schoolyard, a stack of books in her hands. Then he'd watched Tim and his gang bully her and how she'd held her own verbally against the bullies, and he'd been even more impressed.

She was smart, cute, and pretty back then. Now, as a woman, she was downright sexy and even smarter, something that drove him completely nuts. She didn't look at him as anything other than a friend, but that was something he was slowly working on changing.

After dropping off and booking the naked guy, who did in fact have a warrant out for his arrest, he headed back out to help with a traffic accident.

By the time he unlocked the door to his apartment, he was completely drained. Working a ten-hour shift wasn't his choice, but since it allowed him an extra day off a week, he figured he'd suffer through it. Especially since he'd been spending those days off hanging around the resort and Lea.

He'd just lay down when he got a text from Aiden.

-Can you stop by tomorrow? I have a few new cameras and want your opinion on where to put them.

-Sure. Can I get a free breakfast?

-Don't tell anyone that you're just coming around for the food. I'll make sure Isaac whips up something special for you.

-See you at seven then.

-Jesus! Eight will work. Nine would be better, but since I know it's your day off and you plan on hanging around the camp all day, I'll see you when I see you.

He wanted to ask if Lea was going to be working tomorrow but figured it would make him sound too desperate. Besides, Aiden was right, it was his day off and he had already planned on packing his swim trunks and enjoying the pools at the resort.

There was no other place he knew where he could spend his time off without feeling like he was packed in like a sardine.

Not that the camp wasn't busy. But they had three swimming pools, a private beach, and access to the bay, where he could take out kayaks and canoes or even hop on one of the boats to enjoy a sail. They also had a barn full of horses, zip lines, and other fun actives that he could use. He had to admit, it was like visiting Disney World. Each time he went, he tried something new and fun.

The next morning, he showed up at River Camps bright and early. Since he still had an hour to go before Aiden would be in the dining room, he peeled off his shorts and shirt and did a few laps in the larger pool.

He could get used to having access to a pool like this. As his body loosened, his mind cleared. It was wonderful taking in the fresh air, the peace and quiet.

He was taking a turn on what he planned on being his last lap when a splash beside him had him glancing over. He saw the sleek body next to him and smiled as Lea settled into a pace next to him.

Their eyes locked, and he could see the challenge in them. Without thinking, he met her speed and as she carved through the water smoothly.

He hadn't planned on working out so long, but there was no way he was going to let her win. Not after he realized he was having a difficult time keeping up with her.

After another fifteen laps, she kicked into overdrive and the race to the finish line was on. He'd like to tell himself that he had easily won, but the truth was, he'd done over a dozen laps already and his muscles were burning. He pulled up to the wall just as she did.

Breathing heavy, he smiled over at her.

"You should have been here half an hour earlier," he joked.

She smiled over at him as she pulled off her swimming cap, letting all that jet black hair of hers fall around her face.

"You're just saying that because I beat you," she teased.

He laughed. "You did no such thing."

Her eyebrows shot up. "Oh? We can have a rematch?"

"There you are." They both turned and looked up at Aiden and Aubrey standing at the edge of the pool.

Aiden was dressed in his standard work jeans and shirt, while Aubrey wore yoga pants and a camp T-shirt.

"Morning," he said cheerfully.

"Morning. Did you two just race?" Aubrey asked.

"I won," Lea said.

"Did not." He narrowed his eyes towards her. She smiled in response and shrugged her shoulders.

"He's just a sore loser," Lea replied. Aubrey and Aiden smiled down at them.

"Well, I've got to get going to my class," Aubrey said to Aiden. "See you for lunch?"

"Yeah." Aiden reached over and pulled Aubrey into his arms and kissed her.

He thought he heard Lea make a sound and tried not to feel a wave of jealousy hit him. After all, he'd known forever that Lea had a thing for Aiden. He had believed that she'd gotten over it years ago, but maybe she hadn't?

After Aubrey left, he watched Lea duck under the lap ropes and climb up the ladder of the pool. It wasn't the first time he'd seen her in a swimsuit, but still, he felt his heart skip at the sight. She looked perfect in a black one-piece trainer swimsuit. The back of it had a crisscross pattern and when she turned and wrapped a towel around her, he noticed the front had a zipper that went all the way down to where her navel was.

"Earth to Brett," Aiden said, getting his attention.

"What?" He turned towards his friend. Aiden laughed.

"Breakfast?" he asked again.

"Oh, sure." He held the side of the pool deck and pulled himself out of the water quickly. He glanced over and noticed that Lea was watching them. Again, he wasn't sure if she was looking in the direction of him or Aiden.

He pulled on his shirt and flip-flops and followed Aiden down the pathway to the main dining area.

"We'll sit outside since you're still wet," Aiden said, motioning to his shorts.

"I had planned on being dry, but then Lea challenged me to a race," he joked.

"I did no such thing," Lea said from behind them. He hadn't realized she'd followed them and stopped to let her catch up. She'd pulled on a black swimsuit coverup, which hugged the top part of her body and flowed around her legs.

"Sure, you did." He chuckled. "Even if it was unspoken," he added as they walked to the patio dining area.

"Care to join us for breakfast?" Aiden asked her.

"Sure. I was going to meet…" Lea started.

"Lea, over here," Elle called out.

They all glanced over to see Elle, Scarlett, Zoey, Dylan, and Liam sitting at a couple of tables that had been pushed together. Zoey was just shy of nine months pregnant and looking very happily miserable. They pushed another table close to theirs and made room for them all.

Brett held out a chair for Lea and then took a spot next to her while Aiden sat on the other side of the table.

Levi was just coming through the back door and, after spotting them, headed over.

"The gang's almost all here," Elle said cheerfully. "Owen's at work, which means Hannah will be here soon."

"There she is," Zoey said, motioning to the pathway.

"Aubrey has her morning class," Aiden supplied as Dean, one of the waitstaff, delivered cold carafes of cucumber lemon water to each table.

"Is everyone doing the buffet this morning?" Dean asked.

Dean was roughly his age and had lived in Pelican Point since his freshmen year of high school, after his parents' divorce. Even though he was a flirt with all the women, he was honest and had a kind heart under the macho exterior. Brett liked the guy.

"I'm ordering," he spoke up after several people chimed in that they would be having the buffet. He was pleased when Lea claimed she was ordering as well.

As most of the people shuffled inside to join the line at the employee's buffet, he ordered his favorite breakfast after Lea placed her order of an egg-white omelet.

"That's not a breakfast," he told her when they were alone.

She arched her eyebrows. "And I suppose sugar-covered carbs is?"

"Hey, the French toast Banana Fosters is a specialty here. You can't get anything like it unless you head to Hawaii."

She tilted her head. "When did you go to Hawaii?"

"Senior trip." He shrugged and poured her some more water. A look crossed her face that had him setting down the carafe. "Problem?" he asked.

"No, it's…" She shook her head.

"What?" He leaned a little closer and lowered his voice. "You can tell me. We're friends, right?"

He watched another look cross her face and then it was gone quickly, and she was smiling. "I didn't get to go on my senior trip."

"Of course not. You were probably at Harvard dissecting something," he replied with a smile. "So, Dr. Lea Val, was it worth it?"

Her smile brightened. "Yes, it was."

"So, you go to Hawaii when you want." He waved his water glass around. "Once you take over the world, that is."

She laughed. "Do you know how long you've been telling me I was going to do that?"

He thought about it for a moment then shrugged. "Since I saw you berate Nicole Flanagan for holding the scalpel wrong in biology class."

She stilled, her eyes going to his. "You… remember that?"

He laughed. "Who could forget?" He shook his head, then picked up the knife from the table and held it up like Nicole had. "No, not that way," he said clearly, mimicking her softer tone. "One simply doesn't hold a scalpel like a dinner knife. You must hold it as if it were a paint brush." He switched his hold on the knife and Lea laughed.

"Oh my god, that's a perfect recreation of Lea in fifth-grade biology," Aiden said, sitting down with a full plate of food. "Do you remember when Lea schooled Mr. Colins on human anatomy?"

"Oh, are we boasting about how smart Lea is?" Elle said, sitting down beside Lea.

Lea rolled her eyes and then groaned. "Let's change the subject."

For the next few moments, while they waited for their food, stories of when they were young were shared around the table. The stories turned away from Lea, which he could tell she was grateful for, and moved to the five friends who called themselves the Wildflowers.

He'd always thought it was a perfect name for the five best friends, even back when Elle had first told him and Aiden about her friends. Not that he'd met any of them until they'd all agreed to reopen the summer camp together. Still, just the way Elle had described them, he knew the nickname had fit perfectly. Now that he knew all of them, he realized just how perfect it was.

They were just finishing up their breakfast when Dean rushed out and called for Lea.

"Someone's choking," he barked out.

It was like watching a dancer at the peak of her career. Lea sprang into action, racing from the table and pushing through the crowd of people who had gathered around the woman. She grabbed the woman, who was easily twice Lea's size, and perform the Heimlich maneuver until the grape she'd swallowed went flying out of her throat and the older woman gulped in a deep breath.

"Sit." Lea moved the woman into a chair. "Take several deep breaths." She knelt next to her and grabbed the woman's wrist as she took her blood pressure. "How do you feel?"

"You..." The woman blinked a few times. "You saved my life. Thank you."

Lea smiled just as the woman's husband pushed through. "Carmen? What… What happened?"

It was hard not to feel pride for Lea as the crowd erupted in cheers and then dispersed.

He wanted to stay longer, but he knew that the woman and her husband might want some privacy. Besides, Lea was trying to convince the woman to come back to her office just to make sure everything was alright.

"Wow, does that happen a lot?" he asked Aiden.

"No." Aiden shrugged. "No more often than you probably see at any school cafeteria." He smiled and slapped him on the back. "Which is why we're trying to convince Lea to stay on full time."

"You are?" he asked, only realizing too late that he sounded eager.

Aiden chuckled. "Her and you. We could use someone to oversee security just as much as we need a full-time doctor around here. I've been far too busy at Hammock Cove to deal with a lot of the issues around the campground."

Hammock Cove was a housing project that Aiden was in charge of for Owen Costa, the developer and Hannah's fiancé. It was a large new subdivision not far from the camp. The first phase of the housing project was completed, and Aiden and Owen were starting the second phase. He'd thought of purchasing his own home in the neighborhood, once he could afford it.

Brett glanced around as he followed Aiden down the hallway towards his office. He knew that there was a room with wall-to-wall monitors showcasing all the cameras he'd help Aiden set up over the past couple of years.

There were now more than forty private cabins, which were completely booked more often than not, so the number of guests coming in and out of the camp was growing. Aiden and his team were working on building several more cabins as well as a new Frisbee golf course, some pickleball courts, and even a miniature golf course.

By the time they were done, the place was going to have everything anyone would ever want in an adults-only vacation spot.

Brett knew that their security concerns were real. After all, since they'd reopened the doors, they'd had to deal with a crazed employee who had tried to shoot Dylan and had stabbed Hannah, a psycho killer who had kidnapped Hannah, and the hurricane that had ripped through last year when Zoey and Scarlett's crazy stepmother, Bridgette, and her mother, Martha, had tried to kill Aubrey and Aiden. They would have succeeded if Aubrey wasn't such a badass and knew self-defense.

After that ordeal, they'd made it a requirement that all employees take her basic self-defense class once a year. They had asked him to come in and help out last time, and he'd gotten to spar with Lea, something he'd never forget. He still dreamed about doing it again.

CHAPTER 3

$\mathcal{N}$ormally, Lea's days weren't this busy. A few bug bites, some scrapes, or a minor health issue to deal with. But today had been downright chaotic. It had started with Mrs. Helms choking on the grape and had ended with Mrs. Wilkinson twisting her ankle on the beach during a sunset stroll.

By the time she crawled into bed that night, she was beginning to wonder how they'd ever survived around the camp without her.

Far too soon after she'd fallen asleep, her phone rang, waking her up. Holding in a groan, she saw the hospital's emergency number and answered it quickly.

"Dr. Val," she said, blinking the sleep from her eyes.

"Dr. Val, it's Karen. I hate to call you in, but I have a patient down here who claims he knows you personally. He won't let Dr. Rufkin see him."

"Who?" she asked.

"It's a police officer. The one—"

"Brett?" Val sat straight up. She felt her heart skip. "What's

"

wrong?" She thought back to the last time Brett had been injured on the job. Then she remembered that yesterday had been his day off. He shouldn't have been working.

"Gunshot to the upper thigh," Karen replied quickly. "His vitals are good. He's awake and coherent."

"I'll be there in ten," she said, sliding on her scrubs.

"I'll let him know, but hospital policy says..." Karen started.

"I know, I'll just assist," she said quickly, and hung up.

She made it to the hospital in less than ten minutes, making sure to call Aiden and Elle as she drove.

She knew that before Brett was out of surgery, the waiting room would be full of their friends.

"Fill me in," she said to Karen as she rushed into the ER.

"Dr. Rufkin's in there with the patient now," Karen said, looking a little concerned.

Then she heard the shouting and instantly recognized Brett's raised voice and rushed down the hallway.

"I don't give a damn. I'm not letting you knock me out until..." Brett stopped when she stepped into the small room.

"What on earth have you done to yourself?" she asked, her temper flaring at seeing his left leg soaked in blood. She'd been right, he wasn't wearing his uniform. Actually, he was still wearing those damned flowery board shorts he'd been wearing when they'd raced in the water that morning. At least now he had on a T-shirt. His flip-flops were missing though.

"I didn't do anything," Brett said in a much calmer tone. Actually, now that she was there, he'd gone from angry and agitated to looking exhausted in a blink of an eye.

She walked over to the side of Brett's bed and looked over to Dr. Rufkin. "Do you care if I assist on this one? I want to make sure he doesn't heckle me for the rest of his life if he walks with a limp."

Sanjay nodded as his eyes went between her and Brett. She

could tell what he was thinking and at this point didn't care. Let the man think she was involved with Brett. Maybe then he'd leave her alone and stop asking her out all the time.

"You're going to be okay," she said to Brett.

"Just a flesh wound," Brett said before closing his eyes. She could tell he was in a great deal of pain. His coloring was off, and the monitor was showcasing his elevated vitals.

For the next three hours, she focused on helping Dr. Rufkin out as he patched Brett's leg up, removing every speck of metal from his skin, bone, and muscle.

His leg looked like it had been through a shredder. She knew that he'd have months of physical therapy to deal with. Not to mention he'd be off work indefinitely. Maybe permanently.

Whatever Brett had just gone through was going to change his life forever.

When they wheeled him into recovery, she walked out and met their friends. As she thought, the waiting room was full of faces she knew.

"What's going on?" Elle rushed forward. "How is he?"

"He's in recovery," she said loudly enough for everyone to hear. "We've removed the bullets and all the fragments. He'll be down for a while, and we'll need to keep him in the hospital for a few days. After that"—she met Aiden's eyes— "he'll need someone to watch out for him."

"How long will he be down?" Aiden asked, concern flooding his voice.

She sighed. "I think now's a perfect time for Brett to rethink his career," she admitted. A tear slipped down her cheek before she realized she was crying.

Elle pulled her into her arms and held onto her.

"He's okay. You did a wonderful job," Elle whispered to her.

She'd never lost it at work before. Had never allowed herself to, even when she'd lost patients. This, however, was different. This was Brett. Their Brett. Her Brett.

"Can we see him?" Aiden asked.

She wiped her face clean and nodded. "One at a time. I'll take you back. He's probably still asleep." She turned to go, but then stopped. "Does anyone know what happened?"

Everyone was quiet for a moment. "You…" Elle started and then shook her head. Instead of answering, she motioned to the television screen.

Brett's face filled the set in the waiting room. Below his image, in bold letters, it read, "Local off-duty cop gets shot saving a family of three in a botched carjacking."

She closed her eyes. "He's a fool."

"Yes, but he's also a hero through and through," Aiden said, wrapping his arms around her shoulder. "Now, show me to the idiot so I can tell him how proud I am of him."

At half-past six in the morning, Aubrey found her in the post-op and handed her a breakfast sandwich.

"Is this…" She opened the container.

"Isaac made it special for you." Aubrey hugged her. "You must be exhausted."

She was, but at this point, she'd already gotten her third wind. She figured she had another two hours before she'd need to escape to the break room and shut down for a few hours. Even though she wasn't technically on duty, she figured she'd stick around until Brett was fully awake.

"I know you don't drink coffee, but Elle says you liked this tea." She handed her one of the camp's signature thermoses.

"Thanks," she said.

"Everyone's going to head out. I'm sure we'll be taking turns coming back to check on him while he's here," Aubrey said.

She glanced towards the room where she knew Brett was recovering. Aiden was still in there with him.

"I'll let you know if anything changes." She hugged Aubrey again.

"Get some rest," Aubrey said softly. "If you need anything…"

Lea nodded. "Thanks."

She noticed the entire gang leaving, and a few minutes later she carried her sandwich and tea into Brett's room to sit and eat there while listening to him breathing and the sound of the machines humming. He didn't snore.

Her eyes ran over his face as he slept. If she didn't know better, she'd believe he was just taking a nap instead of being in a medicine-induced sleep state.

Instead of eating, she sipped her tea and watched Brett's eyelashes, willing them silently to open. For him to spring out of the bed and tell her that it was all a sick joke he was playing on her.

At some point she fell asleep, waking when Karen stepped into the room to check on Brett.

"Sorry," Karen said softly. "I didn't mean to wake you."

"You…" She was about to deny that she'd fallen asleep, but then realized there was no point. "It's okay. I needed to get up anyway." She sat up and picked up her sandwich, feeling her stomach growl. "What time is it?"

Karen glanced at her watch and answered. "Just past nine."

"Nine?" Lea balked. She'd slept for close to two hours.

"You needed the rest," Karen said as she moved around the room to check Brett's vitals and change out his saline bag.

"How's he looking?" Lea asked.

"He's improved." She handed her the chart, and Lea ran her eyes over his numbers. Karen was correct. Brett's vitals were much better.

When she glanced up from the chart, she was slightly shocked to see Brett's eyes on her.

"What's the verdict, doc? Will I survive?" he asked, his voice slightly slurred.

She handed Karen his chart and moved over to his side to take his hands and check his pulse herself.

Before she could, he took her hand and tugged her down until she sat next to him, his good leg pressed up against her hip.

Out of the corner of her eye, she saw Karen slip out of the room.

"There, that's much better." He took her hand in his.

"Brett, I need to check—"

He hushed her. "That's what the machines are for. Just… talk to me," he said with a sigh.

At first, she didn't know what to say, then she smiled.

"You're a national hero." she teased.

His eyes opened a little wider. "I am?"

She chuckled. "Yes, your silly face is on every news channel. The family you saved has requested to see you once you're up to a visit."

"Later," he mumbled.

"How are you feeling?" she asked, worried as she watched his eyes close.

"Drugged," he replied. "How bad did it turn out?" She was silent for a minute until his eyes opened and locked on hers. "That bad?"

"You won't be racing against me for a while," she teased.

He winced. "Will I be walking anytime soon?" He glanced down at his leg.

"Yes," she said, holding him still as he tried to sit up. "With some therapy."

He closed his eyes again, and she thought for a moment that he'd fallen back asleep.

"I'm sure that when I'm not drugged, I'll have a different reaction," he said. "Did someone call my parents?"

She stiffened a little, remembering how strained his relationship with his folks was. "No," she answered. "Aiden thought… We all thought you'd want to call them yourself. But with your face being all over the news, there's no way they don't know what happened. Not at this point. It's nine in the morning."

His eyes opened and he stared up at the ceiling, then reached out his hand and took hers again. "Did someone get my cell phone?"

She nodded. "Your stuff is in the bag." She motioned to the overbed table. Reaching over, she pulled it towards him with her free hand.

"From what I can remember, it was just my leg?" He glanced down at himself. "Everything is a little too numb right now. Is the rest of me in the same place?"

She smiled. "If you're asking if you're still a complete man, yes. The damage is confined to your upper left leg. It nicked your femur and tore a hole in your rectus femoris and vastus lateralis muscles." Since he was giving her a look, she sighed. "Right here." She ran a finger over her thigh to show him the area. "You'll have problems walking and squatting or sitting down until you've healed and gone through therapy."

"That's not so bad." He relaxed. "Like having a broken leg, I would suppose." He shrugged.

She wanted to argue with him, but she could tell he was growing tired. When she tried to take her hand from his, he nudged her closer.

"How about another kiss? I've thought about kissing you since the last time." His words were slurred. She'd heard the machine dispense another dose of meds to him a few moments ago and knew he was feeling the effects already. "Come on, Lea.

Pretty Lea. What does a man have to do to get a kiss from you? Get shot?"

She smiled and leaned forward and brushed her lips over his. When she pulled back, she could tell he was fast asleep. She brushed her fingers over his face, pushed a strand of his blond hair away from his eyes, and cupped his face.

He was so pleasant to look at as he slept that she lost track of time once again. How had she overlooked the man for most of her life? Sure, when they'd been younger, he'd been a tease. Well, actually, he was still a tease.

She smiled remembering the kinds of things he teased her about. Had that been his way of flirting all along?

He had said he'd dreamed of kissing her since last time. Truth be told, she'd dreamed of kissing him too. If she was being honest with herself, it was because the first time, she'd been a little too drunk to enjoy the feeling of his mouth on hers.

The chaste kiss she'd just given him was nothing like the first, she was sure of it.

When her phone buzzed, she stood up and walked out of the room. She wasn't able to check up on Brett again for another three hours. By then, Aiden was back, along with Brett's parents. When she stepped into the room, she could tell instantly that tensions were high. Brett's eyes were closed, yet she doubted he was asleep after seeing his heart rate on the monitor.

"Morning," she said cheerfully.

"What are you doing here?" William R. Jewel Jr. asked with a scowl.

"Mr. Jewel," Lea said without answering his question. She turned to his mother, Clara, and gave her a pleasant smile. The woman worked at the local library and, as far as Lea could remember, had been nothing but nice to her. "Mrs. Jewel, Aiden." She nodded to her friend.

"Morning, Lea," Aiden said. Even though there was a cheerfulness to his tone, she could see the agitation on his face.

"I said, what are you doing in here?" Mr. Jewel said a little louder. "Don't you fucking understand English? Damn gooks."

"Hey," Aiden stood up. "I've warned you…"

"Dad." Brett spoke firmly, getting everyone's attention. "Get out." He practically barked it, causing her to jump slightly at the tone of his voice. She'd never heard him raise his voice.

Lea braced for the fight she knew was coming. But Clara grabbed her husband's arm.

"You don't want to be late for work," Clara said softly.

Brett's father jerked his arm free from his wife's hold and glared at Lea as he walked out of the room.

"I'm sorry," Brett said softly. She could hear the pain in his tone and walked over to the side of his bed to check on him.

"It's not your fault your father is…"

"A racist asshat?" Aiden finished.

"A bigot," she finished smoothly, gaining a smile from Aiden.

"I'll go see about that breakfast," Aiden said.

"Cheeseburger, fries, and a Coke," Brett called after Aiden. "Don't come back if you don't have all of those."

Aiden chuckled and waved as he walked out of the room, leaving them alone once again.

She smiled down at Brett, knowing that he would get none of those things. Most likely his first meal would be Jell-O or pudding.

"You've got some pull around here," Brett started as she checked his fresh bandages. "What does a man have to do to get some real food?"

"Not get shot," she replied smoothly.

"Ha ha." He rolled his eyes. "You're a comedian, just like Aiden."

"How are you feeling? In pain?" She looked into his blue eyes and saw the answer herself.

"No," he lied. He was sitting up in the bed with his left leg elevated slightly. Someone, most likely Aiden, had brought him a T-shirt, which he'd thrown over the hospital gown.

She walked over to the infusion pump, but before she could give him another dose, he stopped her.

"No, please." He took her hand. "I'd rather deal with the pain than be knocked out again. Isn't there something else you can give me to knock the edge off?"

She took his chart and ran her eyes over his vitals. If he was willing to deal with the pain, there was nothing in here stopping her from allowing it. He wasn't in distress; his heart rate and other vitals were good.

"I'll get you something." She turned only to have him tug her again until she sat on the edge of his bed, being extra careful since she was on his left side.

"I really am sorry for my father. The way he treats you and anyone else not..." He shrugged.

"White?" she offered.

"I was going to say pale-skinned, but yeah." He sighed. "There's no excuse for it. We've tried over the years to enlighten him, but..."

"Some people fear others' differences because they're ignorant." She smiled. "No one can make you feel inferior without your consent. Your father is as ignorant as they come. I'm one of the youngest people to receive my medical degree in the entire country. He feels threatened by me. That's all." She shrugged.

"Eleanor Roosevelt." He tilted his head. "You're a lot like her, I would think."

She smiled. "I wasn't aware the ex-president's wife had been a doctor?"

He chuckled, then winced slightly. "No, you're both strong women with more brains than the men that surround them."

She smiled. "Flattery will get you anything," she said with a chuckle.

He smiled. "Will it get me a cheeseburger?"

She laughed and leaned in to place another soft kiss over his lips. "It just might."

CHAPTER 4

*I*f you didn't count the pain and the possibility of never walking normally again, things were looking up for Brett.

It had been a full week since he'd jumped in front of a bullet, so to speak, for the family of three. He hadn't thought about it at the time. It had been instinct.

He hadn't seen the color of their skin, the style of clothing they were wearing, or what model of car they were driving. All he'd seen was a young couple with a child under five, cowering from a bully with a gun who had wanted something that wasn't his and was willing to kill for it.

The fact that the gunman was white and the family wasn't hadn't even registered to him at the time. Nor, he thought, would it have ever. But of course, the news anchors played on those key points over and over, choosing to use this story to highlight the near pandemic of racism that was spreading around the country, especially in the southern parts.

He was being played up as the all-American hero, a Captain

American sort who stood up for all and any. Okay, that part was true.

Which of course led to the haters coming out of the woodworks. They started when he was still in the hospital. Lea and her team had blocked the messages. He'd only gotten wind of them after Aiden had overheard Lea dealing with one on the phone outside his room.

When he'd been well enough to move out of the hospital and into a cabin at the campgrounds so that he could be watched over by his many friends, more calls and messages had leaked through.

But staying at the camp wasn't even the best part. The best part was that he got to see Lea every single day. Especially now that he'd moved into the Cruiser, which was the name of the cabin Elle and the rest of the gang had forced him to live in until he was back on his feet.

The Cruiser, so named because it was one of a handful of cabins with wheelchair access, was one of the newer cabins, so he hadn't complained.

Nor had he complained when all his meals were delivered to him along with his every wish or desire. Well, almost every.

He wanted to go swimming. A few laps in the pool would stretch out the tight muscles he had from lying in a bed twenty-four-seven.

But Dr. Lea Val was there to stop him every single time he worked up the nerve to try and make it down the pathway in the damned wheelchair he'd been given to head to the nearest pool.

She claimed that it was only a matter of days before his incisions would be healed enough to allow him to take a dip.

Until then, he'd sat back and enjoyed the hot showers or baths he could take after he'd wrapped up his leg with a trash bag like his new physical therapist had shown him to do.

Since their short visit to the hospital, his parents had come back to see him once. He'd doubted his father would after the interviews Lea had done updating the press on his condition and the one that he had done when the Hernandez family had wanted to thank him personally for saving their lives.

Not that he minded. Actually, when he'd opened his eyes that day in his hospital room, it had been the first time he'd seen his father since he'd graduated from high school.

His mother worked at Pelican Point Public Library, which he frequented a few times a month. She always asked how he was doing and was cordial like she would have been to anyone else in town.

He knew it was his father's doing that his mother had to remain distant. After all, years of the man yelling that she babied him too much had carved the path that their relationship had taken long ago.

It was one more area where Aiden's parents, Robin and Carl Stark, had stepped up in his life. If he ever missed having normal parents, he'd head over to Aiden's house and get his fill. The Starks had spoiled him like he was one of their own.

Actually, their visit to the hospital had been far better than his own parents' brief visit. Plus, they'd come out to the cabin the other night and brought him some of Robin's homemade chili. He'd enjoyed it so much. It brought back a lot of memories of when he'd spend the night—or a few nights—at their house when he was younger.

They'd often joked that he spent so much time at their place that they were going to designate their spare bedroom as his own room.

He didn't ever know if they understood why he was always requesting to hang around. He didn't know if Aiden had ever mentioned how terrible his homelife was, nor did he care. They treated him like family, and he ate up the attention.

Becoming a cop was the one thing he could do to stick it to his old man. Growing up, he'd told himself that if he was the law, his father would have spent more than a couple of nights behind bars for the things he'd said or done.

The fact that he had yet to arrest his father himself once irritated him. His old man had gotten away with so much hate over the years that surely he'd broken at least one law. That hate hadn't just been pointed at him and his mother but at anyone and anything that got in the way —or even hinted at getting in the way—of Willy Jr, as he liked to be called.

"What are you doing out here?" A voice broke into his thoughts.

He looked up and noticed Lea walking towards him on the narrow pathway.

"Getting some fresh air." He smiled at her. He'd hobbled out to the front porch of the cabin. It wasn't one of the best views, but it was quiet, and the trees were nice to look at. Especially since they were swaying with the breeze. He really enjoyed watching the birds and squirrels playing in the pine trees.

"Fresh air?" She stopped at the base of the ramp and looked up at him. "It's got to be close to a hundred out here."

He glanced down at his phone and smiled. "Ninety-eight." He shrugged. "It beats sitting inside, watching television all of the time."

She was quiet for a moment. "I thought you might like to get out of here for a while."

His eyebrows shot up. "Yes."

She laughed. "Don't you want to know where—"

"No." He shook his head and started to stand up.

"Hang on." She laughed and rushed to help him. "You'll want to change first."

"Okay." He glanced down at the sweat shorts and T-shirt he was wearing. "Into what?"

She smiled. "How about some swim trunks?"

"Hell yes," he said with a sigh. "I'll be just a moment." He grabbed his crutch and did his best to rush into the cabin and change.

The prospect of taking a dip, of letting his entire body relax in the water, was so predominant in his mind that instead of sitting on the edge of the bed to pull off the sweats, he tried pulling his bad leg out of the shorts while he stood. That ended with him flat on his ass on the hardwood floor.

"Are you okay?" Lea rushed into the cabin and saw him sitting on the floor. She shook her head and walked over to help him up. "I thought you were smarter than that," she said as he pulled himself up off the floor.

"I guess I was just too excited," he murmured, trying to hide the pain the fall had caused him. He didn't want her to have any excuse to cancel the swim.

"Here, let me." She knelt before him and helped him step out of his sweat shorts. "Now your boxers." She motioned for him to pull them off his hips.

"Um." He shook his head and made a motion for her to turn around.

She rolled her eyes at him. "I am a doctor."

"Yeah, I get that, and I'm a cop. That doesn't mean I strip search you every chance I get," he retorted.

He could tell she was thinking about it and watched her eyes flood with embarrassment at what he'd hinted at. Her eyebrows shot up and a slow smile formed on her lips as excitement crossed her eyes.

"Oh, you are in deep trouble." He'd meant to say it in his head, to himself, but when she laughed at him, he realized that he'd said it out loud.

"Promise?" she asked softly.

He felt his entire body grow hard. Harder than it had been in years. Damn, why was she still standing there, looking at him? Did she know what she was doing to him?

"As much as I'd like to…" He glanced down at the bandages over his thigh and knew that he'd probably last two seconds before moving wrong. The pain had become a standard part of his life. If he moved wrong, it overcame him, and he would double over or fall into the nearest chair.

At this point, he couldn't imagine doing anything more than walking or, as he'd been dreaming about, swimming and becoming weightless for a while.

"As much as I'd enjoy having you try to strip search me"— she nudged him slightly until he fell backward to sit on the side of the bed, and her eyes laughed at him when he sat there breathing heavily— "I'll let you change in peace. Just yell if you need help." She turned around and walked out.

Damn. He *was* in trouble. Had Lea always been this… frisky? Sexy? Double damn. He glanced down at his leg and silently cursed it while knowing that he wouldn't be this close to her if he hadn't gotten injured.

There was nothing more he could do about it until he felt stronger, but he figured swimming was the best path to his recovery.

He pulled off his boxers and slipped on his swim trunks. He figured he'd have to remove the bandages if he planned on getting in the water.

He had just cut off the last bandage when Lea stepped back into the room.

"Ready?" she asked, her eyes going to his thigh.

"Yeah." He tossed the soiled bandages in the trash.

She walked over and knelt in front of him, her eyes zoned onto where he'd been stitched back up. He stood still while she ran her fingers over his scarred skin.

Her fingertips brushed over him lightly, and he had to close his eyes as thoughts of taking her crossed his mind.

He tried to be patient, but the more she examined his leg, the more he convinced himself that he could chance the pain. For her.

"Lea," he groaned, "you're killing me."

She glanced up at him and understanding crossed her face. She stood up quickly. "If you're ready." She moved towards the door.

As they walked down the pathway towards the nearest pool, they remained quiet.

"Your wound looks good," she said once they'd reached the pool area. "Good enough that you can start swimming every day. I brought some waterproof tape; we'll have to make sure your sutures are kept dry. Besides, the exercise will do you good."

"Calling me fat?" he joked.

She chuckled. "No, not yet." She tossed off the coverup she had on, and he enjoyed the one-piece swimsuit she was wearing. It was his turn to run his eyes over her as she sat down to remove her sandals.

He stepped out of his flip-flops, set his crutches down on the edge of the pool, and stepped into the water.

"We're going to take it easy this first time." She stepped into the water next to him.

"Why can't I just...relax." He sighed when he started floating in the water.

"You can if you want to take longer to walk on your own or with a limp." She shrugged.

He sighed and motioned for her.

"Okay, show me what I need to do," he relented.

Half an hour later, he grunted.

"I didn't think it was possible to sweat while you were in a pool full of water." He felt his leg muscles scream at him.

"This is the first time you've moved like this in over a week," Lea said, pushing his left leg up to his chest. Well, okay, about a quarter of the way up to his chest. His torn muscles wouldn't allow him to move it up any further. He winced when pain shot through his entire leg and back, and Lea backed off.

It would have tortured him, having her touch him and be so close to him like this, but the truth was, he was in far too much agony to think of anything other than breathing through the pain.

"I think that's enough for today." She released her hold on his leg. "Want to relax a little?"

Hell yes, he did. But now he was so exhausted that he thought he might drown if he tried to float around in the pool. Besides, there was a group of guests that had arrived, and the pool was almost completely full.

"No, I think I'll head back to the cabin. Maybe come back a little later."

"Drink plenty of water," she said as he moved towards the stairs and his crutches. He was going to need to lean heavily on them to get back to the cabin.

"Here." A woman met him at the stairs and handed him his crutches. "Let me help you."

"Thanks," he mumbled.

"I've got you," Lea said behind him and wrapped her arm around his waist.

He was too tired to care about the look the two women exchanged. Instead, he hobbled as best as he could towards a chair so he could slip on his flip-flops and shirt.

Lea was there to help him.

"I can call and see if someone can give you a ride to your cabin," she said, pulling out her walkie-talkie.

He didn't want to seem so fragile, so he shook his head. "No, the fresh air will help. Besides, it's not that far."

Her eyes narrowed slightly as she scanned his face. "Are you sure?"

He nodded and slipped on his sunglasses. "Yup," he answered quickly and stood up.

"We'll do this again tomorrow," she called after him.

Thankfully, he was far enough away from her that she couldn't hear his groan. Or so he'd thought. Her soft chuckle floated in the breeze behind him.

He'd made it a quarter of the way back to his cabin when his leg seized up on him and he had to find a bench and take a break. He hadn't expected to be light-headed and had to breathe through the pain until his vision cleared.

"Are you okay?" a soft voice asked through the haze.

He glanced up and spotted the same blond woman who had handed him his crutches at the pool.

"Yeah," he said, standing up again. "Just... taking in the view."

Her smile told him that she didn't believe him. He turned to head back down the pathway, but she fell into step with him.

"Are you a guest?" she asked him.

"Sort of," he said, wishing instantly to be alone again. The pain was becoming unbearable, and he didn't want anyone to see how much pain he was in.

"I just got in this morning," she said with a sigh. "I hadn't realized how wonderful this place could be." She giggled.

When he'd first seen her, he'd expected her to be like the rest of the guests. Older. Now, as he looked at her, he could tell she was roughly his age. It threw him off.

She was young, extremely pale, and had almost white-blond hair, blue eyes, and an impressive double-D hourglass figure that would normally get any man's attention.

"Are you a guest?" he asked.

"No." She shook her head and giggled again. "I'm the new massage therapist."

"What happened to Andrea?" he asked as he stopped on the pathway. Her eyebrows shot up slightly.

"Oh, she's still here. Actually, she's my boss, in a way." She shrugged. "I noticed that you were working on your injured leg." She motioned to his left leg. "Was it a car accident?" she asked. When he didn't reply right away, she continued, "If so, I know the rest of you must be as sore. If you need to schedule a session…" She let the rest of her statement hang in the air.

Hell yes, he thought. That's just what he needed. A massage. But at that moment, the way Lea had looked at the blonde played over in his head.

"No, thanks," he said with a sigh. "For now, I'm going to do what the doctor orders." He smiled.

"Oh." She pouted a little. "Okay, well, if you change your mind, I'm Kara." She held out her hand.

"Brett." He shook her hand. "Welcome to River Camps."

"Thanks," she said with a slight frown. "Brett… Jewel?"

"That's me." He nodded.

"Gosh, it is you. I don't know why I didn't recognize you." She tilted her head. "You've got more facial hair than the pictures they used on the news."

He held in a groan and ran his hand over his stubbly face. "They used my rookie pictures from five years ago." He shrugged.

"Well, it's nice to meet you." She motioned to the pathway. "Need any help getting to where you're going?"

He wanted to agree but didn't want to let a stranger in on how much pain he was in.

"No, thanks. It's not far." He motioned back to the pathway she'd come down. "The main building is that way. If you get lost."

She glanced over her shoulder and then turned back to him and nodded. "Thanks. I'll see you around, Brett Jewel." She started walking down the pathway he'd just pointed out for her.

He didn't reply and continued back to his cabin. By the time he walked up the stairs, sweat was dripping down his arms, his legs, and his back. He wanted—no, needed—a cold shower.

Instead, he dropped his crutches on the floor and fell face-first onto the bed, and passed out asleep.

He woke when someone knocked on his door. He was instantly in a foul mood, as the pain was unbearable. His entire body had tensed up and even the muscles in his fingers ached.

"Go away," he murmured. Instead, the door opened. He didn't even have the energy to look over to see who had come in. If it was someone there to kill him, he'd just lay there and let them put him out of his misery.

When a platter of food was set on his nightstand, he figured he wasn't going to get so lucky.

"You look terrible." Lea's voice sounded from directly beside him.

He closed his eyes and turned his head away from her. "Thanks," he said sarcastically. He wanted to tell her to leave, but he didn't even have the strength to.

When her hands landed softly on his shoulders, he tensed for a split second, until she started rubbing his muscles.

"You really should have taken Kara up on her offer," she said softly.

He glanced over at her. "Spying on me?" he mumbled.

She smiled. "No, just walking down the same pathway and overheard." She shrugged.

"I like this private session with my doctor much better." He motioned for her to continue rubbing his shoulders. She narrowed her eyes at him but continued to rub his shoulders.

"You're really tense," she said after a moment.

He moaned and tried to breathe through the pain when she ran her hands down his back.

"You're overcompensating for your leg," she said.

"Over...?" he mumbled into the mattress.

"You're tensing up every muscle when you walk," she explained. "You need to learn to relax when you walk."

"It hurts too bad," he admitted, feeling groggy again. Her hands were doing wonders to his muscles. He hadn't realized what he'd owned up to, not until he felt her fingers still on his body.

"Are you in that much pain?" she asked.

He took a deep breath. "You worked me pretty hard in the pool," he admitted.

She sighed and started rubbing again. "I'll go easier on you tomorrow."

"No, don't. I want to recover as quickly as possible. A little pain will be worth it."

Her hands moved over him, going down to work on his lower back. He felt the tension melt away. His stomach chose that moment to let out a loud rumble.

"I brought you some food," she said with a chuckle as her hands stilled on his lower back.

"Later. Right now this is doing more for me than food will," he mumbled as she started working on him again.

CHAPTER 5

This was pure torture. Lea's hands ran over Brett's hard muscles, feeling his tension melt away like butter under her fingertips, while her own body started to ache in places that she'd ignored for longer than she cared to admit.

While she worked on releasing the tightness from his abused muscles, he made deep sexy sounds that had her wondering what it would be like to be with him. She pondered if he was a selfish lover, like the only other person she'd ever been with had been.

Her mind kept playing over scenario after scenario of what it would be like to enjoy the man that she was running her hands over. Of course, now, she was trying desperately to keep her movements professional, therapeutic, but her eyes, well, she ran them all over him. His powerful arms were easily as thick as her thighs, and his rugged shoulders were filled with cords of muscles that he spent a lot of time working on. His back was full of lean, toned muscles that led down to his narrow waist, a true athletic swimmer's build. His legs—well, at least his right leg, at the moment—were powerful, like the rest of him. His swim shorts, which had dried and sucked tight against his form, allowed her to admire the tightness of his butt. She wanted more than anything to dip her hands lower and feel just how firm and potent he was there.

"You're not listening to me," Brett said with a chuckle, getting her attention.

She jerked her eyes away from his ass and up to the back of his head as her hands stilled on his shoulders.

"Sorry, what?" she asked, feeling her entire body heat.

"I think you've worked out the worst of it," he repeated.

She yanked her hands away from him and stood up suddenly. "Sure, um…" She looked around, trying to remember where she was and why. She spotted the tray of food that she'd brought for him and took it over to the kitchen table.

The Cruiser cabin was one of the smaller cabins that Aiden and his crew had built in the past few years. It consisted of one giant room, a small kitchenette area with a dining table, a sofa, a television, a queen-sized bed, and even a gas fireplace. The bathroom, she knew, was well equipped for guests with physical limitations. It was one of the five wheelchair-accessible cabins.

This one had large windows that overlooked the surrounding forest of tall pine trees. It still had a view of the bay but wasn't directly on the water itself. Instead, it was across from a small grassy meadow. The pathway leading to the cabin was wide and handy for anyone with physical restrictions.

"Here." She set the tray down on the table. "I brought you lunch."

She heard him moving behind her but didn't look back to see what he was doing. When his hands landed on her shoulders, she jumped slightly.

"Sorry," he mumbled. She realized she'd been blocking the chair and stepped aside to let him sit down. "Thank you," he said, lifting the lid to the tray. "Chef Isaac strikes another home run." He chuckled. "Sit, have some lunch with me. There's plenty of it." He motioned to the full tray of food.

She opened her mouth to turn him down but realized she'd been so preoccupied with getting his food that she hadn't grabbed any for herself. Sitting, she reached over and grabbed a few fries from his plate.

"How's it going out there? Have you had to rescue anyone else today? Other than my sore muscles?" he joked.

"Just you, today." She took the bowl of fruit he offered her.

"Want half this burger?" he asked, cutting it in half.

"No, I'll stick with the fries and fruit."

"There's some drinks in the fridge." He motioned behind them. She stood up and walked over to the mini-fridge. Most of the cabin's fridges were restocked each day with basics for all the guests.

"What do you want?" she asked.

"I want a beer…" he started, but when she gave him a look, he sighed. "I'll have a Coke instead."

She smiled and reached in to grab two drinks, then returned to sit next to him.

"You've been hanging around a lot at the campgrounds." He glanced sideways at her. "Sticking around here just for me?"

She wanted to deny it, but she *had* requested a cut in her hours at the hospital since Brett's injury. It hadn't necessarily been because of him, or had it? She had been thinking of shifting her work schedule to be more available at the camp than the hospital. After all, they had enough interns and personnel to deal with the patients at the hospital. But she was the only medical staff at the camp, which meant that she was needed more here.

Not to mention that this job was far more relaxed and beneficial to her, in terms of both her pocketbook and her emotional fulfillment. She wanted—no, needed—to be needed.

Besides, if she was planning on opening her own practice, she needed to have more free time to plan.

"It was past time for me to cut back my hours at the hospital anyway," she said with a shrug.

He reached over and placed his hand over hers. "I never expected you to have to keep an eye out for me."

She smiled. "That's what friends do." She saw something close to sadness cross his eyes before he looked away. "What about you?" His eyebrows shot up. "Work," she hinted.

He sighed. "My captain says my job will be there for me when I've healed. If I want it."

"Do you?" she asked, trying not to sound too eager. He shrugged and set the burger down and took a drink.

"Part of me does. It's what I've wanted to do since..." He shook his head. "For as long as I can remember," he added softly.

This time it was her hand that touched his. She knew about his past. Well, most of it at any rate. It didn't take a genius to understand that being raised by a man of William Jewel's caliber would take a toll on any kid.

She had suspected that Brett had leaned towards law enforcement to stop bullies such as his father. The man had always heckled her, dating back to the first time she'd had a run-in with him at a football game, when he'd called her a gook for the first time. She hadn't understood him, since she'd never heard the derogatory slang before.

When Brett had started apologizing to her, she'd understood that his father had meant to be offensive. She'd been excited to run into his and Aiden's parents at the game, but after that, she'd steered clear of Brett's father.

Over the years, she'd had a few more run-ins with the man. Each time, he'd throw more curses her way, and she'd somehow grown numb to them. To him.

It wasn't as if he'd been the only one. Not that she'd been

verbally attacked on a regular basis. But living in the south, it happened more than it had when she'd been away at college.

"Now?" she asked Brett, holding her breath slightly as she waited for his answer.

He shook his head and glanced down at his leg. Then he glanced up at her. "What are the chances I'll shake this off soon and return to my old self?"

As a doctor, her gut reaction was to tell him the truth. Tell him everything. As a friend and someone who cared for him, she wanted to lie to him and tell him his chances were good.

"Odds are always fifty-fifty," she started, but he held up his hand to stop her. Then he leaned closer, took her hand in his, and lowered his voice slightly.

"Give it to me straight. None of this medical bull. You know what I can do. You know me," he said in a deep voice that had her insides jumping around like a kid on a trampoline. "Do you think I can get back to one hundred percent?"

She took a deep breath and shook her head. "You have extensive muscle and nerve damage in your leg. I believe you'll have to work the rest of your life to rebuild what was damaged and what you lost. If you're asking me if you can get back on the force, yes. There's no doubt in my mind that you could work… a desk job." She hated adding that last bit and felt his hand tighten around hers for a split second. "But the physical ability to return to what you were doing before?" She shook her head once. "I don't see that as being possible for a long time."

He sighed and dropped his hand from hers. "Thanks for your honesty." He stood up, took up his crutches, and leaned heavily on them. "I'm tired," he said. She jumped up from the table.

"I'll… let you rest," she said, feeling heavy-hearted. She walked over to the door and stopped to look back at him. His eyes were glued to his left leg, so she couldn't see how he was feeling. "Brett?" He glanced up at her, and she saw the heartbreak in his expression. "For what it's worth, I have faith that you will someday get back to one hundred percent."

He nodded quickly without saying anything, so she turned and left.

As she walked down the pathway towards the main pool area, she thought of how far her emotions had just swung. She'd gone from hot and heavy to sad and depressed in the span of a few heartbeats.

How had she allowed herself to build up her thoughts towards Brett so much? Seven days ago he'd been lying on the operating table with his leg wide open. She'd seen the damage a gunshot could do to a man.

She'd watched Brett grow from an awkward funny boy to a seriously potent kind-hearted man. Seeing him weak was like seeing Superman shot out of the sky.

She sat on a bench at the fork of the trail and wished she could have the rest of the day to think about what being around Brett had done to her. How she could possibly cheer him up. But she was due to make her rounds, which consisted of visiting the handful of guests that had physical needs. Most of the time it was just to check in on a diabetic or someone with limited mobility.

Today, there were four such guests that had checked in, and she wanted to introduce herself to them, if only to ensure them that she was on hand should any need arise.

"Lost?" someone asked her.

Glancing up, she smiled at an older man.

"No, just taking a break." She stood up.

The man smiled at her. "I'm lost. I was heading to the pool..." He glanced around at the many signs marking each pathway. "Left my glasses in my cabin."

She nodded. "I'm heading there myself. I'll show you the

way." She started walking and the man fell into step with her. She didn't have to slow her pace since her shorter legs easily allowed for his leisurely stride.

"Are you a guest here?" the man said.

"No, I'm the on-call doctor."

The man stopped and looked at her in surprise.

"You are?" he asked. She braced herself for what she assumed was coming, but instead, the man chuckled. "Damn, they're making doctors younger and younger these days. Prettier too."

She laughed and took his arm in hers. "Flattery will get you everywhere," she joked as they started walking. "Are you here alone?"

"No, my wife, Mia, went to one of those fancy classes up at the main building while I slept in like a baby." He sighed. "First time I could do so in years." He chuckled. "I'm meeting her for a late-morning swim and lunch."

"May I suggest the Mahi-mahi sandwich? It's superb," she suggested.

"It was on my list to try." The man patted her hand.

"Here we are now," she said when they stepped into the patio area for the pool. There were more than a dozen tables set up where food and drinks were served all day long.

She spotted an older Asian woman walking towards them with a big smile on her lips.

"There you are, Henry. I was getting worried you'd gotten lost." The woman's eyes turned to her. "I see you've already picked my younger replacement," she added in a joking tone.

Henry laughed and took his wife in his arms and kissed her. "Mia, there is no replacement for you." He kissed her again. "I was just meeting the camp's on-call doctor." He turned towards her. "I didn't get your name?"

"Dr. Lea Val," she said easily.

"Val?" the man said, his eyebrows going up. "As in Ken Val?"

Lea nodded. "Yes, he's my father."

The man laughed. "Then we're in luck. We're here to meet your father on some business. He suggested while we're down here to check this place out and take some time to enjoy ourselves."

"We were just lucky to get in when we did. Apparently, there was a cancellation that opened up a cabin for us," Mia said with a smile while she held onto her husband's arm. "We've only been here a day and I can already tell we'll be back again soon," she joked.

"That all depends on how well my meeting goes with Ken." Henry laughed.

"Have you known my father long?" she asked.

Henry laughed again, and she followed him over to sit at one of the tables. He motioned for her to sit, and she did so, along with Mia.

"I've known of Ken Val for over thirty years. I've met the man all of zero times," Henry said, causing her eyebrows to shoot up. "Tomorrow's meeting will be our first face-to-face."

"Wow, why haven't you two met before?" she asked.

"They were sworn enemies," Mia added.

Henry waved his hand. "Nothing as ominous as that. We were simply competitors. I own FLD, Flemings Lighting Distribution. Your father owns Val Industries." Henry shrugged. "Until now, we never had to meet."

"Why now?" Val asked, feeling her stomach roll. Her father had been grumbling about financial issues lately. But then he'd been complaining most of her life how his business was hard.

Running a large lighting company that supplied most of the office and home light fixtures in several states had been a good business for her family. Not that her mother hadn't made her own contributions. Being a lawyer had some benefits, but her mother had chosen to be a public defender, which had left her father's business as the bigger source of income.

For as long as Lea could remember, her mother had loved her job and had been a huge role model for Lea.

"Your father has finally agreed to meet with me," Henry added.

She wanted to ask him more, but just then Dean, one of the waitstaff, showed up and handed them menus.

"I'll let you enjoy your lunch." Lea stood up.

"Thank you for helping me find my way," Henry said.

"You're welcome. Enjoy your stay." She turned to head towards the main building, all the while worrying that her father's business was in jeopardy.

Maybe now wasn't the best time for her to cut her hours at the hospital. After all, it was good money. Not private practice money, but good enough to help her save up for her own place.

But if her parents were in trouble, she knew without a doubt that she would step in and help them.

She finished making her rounds and decided to swing by their house on the way home. Her parents still lived in the older home in downtown Pelican Point. The massive three-story place had killer views, a swimming pool her parents had put in when she'd been a pre-teen, and a dock that her father's pride and joy could be launched from. The fishing boat's name was *Quiet Time*.

The home was less than two miles from her old school and was easily one of the largest homes in Pelican Point.

Before leaving for the day, she thought about heading back out to talk to Brett, but she wasn't sure what she would say to him. She didn't have an excuse to see him again, other than to check up on him, and she didn't want to become the nagging doctor type.

She was walking towards the parking lot when she spotted

Brett and Kara talking on the pathway closest to the parking lot. It was difficult not to let jealousy consume her. She had to take a couple of deep breaths to stop herself from stomping her foot in frustration as she watched the pair flirt.

When she'd finally calmed down, she made a decision to divert away from the couple and take a shortcut to her car through the trees. That was until she glanced back and saw Kara playfully slap at Brett's shoulder, which sent him toppling backward.

Lea was beside Brett, holding him upright, in less than a heartbeat. She berated Kara for her carelessness.

"Easy tiger," Brett said, interrupting her calmly, shifting his crutches. "I'm okay," he assured her.

CHAPTER 6

 atching Lea shift into full-time protection mode was a sight he would never forget.

"She almost made you fall over." Lea turned her eyes towards him, and he could see the anger in them.

He glanced over at Kara, who looked upset. She started apologizing.

"I didn't think…" the woman was saying. "I'm so sorry."

"I'm fine," Brett told both of them. "I just wasn't ready for it." In truth, he doubted at this time he could have stood up if anyone tried to blow on him.

After Lea had left earlier, he'd pulled out the weights he'd convinced Aiden to bring him and had worked out until he couldn't lift his arms or his good leg anymore. He knew better than to try and work on his left leg at this point. Just the physical therapy he did twice a week was enough exercise on that leg for now.

After working out, he'd looked at the time and had known that Lea would be getting off work soon. So he had made his way towards the parking lot, after a quick shower. He'd hoped that he would catch her, if just to tell her thanks for the meal. Instead, he'd bumped into Kara. Again.

It wasn't as if the woman wasn't attractive. But he'd never really gone for the blond, busty, straight-off-the-cover-of-a-magazine type. She was nice enough that he figured they could be friends, though.

It was obvious, however, that she'd gone out of her way to hunt him down. He'd have to break it to her gently that he wasn't interested in anything other than a friendship, which he'd been doing when she'd playfully slugged him on the shoulder, causing him to lose his balance.

Watching Lea turn on her defensive mode had an odd effect on him. He felt his libido stir and mentally kicked himself for coming all this way. He doubted he had enough energy to do anything about the attraction he felt. Another reason why he should have stayed in the cabin and not come out into the heat of the night to find Lea.

"You should be resting." Lea turned on him. "You look like death."

He chuckled a little. "Thanks. I think."

Lea gripped his arm and started walking—no, scratch that—marching him back down the pathway. He didn't even have a chance to say goodbye to Kara. When he glanced back, Kara was watching them with an apologetic look on her face.

He would have to make a point next time he bumped into her to reassure her that she hadn't done anything wrong. After all, it wasn't her fault that he was as fragile as a newborn. No, that was on him for barging in on a carjacking.

"I worked out," he heard himself telling Lea as they walked towards his cabin. He must be delirious if he was admitting everything to her.

"Good," she mumbled. "Next time, however, stop before you fall over," she said as they reached his cabin.

"I'm not..." he started to say as he tripped on the bottom step. He shifted with his crutch as she caught him and held him firmly upright. "How are you so strong?" he asked as she pulled him through the doorway.

"I'm not. You're just weak right now." She nudged him onto the sofa. "Sit, I'll get you some water." She disappeared into the kitchen area before he could argue.

He hadn't realized how thirsty he was until after he'd had a drink of the ice-cold water Lea handed him. Nor had he realized just how sore he was until he'd sat down. His right leg was throbbing, which threw him off until he thought about how much he was having to rely on it to compensate for his left one.

He realized Lea was watching him, her eyes running over his face, and he shifted slightly, holding back a slight wince as he did so.

"You pushed yourself too hard," she said suddenly with a frown.

"No, I'm—"

She waved her hand in the air, stopping him. "Don't deny it. I'm trained to spot it." She pointed at him. "You pushed yourself too hard. Why?" Her eyes narrowed. "Is it because of the blonde?"

"No," he burst out and almost laughed. There was no way he was going to tell her it was because he hated feeling helpless. Hated not being able to trust his body to do simple things like walk or, hell, stand up even.

He felt like a child. His damn leg hurt whenever he did anything. He even had to sit to take a piss now because he'd almost fallen on his ass when he'd tried to stand and do it. He was thankful there was a large bench in the shower, so he could at least take his time and clean up properly.

"It seems like the two of you keep bumping into one another," Lea said, a look crossing her face that he just couldn't pinpoint.

He was silent for a moment and then a slow smile curved his lips.

"Jealous?" he teased.

There was a moment of silence before Lea burst out laughing. "You're delusional." She moved over to take his water glass and pour him more, but he stopped her by taking her wrist. Before he knew what he was doing, he pulled her onto his right thigh and kissed her.

If he'd been thinking about it, he would have realized it was a terrible move. Like when he'd kissed her that first time last year when she'd been drunk and had looked sexy as hell in the little black dress that she'd worn that night.

This, this was something different. Maybe he *was* delusional. Maybe almost dying had caused him to throw all caution to the wind.

Whatever the reason, he allowed his body to take over as he took her mouth and enjoyed the taste and feel of her plastered against him. Her fingers dug into his hair, ensuring him that she was enjoying the kiss as much as he was.

His body came alive under her, and he thought maybe he did have enough strength for a little pleasure. But then she pulled away suddenly and jumped off his lap.

"I..." She looked around and, without saying anything further, bolted for the door. Before he could recover his voice or his thoughts, he was alone in the cabin.

He must have sat there for fifteen minutes before he had the strength to get up and fall face-first into bed again.

He woke to the sound of rain and thunder, which meant that he'd have to skip his planned morning swim.

As he made his way, carefully, down the wet pathway

towards the main building, he realized just how nice it was to get out of the cabin more often.

For the past week, Lea or Aiden and all his other friends had delivered his meals to him. But since he'd woken up early enough, he figured he'd beat them to it that morning.

When he walked into the employees' dining room, he spotted the gang of friends sitting at their usual table. Since he knew he wouldn't be able to carry a tray of food and use his crutches, he made his way towards them and stilled when he spotted Lea in the middle of everyone.

Her eyes met his, and he could tell when they darted away that she was going to avoid talking about what they'd done yesterday.

Actually, the entire table grew quiet as he approached. He didn't need to be a detective to surmise that the group had been talking about him.

"Morning," he said cheerfully.

"Brett." Elle stood up quickly and pushed out a chair for him. "What are you doing here? Aubrey was just going to deliver your breakfast." Elle motioned to Aubrey.

"I needed the fresh air," he admitted as he sat down. "Besides, I was going stir crazy being cooped up like that."

He noticed a few looks across the table.

"Want me to grab you some breakfast?" Aubrey jumped up and motioned towards the buffet.

"Sure," he said. "Lots of bacon," he called after her. When he turned back to the table, everyone was looking at him, and he figured there was only one way to get to the bottom of what was going on—to ask. "So, what's the latest gossip on that Brett guy?" he asked with a whisper as his eyes met Lea's again. "I hear his doctor caught him taking a walk last night."

Scarlett laughed as Lea choked on her coffee.

"Sorry," Scarlett said, clearing her throat. "At least his humor didn't get damaged," she added as she sipped her water.

"No, but his brain obviously did," Lea added under her breath, causing his eyebrows to shoot up.

"Problem?" he asked her directly.

"Yes." She set her mug down with a slight bang, causing the coffee she'd been drinking to slosh over the rim. "Do you think this is some sort of joke?" Lea put her hands on the table, and her knuckles turned white as she gripped the edge of it. "Less than a week ago, you almost lost your life, or your leg. Now you're galivanting around the campgrounds, chasing women."

"Women?" His voice cracked and he cleared his throat. "Really?" He narrowed his eyes at her, trying to assess her mood. "You know very well I wasn't… chasing women."

"Just one woman then," Lea countered as she crossed her arms over her chest.

He felt his temper grow as well as his desire. How could the woman infuriate him and turn him on at the same time?

"I told you we just bumped into one another," he responded.

"Oh?" Lea laughed. "How many times over the years have I heard that one from you or Aiden?"

"Hey, don't bring me into this," Aiden said, and quickly earned an elbow to his ribs from his cousin Elle.

"You had no business taking long walks in your condition," Lea said, ignoring Aiden's comment.

"I seem to remember my doctor mentioning it was a good idea to take walks."

"Short walks. To the pool or to the dining hall, but not the parking lot."

"Your food," Aubrey said, interrupting the argument. "Why were you out at the parking lot?" Aubrey asked innocently. She'd missed the first part of the conversation and, since he was in a foul mood, he answered her truthfully.

"I wanted to see Lea," he said before he shoved a piece of crispy bacon in his mouth.

The entire table turned to Lea, who sat there, watching him.

"You… did?" she asked after a moment.

"Yeah, I wanted to thank you for helping me out earlier." He shoved another piece of bacon in his mouth. "Bringing me food, helping me out with the exercise in the pool, the back rub." He shrugged and suddenly felt stupid. "It really helped yesterday. I finally felt good enough to work out. Which is why I was exhausted when I finally caught up with you."

"You should have called or texted me instead of walking all the way out to the parking lot. Alone," she said softly.

"Believe me, I will next time. I slept like the dead." He sighed. "I was hoping for another session in the pool today, but…" He glanced towards the large windows that looked out towards a large grassy area, the main pool and pool house, and the water of the bay beyond. Normally you could see it all. Today, however, it was nothing but gray and white haze as the rain continued to stream down.

He normally liked the rain, but today it was just another reason he was feeling trapped. A feeling he had all too often when he'd been a kid, living at home with his father.

Now he was trapped inside his own body. One that just wouldn't do what it could have easily done over a week ago.

"There's still plenty of therapy we can do," Lea assured him. "If you want, we can check and see when one of the rooms is open and hit the mats?"

He couldn't stop the images of him and Lea rolling around on a mat. Every other man would have thought the same about getting the woman he was hot for naked and on a mat under him.

Her eyes went wide as if she understood what he was thinking, and she turned away from him.

"I'm done with my next class at eleven in the blue room," Aubrey offered cheerfully. "The room won't be used again until after two."

"That will work," Lea said. "If you're up to it. You should go back and rest some more, then we can meet there at eleven thirty?"

"Works for me," he said without really thinking about it. He didn't know what she had planned for him but figured anything was better than being cooped up in the cabin alone for the entire day.

"Good, then eat your breakfast." She pushed a plate of fruit Aubrey had gotten him towards him. "You'll need the energy." Lea stood up and, without waiting for a response, walked away.

"Oh, you're in trouble now," Aiden said, slapping his back slightly.

For the rest of the meal, he listened while the friends did what they normally did—gossiped about everything. Zoey and Dylan's baby, and Hannah and Owen's wedding were the top two subjects.

The wedding, it seemed, was all planned. Brett was kind of sad that he'd be missing the bachelor party, since they were heading into Destin for a guy's night out. There was no way he would be able to keep up with everyone.

The wedding was the following weekend, and he even doubted he'd be able to sit through the services, unless he started building up his tolerance again.

Zoey and Dylan's baby, —little junior, as they called it—was due to arrive any day now. The topic changed to shifting schedules so that both Zoey and Dylan could be off work for the foreseeable future to care for the newborn.

Since he was an only child, he hadn't been around kids a lot, not ones fresh from the oven, at any rate. Being a police officer, he'd volunteered his time to stop off at the schools and talk to youngsters about drugs and crime, though.

He liked kids. Really. Had always thought he'd have a few of them running around one day himself. But with his friends getting married and starting families of their own, it seemed as if everyone was ready for them while he was still in the "someday" mindset.

At some point, Aubrey and Elle disappeared to teach their many classes, leaving him alone with Dylan and Zoey.

Since their marriage, Dylan had taken on more of a management role around the camp. When he'd first come to River Camps, he'd been in charge of the zip line and a few other attractions. Now, however, he oversaw most of the grounds. He made sure all the attractions were working and that the employees were skilled at doing their jobs.

Brent didn't know much more about what he or his brother Liam did around the campgrounds. He knew that Liam had built most of the benches and other wood furniture on the grounds. He also ran a wood shop class for the guests.

The brothers always seemed to be busy and happy. He figured that was in part due to the ability to work with their fiancées.

The story of how they had come to the campgrounds in the first place was a rumor that drifted among the employees and the guests still. He knew the legal side of things, as he'd been the one to arrest their cousin, Joel Copeland, for both kidnapping Hannah last year and murdering his father and stepfather in the years previous. The man was rotting in a jail cell, much like Zoey and Scarlett's stepmother, Bridgette, and her mother, Martha, for almost killing Aiden and Harold Smith, one of the richest men in the world.

He still found it odd that Aubrey was Harold Smith's daughter. That was one rumor that hadn't floated around the camp.

He doubted many people, other than the Wildflowers, knew about it. Knowing how private of a person Aubrey was, he didn't question that she kept that bit of information to herself.

Once he was done eating, he'd stick around the pool area, under the awning, and enjoy the rain until it was time to hit the class.

"Where are you heading to?" Lea asked him when he caught up with her just outside the doors. Her eyes traveled quickly over him.

"I was…" he started, but her eyebrows arched up. "Where do you want me to be?" he asked, hating that he sounded too tired to argue with her. It was normally the highlight of his day.

"I booked you a massage," she answered. "We need to limber you up again before we build up your muscles."

A massage sounded… wonderful.

"You did?" he asked, then he smiled. "Thanks."

She nodded and took his free arm. He tucked both crutches under his left arm and walked slowly with her towards the pool house, which also housed the massage rooms.

While they walked, she talked about getting him a scooter.

He stopped walking. "Like they have in Italy?" he asked, causing her to laugh.

"No, it's one of the kinds that you push yourself. There's a platform for your leg, so you don't have to use the crutches," she answered.

He'd seen them around and glanced down at his leg. Since it was his thigh that had been damaged, he figured he would be able to tolerate scooting around the grounds on one of those. It might make him move faster, not to mention take less of his energy to get around.

They'd given him his very own golf cart to get around, which he used when he wasn't on the walking pathways.

They hurried together through the rain under a large

umbrella, as much as he could hurry, and stepped into the pool house just as the rain grew heavier.

"Torrential rains." Lea rolled her eyes. "It must be spring in Florida."

He chuckled. "Thanks for getting me here safe." He spotted Kara standing behind the counter in front of the massage rooms.

"Oh." Lea turned to him. "I didn't just get you here. I'm the one giving you the massage." She walked over and opened the door to the private massage room.

Images of Lea running her hands over him once more had him holding in a groan.

He'd been hoping for Kara since he knew he could keep it professional. Sure, the woman was pretty, but he wouldn't have to fight all the feelings he had for her because he had none. But Lea… There was too much between them. Too much he thought of her. Too much he felt for her.

The next hour of his life was going to be pure hell.

CHAPTER 7

"Stop tensing," Lea said, trying to keep her tone soothing.

"I'm not." Brett groaned, and she felt his muscles tense even further.

"You are too." She sighed and started to work out the new tension she felt in his shoulders. This was a bad idea. She knew it, but when she'd texted Andrea to schedule a time for Brett, Aubrey had mentioned that she was out for the day and that Kara was booked solid, but the room was available.

How hard could it be, giving someone a massage? After all, she knew more about the human body than either of those two women. So she'd booked the room for herself. She hadn't planned on Brett fighting her all the way.

"Stop it," she hissed when she felt him tense again.

"This isn't working." He started to get up. She placed her hands squarely on his shoulders and held him down. He was lying face down on the massage table, with nothing but a white towel laying low over his hips.

"You just need to relax," she suggested.

"How can I?" he groaned. "You're killing me."

She took a deep breath. "I'm barely touching you."

"Yeah, and it's killing me," he mumbled.

"I can apply more pressure if you think you can handle it," she offered.

He was silent. "No," he finally added. "Distract me by talking to me. Tell me about work."

She bit her bottom lip as she started running her hands over him again. She glanced up at the ceiling, hating to keep the truth from him. "Well… work's work. Oh, the other day I pulled a two-inch sliver from under a man's toenail." She smiled.

"Ouch," he replied, and she felt him tense once more. "Okay, maybe don't talk about work. Tell me how Raya's doing in Orlando. Is she still Mulan?"

"Yes." Lea smiled. "And loving it. She's gotten another acting job at the shows in Hollywood Studios. She gets to sing and dance instead of just take pictures with kids. She's in heaven."

"She was a big hit in the school plays," Brett said, and she felt him relax a little.

"She's met a man," she added and for the next few moments she talked to him about her sister's love life. The more she talked, the more he relaxed his shoulders. When she moved her hands to his lower back, he tensed.

"Let's just stick to my shoulders today," he suggested.

"I wanted to look at your thigh," she said, taking a step back. "Flip over."

"No," he surprised her by saying quickly. "I'm done." He sat up, facing away from her, and wrapped the towel around his waist. "I think that's good enough for now."

"Brett." She moved around the table. "I'm your doctor. I'll need to look at the incisions and—"

"Later," he said quickly, reaching for his shorts and shirt.

She placed a hand on his chest, holding him onto the table.

"Lea." Her name was a warning growl. "I said…later."

Her eyes moved down to his lips, and she dreamed of kissing them. Then, before she knew what she was doing, before she could help it, she moved closer.

The entire time she'd been running her hands over his muscles and talking, she'd dreamed of being with him.

Before she could decide what she was going to do next, he pulled her between his thighs and kissed her. It wasn't like before, when he'd run his lips slowly over hers. This time it was all heat and speed, as if it had been building up for years.

She was so shocked at the urgency in his movements that she couldn't respond, only enjoy as he took her mouth deeper. He moved his mouth over her lips while his hands gripped her hips, holding her firmly against him.

She scraped her nails against his bare shoulders and heard a low moan emanating from his chest.

"Lea." This time her name was a plea, and she was desperate to give him anything he wanted. A flood of brazenness washed over her, and she pushed him back onto the massage table and covered his body with her own. Her legs were on either side of his hips as she took control of the kiss.

His hands had stilled on her hips, until she started gliding over him, feeling just what the kiss and the massage had done to him.

He was so hard under the towel against her that she couldn't stop from gliding over him, enjoying the way her cotton shorts rode up. His fingers nudged the material even further until he cupped her ass.

She arched for him, willing him to take it further. When his fingers scraped under her shorts and found her, she moaned his name, encouraging him on.

Moving just slightly, she reached down and pushed the towel away until she could wrap her fingers around his length.

"Lea," he groaned, and she was afraid he'd stop her, but instead, he shifted slightly until he nudged her shorts off her hips.

She kicked them onto the floor and smiled down at him.

"Come here." He pulled her back on top of him.

This time, when her fingers wrapped around him, he rested his hand over her panties and rubbed her through the light material.

"God, you feel so good," he said between kisses.

She went back to rubbing herself against him. He slid his finger under the silk of her panties, and she held perfectly still as he dipped a finger into her.

She could have never expected the intensity of the explosion that wracked her entire body.

"Brett," she said against his lips as tears slipped out of her eyes. "I..."

Just then there was a knock on the outer door, signaling that their time was almost up. She froze in place.

There she was, her shorts on the floor, his fingers still embedded deep within her. Her camp shirt was hiked up, exposing her bra, while she straddled a very naked man. She glanced down and could see the bandages on Brett's thigh. She carefully but quickly jumped down from the table.

Before he could say anything, she pulled on her clothes and tossed the towel back at him. "I'll see you at eleven-thirty," she said and left quickly.

Her face heated when she noticed Kara standing outside the door.

"So?" the blond said cheerfully. "How's your patient doing?"

"Good," she said quickly and left. She wasn't in the mood to chat nor explain why she was breathing so heavily.

Oh god, had Kara heard her cry out Brett's name when she'd come?

Hell, she needed the cool spring rain and a very long walk to cool her off.

She was trying not to think about Brett, so she called her father once more to see how his meeting with Henry from FLD had gone. She'd stopped by her parents' place, worried that her dad's business was failing in some way.

Instead, he'd informed her that he was thinking of merging his business with FLD and that it was going to be a very lucrative deal.

It appeared as if both her father and Henry were tired of running their separate businesses and had finally decided on a mutually beneficial agreement.

When she called him, her father had informed her that they had come to terms and had gotten along well enough that the Flemings would be returning to the area in a few weeks' time to officially seal the deal.

Her dad even joked that this could be the perfect time for him to retire. Again.

She felt more centered as she walked into the exercise room two hours later. She was early and sat in the back to catch the end of Aubrey's judo class.

Lea had always wanted to take judo, but her schoolwork and education had always come first. Actually, she'd put a lot of things in her life on hold for her education.

Like dating and sex. Which was probably why she was starved for attention. It was the only logical explanation for why she was so hot for Brett. Sure, he was sexy as hell and a great guy. Not to mention that he had been there for most of her life.

Even though he'd been annoying those first few years after she'd moved there, he'd turned funny and kind. By a year later, they'd settled into friendship, which had lasted up until he'd kissed her for the first time.

Now, she didn't know how to describe what was between

them or what they had done in the massage room. What was that, anyway?

Maybe he was just as horny as she was? Maybe she had been just a convenience?

Would he have done that to Kara if she'd been the one giving him a massage? That thought had her tensing and upset her stomach.

She'd been so deep in thought that she hadn't realized Aubrey's class had ended and the room had practically emptied out.

"Plotting someone's death?" Aubrey asked cheerfully as she sat down next to her.

Aubrey Smith was the most perfect porcelain-doll type woman. Lea had been jealous of her from the moment she'd met her a few years back. The woman oozed sexuality from the tips of her red hair down to the perfectly manicured pink toenails she showcased each time she wore sandals. She spoke like someone who had been raised in boarding schools and had dined with presidents.

Not that Lea hadn't had her moments in the spotlight. Graduating from Harvard had been fun. At least Lea had been able to dress up in a fancy gown a few times in her life.

"No, just… daydreaming," she answered Aubrey. "How was class?"

"Great." Aubrey rolled her shoulders. "You should join in one day."

"I…" She started to turn her down but then nodded. "I will. Soon," she promised with a smile. "How are the wedding plans coming along?"

"They're coming. We sort of put our plans on hold until after Hannah and Owen's big day next week, but they're coming along." Aubrey's smile grew. "There's a lot to do before the big day." She leaned back and took a sip of her refillable River Camps water bottle.

"Which is?" she asked, glancing sideways at Aubrey.

"Christmas Day," Aubrey answered easily.

"Going for the big day?" she asked with a chuckle.

Aubrey's smile turned slightly wicked. "It'll piss off my dad."

"How's that going?" she asked, knowing all the trouble Aubrey had endured growing up with the cold older man.

"You'd think that after we saved his life he'd be a little grateful. Or at least accepting of our relationship. But Aiden's been great about the entire situation." Aubrey sighed slightly, and Lea heard the love in her tone.

"Yeah, he's been great all his life," Lea joked.

Lea glanced up when Aubrey's attention moved to the doorway. Brett stood just inside the door, looking at them.

"Didn't mean to interrupt," he said a little sharply.

Aubrey jumped up and cheerfully excused herself.

"You didn't have to be rude to her," Lea told him.

"Me?" Brett tossed his crutches down and sat on the mat. "I'd never be rude to Aubrey."

She wanted to say, "Then you were being rude to me?" but instead she sat across from him on the floor and her heart fell a little.

It was true. She had just been a convenience to him. Just knowing that he would have kissed anyone like that had her mood turning foul.

"What do you have planned for me?" he asked after a moment.

She thought of the moves she'd just watched Aubrey do on a fellow student and imagined her holding Brett in the thigh lock and squeezing until…

"Stretches," she said quickly as she shook the thought from her mind. "Lots of them." If she couldn't use judo on him, she figured she could cause him pain in other ways, like he'd just caused in her.

Half an hour later, she watched with pleasure as sweat rolled down his forehead. Still, she could feel the muscles in his legs stretching farther now than when they'd started.

The doctor in her was pleased with his progress. The woman in her wanted to make him suffer even more, but she could see the weariness behind his eyes now and knew she'd pushed him too far. She wished he would complain or at least groan in pain. Just a little. For her own satisfaction. Instead, he'd remained silent the entire time.

"I think you've worked hard enough," she said, getting up from the mat. She handed him a bottle of water. "You should be drinking thirty-five milliliters of fluid per kilogram of body weight per day." She stopped when he glanced up at her and rolled his eyes. "Drink eight fluid ounces more a day than you normally would," she added.

When he was done drinking, she helped him stand up and gave him his crutches. She made sure he was steady before walking over and checking her phone. She'd hoped to have a message to distract her from talking to him further, but her phone was quiet.

"Elle mentioned that you signed on a place to open your own practice?" Brett asked as he moved slowly closer to her.

She'd just signed the paperwork on one of the units in a new building going up on the outskirts of town. She had been waiting for the last of the paperwork to go through before telling everyone else. It was one of the messages she was waiting and hoping for on her phone.

"I'm trying," she said a little dryly.

"Having problems?" He sat down on the bench where she and Aubrey had sat earlier.

"Nothing I can't handle."

"You don't have to go it alone. I know people." He wiggled his eyebrows.

"So do I," she replied. "Probably the same people you do. We did grow up in town together, remember?"

He chuckled. "I remember." He sighed. "So, earlier…"

She shrugged and tried to not let him see her heart beating out of her chest. "You don't have to apologize."

He reached out and took her hand, holding her in place in front of him. She met his eyes.

"I wasn't going to. I was going to say that I want it to happen again." He pulled her a little closer. "Soon." His eyes moved to her lips.

She almost fell into his lap as he tugged her down onto his good knee and kissed her once again. Whereas before the kisses were filled with urgency, this time it was slow, filled with wonder, and extremely passionate. More passion than she'd experienced in her entire life.

Her mind, which had been flooded with a million thoughts moments before, cleared completely. Now she focused only on Brett and what he was doing to her. How he was making her feel. As if for the first time in her entire life.

"Why?" she asked with a sigh as he moved his lips lower to her neck.

The low chuckle that emanated from his chest had her opening her eyes.

"I would think that's obvious," he answered before trailing his lips down her neck and behind her ear, and then taking her earlobe into his mouth and sucking lightly. The move caused her eyes to cross with pleasure.

"Brett." She shifted on his lap and then stilled when he hissed with pain. Jerking up, she stood over him as he began to rub his left thigh.

"I'm okay." He smiled up at her. "Just… sore from the intense workout you just gave me."

She heard his stomach growl loudly and suddenly everything came back to her. She realized where they were. She could even hear voices and music from guests in the next room as they went through one of Elle's Zumba classes.

"You should head on in and get something to eat," she said, turning away and taking up her bag with her change of clothes in it. She had to head into the hospital for her shift.

"Lea?" he said, causing her to stop at the door. She turned and looked at him when he didn't say anything else right away. He was still sitting there, looking hungry and in pain. She wanted to rush to him, to help him, but instead, she gripped her bag more tightly.

"Yes?" she finally said. He sighed.

"Thanks." He motioned to his leg. "For… looking out for me."

Instead of answering, she nodded and left quickly. She didn't trust her voice. Didn't trust that she wouldn't break down and either cry or scream with excitement. At this point, she was so wound up that she was afraid that she'd explode if he touched her again.

She took the back pathway to the parking lot so she could avoid bumping into anyone else and then sat in her car for a moment to collect her composure before heading back to her place to shower before work. Normally, she'd use the showers in the pool house and change into her scrubs, but she was too afraid someone would ask her how she was doing or, worse, see what Brett's kisses had done to her. She knew it was written clearly on her face.

He'd changed her. Just knowing that he wanted her, wanted to be with her, affected who she was and what she wanted out of life. Now she had a new goal to aim for. Brett.

CHAPTER 8

*B*rett must have sat there in the empty exercise room for close to fifteen minutes before his breathing settled. Then he gathered himself and slowly headed towards the dining room.

He'd been going to his regular physical therapy sessions five times a week, but this had been something completely different. Lea had stretched his thigh, moved it in ways that Ken, his PT, hadn't done yet.

After that workout, he was just thankful he had the energy to move around the grounds on his own accord.

He wasn't technically staff or a guest, but he'd been told he could eat in either dining room. Both the staff dining area and the guest dining area were nice. The guest areas included the pool patio dining area on sunny days, the main dining hall, and an outdoor patio area just outside. The guests could also order picnics to take to the private beach or get room service.

Since it was still raining outside, he chose to head to the main dining room. The place wasn't packed, but there were enough guests that he didn't feel lonely.

At night, he knew the massive dining hall could be decorated for dances or big events. It was large enough to house enough people for concerts yet filled with classy furniture that made it feel intimate. There was a long bar near the back set of windows that overlooked the grounds and the bay.

Since he was alone, he made his way back to the bar area and figured he'd watch the game as he chatted with Britt, the camp's main bartender. He'd known the older woman for almost ten years now, ever since she'd moved into town with her partner, Theresa. The two of them were, without a doubt, some of his favorite people in Pelican Point.

Theresa helped out with every event in town, such as holiday parades and book fairs. She was not only on the city council, but she also owned and ran a small local café, Sunset Café, which had the best burgers in town. No offense to the fancy chef they had out here at the camps, but Isaac couldn't hold a greasy spatula to Theresa's bacon double cheeseburger heart attack. Just thinking about it made his stomach growl again.

"Hold on there, boy-o." Britt laughed at the loud sound. "Here, munch on these until you order something." She set a basket of fries in front of him. "They were for me, but since they can hear your stomach in Russia…" She winked at him. "I'll order some more for me."

"Thanks," he said, taking up a fry and shoving it in his mouth. "Burger me," he added. "Loaded." He shoved another fry in his mouth.

"Will do." She nodded. "Drink?"

"Coke. No alcohol until I'm off the pain meds. And seeing as I'm in a lot of pain right now, I plan on taking a few with my burger." He groaned as he ran his hand lightly over his thigh muscle.

Britt punched in his order on the computer screen and

glanced up at him. "That bad? I thought after seeing you hobbling around here that you'd be on the mend."

"I was," he said after a few more fries, "until Lea got her hands on me." He watched Britt's eyebrows shoot up.

"Oh, so it is like that," the woman practically purred as she set his drink down in front of him. "Looks like I win that pot."

"No," he growled out, but at the same time he remembered how wonderful Lea had felt on his lap. How she'd looked when she'd hovered over him. When he'd made her come and with her body plastered against his as her lips…

Britt's laughter had his mind clearing.

"Right." She dragged out the word and leaned on the counter to look at him. "That look"—she pointed to his face— "is the look of a goner."

His eyes narrowed. "You don't know—"

Her eyebrows arched and he shut his mouth.

"I thought so," Britt added with a smile, straightening to take a couple of empty bottles that someone had set on the bar. "You may be a cop, but you have a shit poker face." She chuckled as she walked over to take someone else's order.

He sat in silence and watched the game, trying to get his mind off Lea as he waited for his food. When Britt set a massive burger in front of him, along with a large slice of berry pie, his sour attitude faded away.

"You're a woman who knows what a man needs." He took a bite of his burger.

Britt laughed. "It's not hard. They either want food or beer." She leaned in and lowered her voice. "Anything else you'll have to find another woman for. Cuz I'm taken." She winked at him.

"Theresa's a lucky woman," he said with a full mouth.

"You'll find your own soon enough if you don't already have your eye on her," Britt added.

"Hey there, stranger." Kara stopped and leaned against the bar next to him. "Fancy meeting you here."

He swallowed the bite of the burger and washed it down with a sip of his drink before responding.

"Seeing as I'm being held prisoner and tortured here, go figure," he joked.

"Oh no, we can't have you thinking this is a jail." Her eyes narrowed. "And who is torturing you?"

He opened his mouth but then shut it again and shrugged. "At least the food is good." He motioned to his half-eaten burger.

"It's by far the best burger in town," Kara added.

"A tie, I'd wager," he said. "Sunset Café has one of my favorites."

Kara nodded. "I'll have to give it a try sometime." She leaned further onto the bar. "So, I have a cancellation for my one o'clock session. If you want the spot, it's yours."

His gut reaction was to turn it down since he'd already had a massage that day. Even if that one hadn't done anything to relax him. He also remembered how Lea had reacted towards Kara. But Lea was a professional and he was in a lot of pain after she'd worked on him. Maybe a massage would help him relax since Lea had just tortured him further.

"Sure, I'll take it," he answered.

"Good." Kara's smile doubled. "I'll see you after you're done eating." She grabbed the bag of food she'd ordered from Britt.

By the time he was finishing up with his burger, he had typed and retyped a message to Lea. He didn't want to come across as desperate or as if he was asking permission. Hence all the revisions. In the end, he settled on a simple message.

-Thanks again for the great workout. I lucked out and was able to book a massage to work out some of the tension you built up. Are we a go for tomorrow's session in the pool? Assuming the weather holds.

The moment he hit send, he felt better. He knew better than to keep anything from the woman he was trying to get into bed. Especially if it was about another woman who obviously wanted him there as well.

He made his way through the rain to the massage rooms. Lea hadn't messaged him back. He knew that when she was on shift at the hospital, sometimes she couldn't read or reply to messages for hours, so he didn't worry about it too much.

When he stepped into the massage room, however, that all changed. Seeing Kara's obvious attraction towards him had him on edge.

"Oh good, you showed." Kara smiled brightly at him. "I was afraid I was going to have to entertain myself for the hour until my next session."

He decided to keep things light and responded. "Wow, I get a whole hour?"

Kara giggled and he was reminded of all the young girls he'd flirted with in school. Normally, he would have flirted right back, but the truth was, he just wasn't into Kara. His mind was consumed with a raven-haired beauty with eyes that could somehow see past his defenses.

He initially thought that he would feel strange being mostly naked in front of Kara like he had with Lea. Instead, he felt himself relaxing completely. So much so that, shortly after she started the massage, he drifted off to sleep.

He woke when her hands disappeared, and she said his name.

"Sorry." He woke with a start. "I must have been more tired than I thought."

"Believe it or not, that's a compliment." She smiled at him as he sat up. "You were very tense when I started working. How do you feel now?"

He rolled his shoulders and stretched his good leg. He was more relaxed than he'd been since being shot.

"Great," he admitted, standing up. He noticed pain in his left leg, but none in his right, which had been tense since he'd been shot. Lea had claimed it was because his right leg had been carrying the weight of his body since he couldn't use his left. Now, however, the muscles in his right leg were loose. "Thanks," he added.

"I'm here to please." Kara smiled back at him. "So..." She leaned on the counter and ran her eyes over him. "You and Dr. Val?"

He knew better than to lead a woman on while he was trying to be with another, so he answered quickly with a simple, "Yeah."

"That's cool," Kara added with a sigh. "How long has that been going on?"

He chuckled. "We've been friends since we were ten."

"Oh?" Kara's eyebrows shot up. "That long?"

"No, we were friends up until... well. The rest happened more recently."

"You two are dancing around it right now, aren't you?" she asked, crossing her arms.

"Lea's dancing," he motioned to his left leg. "I'm only working with one leg, so I'm hobbling."

Kara chuckled. "I'll let you get dressed." She turned to go. "For what it's worth, I could see the spark between the two of you the moment we met," she added before leaving.

What did that mean? She'd hit on him even knowing that he was interested in Lea. Why? Women just straight-up confused him sometimes.

That evening, he didn't want to venture out on a muggy

night, so he ate dinner in his cabin. Only in Florida could rain cause a heat wave that brought on a tsunami of humidity.

Since he was running on the last of his energy for the day, he ordered a steak dinner with the works—garlic mashed potatoes, grilled veggies, and, of course, a massive piece of chocolate cake to complete the meal. He wanted to wash it all down with a beer, but he'd taken one of the pain pills at lunch. He knew better than to piss Lea off that way.

After eating, he fell fast asleep and woke to the sound of thunder and pounding on his door.

Stumbling out of bed, he opened the door to a very angry Lea.

"Why haven't you answered your phone?" she said, moving past him.

"I was asleep." He shut the door behind her. He quickly noticed that it was still raining outside. "How can it still be raining?" he thought.

"It's Florida," Lea answered dryly as she removed her jacket, and he realized he'd asked the question out loud. "What are you doing still asleep?" she asked him as she moved around the cabin. He wiped the sleep from his eyes, and he realized she had brought two large plastic containers in with her and was setting them up in the small kitchen area.

"Still?" He glanced towards the clock and frowned. "Is that nine o'clock at night or morning?" he asked, moving slowly over to sit at the table. With the dark clouds overhead, it was hard to tell if it was still night at this point.

Lea frowned at him. "Morning." She set the container down and walked over to lay her hand on his forehead. "You're burning up." She almost jumped away from him. "How long have you been feeling feverish?" She walked over to her bag and looking through it.

One thing he'd noticed about Lea long ago was that she was

organized in every aspect of her life, except for her purse. The thing was bigger than a diaper bag and had more stuff in it than he carried with him when he went hiking or camping.

It took her a few moments to finally find what she was looking for and when she walked back over to him, he realized that she had a thermometer in her hands.

"You carry that in your purse?" he asked.

Instead of answering, she swiped it across his forehead and frowned down at the display.

"One-oh-one," she said as she ran her eyes over him and touched his forehead again.

He closed his eyes and enjoyed how cool her hand felt against his skin.

"Why didn't you call me and tell me you were feeling sick?" she asked.

"I didn't know." He swayed slightly when she removed her hand from his heated skin. "I was asleep."

"Did you take your medicine last night with your dinner?"

"Yes." He groaned and leaned back. When he'd woken, he'd been hot. Now, however, he was starting to feel chilled and couldn't stop his body from shaking.

"Go get back in bed," Lea told him. "I'll bring you something to drink and your pills." She waved him off.

As he slowly made his way back to the bed, he remembered all the times that he'd been sick as a child. His mother had never really pampered him, mainly because his father wouldn't have allowed it. Still, she'd done as much as she could under the very watchful eye of his father.

She'd sneak him some soup and crackers if he had a fever or club soda if he had stomach issues. When he'd been eight and had his tonsils out, she'd stopped off and gotten him some ice cream on the ride home from the hospital.

"Here." Lea's soothing voice interrupted his half-dream state. "Sit up and drink some of this."

He did as she asked and took a sip of the hot tea that she'd made him. There was a hint of honey and lemon, and he realized that his throat was tender.

"Thanks," he said and closed his eyes.

"I shouldn't have worked you so hard yesterday. Your body is fighting off everything that's happened to you in the past week." Her voice sounded strained. "Let me check your wound and make sure it's not infected."

He set the mug down and let her unwrap his thigh. When he saw that it looked fine, he took her hands. "Hey, I'm not as fragile as you think."

"No, you are. At least right now you are," she added. "Trust me, I know. Your body is fighting off infections that we can't even see. The fever is just a symptom of you overdoing it."

"All I did yesterday was work out with you and get a couple of massages," he said before remembering that he hadn't talked to her about Kara. He watched her face closely for any signs of jealousy or anger but didn't see any. Instead, her eyes were filled with concern.

"I pushed you because... I thought..." She looked down at their joined hands, then moved back up to lock on his.

"Because I kissed you?" he asked.

"No," she said quickly.

"Then why are you beating yourself up? You didn't do anything but help me. I need to be able to trust my body again. For it to recover. You're pretty much the only one who is here, willing to help me in that area," he said, meaning every word.

"Kara is willing," she said in a soft voice.

He lifted her chin with his fingers until their eyes locked. "Let me make myself perfectly clear. I want you. Not her." He pulled her closer for a soft kiss.

He felt her relax against him as the kiss continued. Just feeling her body plastered against his had him wishing he was fully recovered. As it was, he was still shaking and feeling even more chilled than before.

Lea pulled back slightly. "Finish drinking your tea." She smiled. "I brought some breakfast, but instead, I think you'll need some soup and rest."

"Thanks," he said, taking the cup from her again. "For everything."

Her smile was more genuine than it had been in a while, making him totally relax.

"When you're happy. I'm happy." He sipped his tea.

She stayed with him, working on her laptop while he drank the tea and nibbled on the fruit and toast that she'd brought for him.

She talked about her work, her sister, and her family while he zoned in and out.

He must have fallen asleep at one point and woke when a cold washcloth fell over his forehead.

"Brett, you've got to help me out here," Lea said.

"I'm here, babe," he said. "Whatever you need," he promised her. Then he drifted back into the darkness.

CHAPTER 9

*H*ell. What was she supposed to do? Lea knew it wasn't a full emergency. His vitals were good. His fever was sticking at one-oh-one, and it was a good sign that he was sweating and had stopped shaking with the chills.

But he was in and out of consciousness. All her medical knowledge kept her calm, but her personal and emotional feelings for the man almost had her in a panic.

She wanted to call an ambulance but knew the only thing she could do if he was at the hospital is push fluids into him. She felt pretty confident that he'd had enough fluids since he'd drank all of the tea, some of the soup, and a glass of water that she'd given him before he'd drifted off.

What his body needed was rest so he could fight off whatever infection he had.

She'd checked his injury for any signs of discoloration or puss. His skin had closed up nicely and was already healed and scarring in some areas.

He still had a nasty bruise running up and down his thigh,

but there hadn't been external signs of infection this whole time.

What his body was fighting off was at least not a wound infection. That made her guilt grow. She knew that his body was weak and that she'd pushed him too hard yesterday. He'd just started feeling better and now this.

She would never forgive herself if this set him back or affected him permanently. She'd watched him sleep and checked on him every ten minutes. He'd been in and out of consciousness, but she'd started really worrying around lunchtime, when she tried to wake him to get him to drink some soup and he wouldn't wake up.

At times his eyes would open and roll around, but she could tell that he wasn't coherent. She kept a close eye on his fever and his vitals and when she worried too much about his temperature, she laid a cool washcloth over his forehead and his neck and wiped down his arms and chest. That helped to bring his fever back under one hundred.

It wasn't until shortly after dark that his eyes opened, and he rolled over to look at her.

"You still here?" he asked, his voice sounding weak.

"Yes." She practically burst into laughter. "I'm still here. How are you feeling?" she asked, trying to swallow the last threads of fear that remained.

"Hungry." He groaned a little as he sat up. "Sweaty," he added. "Hungry and sweaty." He wiped his hands over his face.

"I'll have something delivered while you shower." She stood up, but he grabbed her hand.

"Lea, thanks for staying with me. You didn't have to." He squeezed her hand lightly.

"Yes, I did," she said with a smile.

"Because it's your job?"

She chuckled. "No, idiot. Because you're my friend."

He smiled. "And?"

She rolled her eyes. "And I like the way you kiss." She tugged her hand free from his. "But only when you smell better than you do now."

He chuckled. "Fair enough." He slowly moved to stand up. "I feel like I was hit by a semi." He rolled his shoulders and then stopped and looked at her with a mischievous grin. "I might need another massage."

She held in her chuckle. "Maybe Kara's available."

He stopped her by taking her hand again. "I don't want Kara," he said in a deep tone. "Remember that."

She nodded, not trusting her voice.

"Good." He nodded. "How about you order us the largest steaks Isaac has?"

"Soup," she corrected. "You don't need anything as heavy as..." She stopped when he arched his eyebrows at her. "Fine, steak." She rolled her eyes. "Anything else?"

"Pie, apple if they have it." He used one crutch to get into the bathroom.

She walked over to the computer and punched in their order on the touch screen. Since she had taken the day off, she added a bottle of wine so she could have a glass. She'd earned it.

She knew that Brett was out of the woods as far as the fever went, but she wanted to keep a close eye on him for a while. Was it for selfish reasons? Whatever her deeper motive, she figured she'd at least enjoy a nice dinner with him.

When Brett stepped out of the bathroom, still wet and wearing basketball shorts and a fresh T-shirt, she could no longer hide her reasons from herself. She wanted to be with him. More than she'd wanted to be with any other man in her past.

Not that she'd slept with many men. One. She'd slept with one other man, twice.

Having only exactly two sexual experiences in her twenty-seven years wasn't something she was particularly ashamed of. She could convince herself that she'd had more important things to focus on. Still, she understood that one of the reasons she'd postponed more intimate moments was a lack of interest. The guy she'd been with before just hadn't… done it for her.

Sure, she knew that sex could be magical with the right partner. She watched enough movies to assure her of that. Even her parents were proof that sex and relationships could be mutually beneficial.

Her parents had never been shy about how they felt about one another or how they enjoyed each other both physically and emotionally.

She guessed being with Brett would be very beneficial to her. Especially when he was looking well-rested and sexy as hell like he was right now. Okay, so maybe she'd been starved of physical attention for too long.

"You're looking smug," Brett said, sitting down on the sofa next to her. "What are you watching? Porn?" He glanced at her computer screen. She'd forgotten she was working on her budget to pass the time and shut the screen down with a chuckle.

"No, just happy that I finally have enough saved up to open my practice." She set her laptop back in her bag.

"I remember you saying something about it. You're really going to open your very own place?" he asked her, sounding a little excited.

"Yeah." She leaned back, feeling completely happy. "I've saved up enough for the down payment on the building, all the equipment I need, and to hire employees."

"Wow, that's…"—he frowned— "a lot."

"Yes, which is why it's taken me a few years." She shifted slightly and her leg brushed up against his right thigh. Instantly, a spark of energy zipped up her leg to her core. Just the smell of him had her insides growing jittery, on edge, like a spring coiled too tight.

So she did what came naturally to her—she started talking too much. She'd just gotten to her plans to hire employees when the food was delivered. After an employee set the two meals on the kitchen table, she tipped the young girl and then sat across from Brett to eat when they were alone again.

"So?" he said after taking a bite of his steak. "When are you opening your location?"

"Hopefully soon. I'll be closing on one of the units in the new building going up in town." She took a bite of her salad.

"In Pelican Point?" he asked, his voice going slightly higher.

"Yes." She stopped and looked at him. "Why?"

"It's just… I thought you'd open a place in Destin or Panama City. Someplace filled with…" He shrugged.

"Tourists?" she suggested.

He smiled. "Money."

It was her turn to shrug. "I'm a doctor. We tend to make a lot of that anywhere we set up shop." She smiled when he chuckled.

"True. Okay, then in town it is. That's not a bad location. The new building looks nice. Will it be big enough?"

"I'm getting two units. It should be good enough to start out. If I need, I'll buy more units later on when they become available." She'd thought everything through over the past few months. Well, almost everything. "There is something you can do for me."

His eyebrows shot up. "Shoot." He chuckled again. "Just not in my other leg."

She smiled. "I've got everything planned out, except for a name for my practice."

"Really? You want me to help you name it?" he asked. When

she nodded, he set his fork down and tilted his head. "I mean, Pelican Point Medical is too easy."

"Agreed." She nodded.

"Primary care, right?"

"Yes," she answered quickly.

"I always thought you'd go into pediatrics," he said absently.

"I..." She didn't know how to respond. For most of her young life, she'd always envisioned the same. That or OBGYN. But she'd never told anyone else about her dreams.

What did it say about him that Brett had the same idea for her? Had they really been so much closer all those years ago that he would have picked up on hidden things about her? Things like dreams and desires that she hadn't even known herself?

Wasn't that what friends did? She'd known for a long time that he'd wanted to be a cop. But hadn't most of his friends? After all, Brett hadn't necessarily been quiet about it. Nor had he been mysterious about the reasons. Most everyone in town knew who and what his father was.

She hadn't realized they'd grown quiet until he snapped his fingers, jolting her out of her thoughts.

"Snap, Crack, and Snot Clinic," he said with a chuckle.

"That has to be, by far, the worst name I've heard." She laughed.

He smiled. "Cutting Edge Clinic?" He chuckled.

She thought for a moment. "Give Us a Shot Clinic?" she added with a grin.

"Hurts a Lot Clinic."

"It might be better if I just sick with Pelican Point Medical Clinic," she said after a few more ideas that had them both laughing.

"PPMC." He nodded. "So, Zoey is due any minute now."

"One of the reasons I'm sticking around the camp a lot lately," she said quickly. A look crossed his face, one she knew all too well. Instantly, she added, "And so I can keep an eye on you." His look changed and relaxed.

"I don't mean to be a burden." He leaned back and pushed his empty plate away.

"You aren't." She stood up and took their empty plates to the tray where she knew they'd be picked up the following day. "Besides, I enjoy spending my time here."

"What are they going to do when you leave?" he asked.

"Leave?" She frowned. "Why would I leave?" She turned around and leaned on the countertop. He stood up and, using one crutch, moved over to her.

"You're opening your own practice," he reminded her. "You don't plan on working here and running your own clinic, do you?"

"Why not?" She shrugged. "I'm working here and at the hospital at the same time."

"Yes, but…" He shook his head and leaned against the counter next to her. "I should have guessed. Overachiever. Don't you work hard enough?" He nudged her shoulder as he smiled.

"Me? I'm not the one who got shot when I was off duty." She meant to tease him, but his smile fell away, and she reached out to touch his arm when she noticed the concern flood his eyes.

"They were a family, just trying to get gas." He shook his head and glanced out the dark windows. "I couldn't let them get hurt."

"Of course not." She moved in closer. "That's what makes you such a great cop. And a great person."

He turned towards her, and she realized suddenly just how close they were.

His hand moved up to her hip. "I really wish I was one hundred percent," he said as his eyes moved down to her lips. "If I was, I'd pick you up and carry you over to the bed."

She felt her knees go weak and leaned against him. She

could feel his heart beating in his chest, against her palm, as he dipped his head and brushed his lips across her.

"I never imagined…" he said, in between kisses, "just how good you'd taste and feel." He held onto her as he pulled her body against his. She was plastered against him, desperate to get closer to him, no matter what.

His hands moved up and down her lower back and when he gripped her butt, she pushed herself against his hardness and desperately wished for him to carry her to bed. But, knowing he was still very much not one hundred percent, she took a slight step back until she could look up into his eyes.

"Soon," she promised.

"Not soon enough for me."

"For now, we can enjoy sitting on the sofa and making out." She smiled.

"Sounds like a wonderful night." He kissed her again. "There will be pie too, right?"

She laughed and helped him over to the sofa. "Yes, apple a la mode."

He sat down and sighed. "Perfect."

CHAPTER 10

*D*ays seemed to fly by after that night he'd spent making out with Lea on the sofa in his cabin. He was thankful that whatever infection he'd fought off that day hadn't come back. Somehow, he felt more like himself after it had gone. It was as if his body had flushed out whatever toxins it had been holding onto after he'd been shot.

Even his muscles didn't ache as much. Of course, his left leg was still hurting like crazy, but at least the rest of him was back to normal.

He and Lea spent at least an hour in the pool each day, working on his mobility, and he worked on keeping the rest of his body from going too soft.

Lea had removed his stitches and bandages and claimed that he no longer had to keep the area dry, which was a relief. He was spending a lot of time in the water and hated putting on the waterproof bandages.

He was getting around a lot better on the crutches and had even tried out one of those boot scooters Lea had been talking about. The thing allowed him to go faster on the pathways but slowed him down and caused a lot of issues on the rocky pathways. He opted to stick with the crutches for the most part.

The rain cleared up just in time for Hannah and Owen's wedding. He'd pulled on his best suit and enjoyed sitting next to Lea in the field between the main building and the bay to watch the exchange of vows.

He was thankful he'd asked her to go with him to the event and enjoyed seeing her in the sexy soft teal sundress she'd worn.

At the reception, he had wanted to dance with Lea. Instead, he'd had to sit by while she and the rest of the Wildflowers danced around the floor together.

Thankfully, however, he was able to enjoy a couple of beers since he'd finally gotten off the pain meds.

He had to admit, Hannah and Owen's wedding was just as nice as Zoey and Dylan's and Elle and Liam's had been. All three events had been unique, even though they'd all been held on the grounds.

After sending the couple off on their honeymoon, Lea had come back to his place, and they'd fallen asleep watching another movie.

He was growing tired of not being able to be with her the way he wanted. The way they both wanted.

It was just over a week later when he overheard Damion Wells, the guy in charge of all things aquatic at the camp, talking about a beach party for employees later that next weekend. He'd headed to Lea's office and invited her to join in the fun.

She'd reminded him that Friday night she would be at Zoey's baby shower in the main dining area. He remembered her talking about the party several times in the past few days. Zoey was eager for the baby to come, and it seemed so were the rest of her friends. Hannah was coming back from her honeymoon just in time for the party, which had been planned out perfectly, just like everything else the friends did around there.

He liked seeing Lea in her scrubs and white lab coat with her stethoscope hanging around her neck. The look was somehow sexier than the sundress she'd worn to the wedding the week before.

He hinted to her that she could sneak away from the party and join him on the beach after the baby shower had gotten started.

"It's a baby shower." She giggled. "Not a raging drunken party. Everyone will notice if I sneak away." She held onto him as he rained little kisses down her neck.

"God, you smell so good," he said against her skin.

"I smell like antiseptic." She laughed. "One of the guests stepped on a broken bottle on the beach."

"Under that, you smell like flowers and sin." He trailed his tongue down to her shoulder and pushed her lab coat and scrubs aside to expose more of her skin. "Are you sure we can't lock that door and..."

Just then there was a knock on the closed door, and he sighed.

"Sorry," she said with a smile and pushed away from him. "Duty calls."

He was sitting on her examining table, even though he hadn't been there for a checkup.

"Later?" he asked, sliding off the table.

She glanced down at her watch and sighed. "I'm on shift at the hospital tonight."

He wanted to ask her to call in sick but knew better, as she had hinted that she was trying to work as many hours as she could until she officially quit to open her clinic.

Instead, he took his crutch, kissed her once more, and opened the examining room door.

"I'm heading to the pool to work out. Maybe we can do lunch before you leave?" he asked.

"I can meet you at the pool in an hour," she said as she greeted the older man and woman sitting in the waiting area.

The couple looked slightly embarrassed to see someone else with the doctor. As he strolled past them, the woman blushed and averted her eyes.

He was curious about what kind of ailments Lea saw people for most of the time. He knew that cuts, bruises, and twisted body parts took up most of her time. But did people come to her for other things? Things that their normal doctors should handle when they were at home? He made a mental note to ask her what other issues she dealt with at the camp.

After all, even though most of the guests were older, they weren't ancient. There were all sorts of fun games and activities on the grounds and most guests were very active. He'd heard the rumors of some of the swinger parties that had initially caused some havoc until some simple rules had been implemented.

Just how active could older people be? His parents didn't do anything like hiking or horseback riding. Hell, they had hardly ever talked to one another when he'd been living under their roof.

Which reminded him that he'd been thinking of asking Lea if he could try horseback riding or maybe sailing. Something to keep his mind off his pain and his recovery.

Since the other more adventurous activities were readily available at the camp, he might as well enjoy them. He didn't know how much longer he was going to stick around here now that he was on his feet and could fend for himself. Not that he was eager to return to his two-bedroom apartment.

Stepping outside from the medical cabin where Lea had her office and examining rooms, he took a deep breath and realized that he was thankful he had someplace like the camp to recover.

He doubted he would have enjoyed his recovery as much if he'd been stuck at home, alone.

Being around the camp while he recovered was like taking a vacation instead of just medical leave. Even a few of his buddies from the precinct who visited him told him how lucky he was to get to stay there. Surrounded by nature, not to mention hot women, guests and workers alike.

He was thankful that Kara had made a point to hint to Lea that she knew he was off-limits. Since that night after his fever, the two women had seemed to grow a very strong friendship with one another.

He'd even stumbled upon them having lunch the other day. They'd been laughing together and when they saw him, they'd instantly grown quiet and smiled in his direction.

Lea had suggested that he continue to get massages when he could schedule time. Both Kara and Andrea were great at working out the rest of the tension his injury caused in his body.

For today, the water would have to do the trick since Kara was not on shift and Andrea was completely booked.

As he slipped into the water, he figured he'd swim a few laps instead of trying the exercises Lea had taught him. This pool was half the length of an Olympic-sized pool and had two designated lap lanes.

He started slicing through the water, letting his right leg do most of the work.

He'd been on the swim team when he'd been in high school and had been one of the top athletes in his class. Actually, if he would have chosen to, he was pretty sure he could have gone on to compete professionally.

But he had felt another calling. One that he had thought would help protect women like his mother. His first year on the force, he'd gotten a wake-up call.

He and his then partner George had gotten a domestic dispute call. When they'd shown up at the trashed mobile home, they'd heard yelling and the sound of a crash as they approached the door.

The woman had answered the door, her eyes red from crying. Her husband, a man easily twice her size, stood behind her, anger contorting his face and making his cheeks red.

Half an hour later, George and he had walked back to the patrol car, empty-handed.

"Having no proof sucks," George had said, wiping his hands over his face.

"We both know he hit her," he'd replied.

"There wasn't a red mark on her, and she refused to press charges or even say that he hit her," George had added.

"She was afraid of the bastard. Of course she wasn't going to say he hit her," Brett had pleaded.

"Until we have probable cause or proof of abuse, we can't do anything but wait," George had reminded him. "It sucks, but it's the law. We're only here to enforce it."

"We're here to protect people like her." Brett had pointed towards the trailer and noticed the man standing in the doorway, smiling at them with his arms crossed over his chest, as if he knew that he'd just won the entire war instead of just one battle.

"Until the wife finds the courage to stand up to him, or to run, there's nothing we can do," George added. "In my twenty-some years on the force, I've seen it more times than I can count." He shook his head. "It's not always the woman who is being abused, but the look in their eyes is always the same. Broken." George looked towards the trailer and narrowed his eyes. "As is the look on their faces." He nodded towards the husband. "All this did was empower him. He feels untouchable now. He'll take his anger out on her even more after we leave.

This won't be the last time we get called out here. Mark my words." He sighed.

"Why?" Brett had asked the older man. "Why does she stay?" He hadn't realized at the time that he hadn't been talking about the man's wife but his own mother.

"I don't know for sure. I guess for some it's fear," George had answered. "Others, it's the lack of belief that there is anything better out there. Some stay for the kids, if there are any."

Brett had rolled those words in his head while he waited for the next call.

George had been right; over the next few months, they were called back to the small trailer more than a dozen times. Each time, the woman refused to press charges against her husband and there had never been so much as a red mark on her. None that they could see.

Then, one day, they'd gotten the call that there had been an accident. When they'd shown up, the woman had answered the door. Her hands were covered in blood, and she was hysterical.

Her husband of less than a year lay on the living room floor covered in blood with an eight-inch kitchen knife sticking through his neck.

The same system that had turned its back on her all of those months during her abuse was now the one that locked her up for the rest of her life for her abuser's murder.

The system failed in that case. He had failed her.

That moment defined the way he handled calls like that from then on. Sure, he still stayed within his legal limits, but that didn't stop him from taking extra time on calls.

He studied all the Prevention of Domestic and Sexual Violence policies on how to handle such cases. The PDSV had a lot of good information that he wished he and George had followed to the tee in that first case. The PDSV guidelines had been required reading before he'd gotten his badge, but he'd only really skimmed through it.

It seemed difficult to do your job when criminals knew all the loopholes in the law more than the officers did. After that first case, he made a point to know all the ins and outs of everything he could do. That had helped in the future cases he'd dealt with.

Thinking about work kept his mind off the fact that his left leg was on fire. Instead of pulling himself out of the water after his last lap, he floated there for a while. Watching the white puffy clouds float slowly through the blue sky, he thought of all the good he could continue to do if he was allowed to get back on the job.

Would his leg ever be the same? Could he recover completely? Lea had mentioned that he'd need to continue therapy for a long time and, at this point, he knew that once his month of medical leave was up, he'd have to reassess his own desires. Sure, a desk job would be waiting for him. He knew that.

He could possibly even talk his chief into letting him hit the streets sooner than he was capable of doing. Of that, he had no doubt. But the question was, did he want to?

Being shot had put a damper on more than just his career goals. It had changed the way he looked at life. The longer he hung around his friends here at the camp, the more he realized that there was more to life. There was a lot more he could do to help people, especially the ones he cared for.

After all, in the past three years since the camp had opened its doors, they'd gone through more than most had—a shooting where luckily no one had been shot, a stabbing, a kidnapping, an attempted murder, and even a hurricane.

Maybe River Camps did need his help. He'd never really thought about going into private security before. He didn't even know what they would pay, since he'd always brushed off Aiden or Elle any time they had suggested it to him.

Maybe after lunch with Lea, he would swing by Elle's office and have a chat with her. It couldn't hurt, right?

He felt the water splash as a body cannonballed right next to him, sending water into his eyes and mouth.

When Lea surfaced, smiling and laughing, he reached for her.

"Minx." He held onto her close.

"You looked like a river lily." She laughed and splashed him.

"A… what?" He shook his head.

"A river lily. The flowers." She held onto his shoulders.

"Yes, I know what they are, it's just… I've never been compared to a flower before." He smiled down at her.

"Well, now you have. You float in the water just like one. Bobbing around with no purpose," she teased, causing his smile to grow.

"You're trying to get under my skin." He pushed her body against his.

"Is it working?" she said, a little breathless.

"One surefire way to rile a man is to compare him with a flower." He kissed her.

Her entire body melted against his. Her hands held onto his shoulders as their legs kicked under the water, keeping their heads above the surface.

When he felt himself growing too hard to hide in his swim shorts, he dunked them under the water and they both came back up laughing.

"How was your swim?" she asked as they made their way towards the edge of the pool.

"Good. Relaxing." He sat on the step near her. "How was work?" He remembered the couple and wanted to ask what they had seen her for.

"Good." She tucked her knees to her chest and looked out at the other people enjoying the water.

"I've been dying to know what the couple wanted to see you about?" he asked, nudging her on the shoulder.

"Couple?" She glanced over at him. Then her smile grew. "Barb and Richard Rixton."

"They seemed pretty embarrassed about something." He glanced around, making sure the couple in question wasn't anywhere near.

"Yeah, situations like that can cause some... embarrassment." She smiled. "It wasn't anything serious."

"So?" He nudged her again, causing her to laugh.

"Sorry, patient-doctor confidentiality," she replied, causing him to groan.

"Come on, I told you about the details of the Wilder case. Even though I wasn't supposed to," he prodded.

"That's different. Corey Wilder was found dead, floating face down in the river. The Rixtons are"—she glanced around them — "very much alive and somewhere on these grounds."

"I won't tell a soul." He held up his fingers. "Scout's honor."

Lea tilted her head and then sighed. "I won't tell you the details, but..." She leaned closer and once again lowered her voice. "If you ever have to take pills..." She glanced down at his shorts. "Remember to take only one dose and follow the instructions."

"Oh." He drew out the word and then smiled. "I suppose you see that often." Her eyebrows shot up and she smiled. "I mean, with couples." He felt his face flush. "Happening here, often. Not that you..."

Her chuckle had him shutting his mouth quickly.

"Yes, I get several cases like that a year around here," she admitted. "Typically, the most I have to deal with are sprained ankles or small cuts." She shrugged.

"I've been giving some serious thought to taking the security job Elle has offered me," he blurted out.

"You have?" She turned to him suddenly. A look of excitement crossed her face for a brief moment. "That's... good?" she asked.

He shrugged. "Might be, might not be." He glanced down at the nasty scar on his upper left thigh. "It all depends." He glanced up at her. "Do you think I'll be recovered enough to go back to work anytime soon?" he asked. She bit her bottom lip. Before she answered, he already knew the answer.

"With a lot of therapy, maybe." She looked down at his leg. "I'm going to suggest you start the next level of therapy next week. I think you're ready for the more... strenuous stuff."

He shook his head. "What you and Ken have been doing to me so far hasn't been strenuous?" he asked.

She smiled. "I've been taking it easy on you since I worked you too hard last week," she admitted. "Ken and I both agree it's time to push harder."

He groaned and sank below the surface of the water, only to have her pull him back up as she laughed.

"How about some lunch?" she asked. "I'm starving."

CHAPTER 11

Lea had been looking forward to Zoey's baby shower for weeks. After she'd gotten her invitation, she'd taken her next day off and had gone crazy baby shopping. With her trunk loaded down with the carefully wrapped gifts she'd purchased, she headed towards the camp, eager to spend a night with her friends.

She'd enjoyed Hannah and Owen's wedding, but this party was about a baby, one she'd been asked to help bring into the world herself.

Brett had gotten wind of the employee's beach party that employees Damion, Carter, and Dean— known around the campgrounds as the dynamic trio—were throwing.

Damion was the full-time pool boy and boat guy on the grounds. At one point, Damion had asked her out, but she'd turned him down. Not because she hadn't found him attractive. He had sexy mocha skin and very kind eyes, but he was easily five years younger than she was. Besides, she'd been too busy working back then to date.

Carter was the camp's part-time veterinarian, who looked

after all the horses they owned. He also worked in town at the only veterinary clinic.

Then there was Dean. Dean was the camp's gigolo. Or so all the rumors claimed. He was good-looking enough, with his James Dean hair and sexy bedroom eyes, but Lea knew the guy and just couldn't see him taking advantage of anyone. He and the rest of the trio were really nice guys. They were flirts and liked to party, but who didn't when they had the night off.

She parked next to Elle's Jeep and was unloading her trunk when she heard the gravel behind her crunch and spun around to see Brett walking towards her.

"I thought you could use some help," he said, shifting the cane in his hands.

She looked down at him. "No, I've got this. You should be—"

"If you say resting…" He reached into her trunk and pulled out one of the larger boxes. "What did you do? Buy out the entire baby store?" he asked after seeing all the boxes and bags in her trunk.

"I may have gone a little… overboard," she said with a sigh.

Brett chuckled. "You think?" He shifted the box and reached for another.

"No, you can't carry those and use your cane." She tried to take the box from him, but he held them away.

"I can. They're light." He reached in and took a smaller box; one she knew weighed a little under twenty pounds.

"What is in this thing?" he asked, shifting it in his arms.

She shrugged. "Gifts."

He rolled his eyes. "I got them some baby blankets and diapers. What is this? A car battery?"

She smiled. "You offered to carry it." She took the rest of the boxes and bags and shut her trunk.

"That's before I knew you were going to have me carry the

heaviest ones." He shifted slightly to tuck his cane under his arm.

Letting out a sigh, she grabbed the smaller box from him and nodded to his cane. "Use it. You don't want to piss off your doctor." Then she started marching down the walkway, hearing him following her more slowly.

"You look nice," he said, catching up with her. "I like seeing you in a dress."

She glanced down at the simple silver dress she'd pulled on. "Thanks." She ran her eyes over his board shorts and T-shirt, the same attire he'd been wearing since he'd moved to the campgrounds to recover. "You look ready for a beach party."

"I am." He smiled. "I sure wish you were going."

She glanced over at him. "I might be able to sneak away for a few moments," she said as they walked into the main building.

"I'll look for you."

They walked into the employee's dining area, where the party was just starting. He set the larger box down on the gift table and then gave her a kiss before saying, "See you later." Then he disappeared.

"You two look so cute together," Aubrey said, walking over to help her set the rest of the gifts down.

Lea rolled her eyes. It wasn't the first conversation she'd had with her friends about what was between her and Brett. Nor, she thought, would it be the last.

The Wildflowers liked to gossip. And part of Lea had to admit she enjoyed being included in that group.

"He's coming along so well." Aubrey changed the subject quickly.

"Yes, he is." She glanced back at the door that Brett had disappeared through moments ago.

"We're going to miss having him around when he's gone," Aubrey added.

"Gone?" She frowned and jerked her eyes back to Aubrey, who instantly frowned and took a step back.

"Um, yeah, he's… moving out of the cabin tomorrow. He told Elle that he wanted to get back to his place. I assumed you knew." Aubrey glanced around as if she was afraid to look Lea in the eyes.

"Oh," Lea said. "Right." Brett hadn't told her that he was leaving the camp. Why not?

That thought ate at her as the party started. Here she'd been so excited for the baby shower and now all she could think about was sneaking out to ask Brett why he'd hidden the fact that he was leaving the camp from her.

The more she thought about things between them, the more she realized that, outside of the years of friendship, they had just had a few hot and heavy make-out sessions. Nothing more. No tender words of commitment, no promises for a larger future together.

Whatever she'd believed they'd had was just that, her belief. Here she was once again, thinking that she was nothing more than a convenience to Brett. Why did she always question so much when it came to relationships?

That was the number one reason she'd broken things off with her very first boyfriend, if you could call him that. She'd gone out on three dates with him.

She'd caught him looking at their waitress with interest and… she'd fled the relationship.

Well, Brett was someone she could see herself fighting for. Even if there wasn't anything more between them than friendship.

"You're not paying attention, are you?" Aubrey nudged her shoulder.

"Hm?" Lea snapped to attention.

"The game," Aubrey hissed. "We're losing." She motioned to the tablet Lea had been taking notes on for the game.

"Sorry." She handed the tablet to Aubrey, who quickly jotted down the answer to the last few questions about Zoey and Dylan. "I'm going to..." She nodded towards the doorway.

"Go, I've got this," Aubrey said not even looking up from writing. "I am so going to win that gift card."

Lea slipped out the side door and took a deep breath of the evening air. At this point of the season, it was still cool after the sun went down. She wished she'd thought of sneaking her coat out with her. She made her way quickly towards the beach.

River Camps sat on a peninsula that jutted out between the Gulf of Mexico and Pelican Bay. The bay side housed the boat house and most of the boats and other water recreation equipment. The Gulf side boasted the camp's private white-sand beach, which sat on emerald-green water.

The beach was crowded with employees and guests alike. There were more than a half dozen campfires going in metal bins with people standing or sitting around each of them.

Finding Brett was going to be next to impossible.

"There you are," a deep voice said behind her.

She turned to look up into Brett's blue eyes, which were laughing at her.

"Are you drunk?" she asked, snagging the can from his fingers.

"No, it's..." he started to say.

She held the can up to her nose and sniffed. Smelling nothing, she frowned down at the label.

"Water," he said with a chuckle.

"This?" She held it up to the firelight and frowned at him. "Liquid Death?" The sixteen-ounce can looked like your standard beer can with a gold scull and gothic lettering. "Right." She took a sip and then frowned. It was water. Good water. Cold, crisp, so she took another sip. "Fine," she said, handing it back to him.

"I was thirsty and didn't have my doctor to help me back to my cabin after." Brett shrugged and motioned to two chairs that sat near a fire pit. "Come sit down. It's a little hard for me to stand long in the sand."

She sat next to him, and he grabbed another can of water from a cooler and handed it to her.

"How's the party going?" he asked.

She took a sip of the water and then turned on him. "Are you leaving the camp?" She could have been a little more diplomatic when asking him, but this worked too. After all, she'd mentally talked herself into a fit of anger.

"The camp?" He frowned over at her. "I'm returning to my apartment tomorrow, yes." He nodded. "I overheard that they were completely booked this week." He shrugged and set his can of water down. "I guess I felt guilty for taking away some of the camp's revenue."

"Why didn't you tell me?" she asked.

"I only just told Elle and Hannah an hour or two ago," he said with a chuckle. "I figured I'd tell you when you stopped by here later." He leaned closer to her and lowered his voice "So, um, this is my last night in the cabin. I'm heading back to my apartment tomorrow," he said with a smile as he took her hand. She tried to yank it away, but he held her still. "And..." He paused. "I've agreed to take the head of security job here at the camp." His smile turned slightly strained. "I made sure to stress how important it was that bit of news didn't go beyond Aiden's or Elle's lips or I'd kick their butts with my good leg."

"You..." Her breath was locked in her lungs. "You're not going to go back to being a cop?"

Brett took a deep breath and glanced off to the dark waters beyond the crowd of partiers.

"No," he said softly, then turned towards her. "It looks like I'm going to be a glorified babysitter for this place," he said with a chuckle.

She smiled and squeezed his hand. "Not until your doctor releases you to work, you aren't."

He chuckled. "Right." He sighed and leaned back. "So, how is the party going?"

She glanced behind them to the lights from the main building and sighed. "Good. I shouldn't have snuck out." But she'd wanted—needed—to talk to him.

"You can stay for a few more minutes." He reached over and took her hand. "What time does your party end?"

"I'm not sure," she said, relaxing back. She had to admit, sitting in the dark on the beach by a fire was a lot more relaxing than being in a bright loud room full of women, most of whom she didn't know.

"Want to come over to my place after? Maybe we can watch another movie," he said slowly.

She smiled, remembering the last time they'd tried to watch a movie. They'd watched maybe one scene. The rest of the time they'd spent making out. Pleasing one another. Going as far as they could without hurting his leg.

"I might…" Just then someone burst out from the pathway behind them and shouted her name.

"Here." She jumped up and sprang into action. She couldn't count how many times she'd been called out on an emergency. Expecting blood, broken bones, or worse, she spotted Aubrey scanning the darkness for her.

"Here," she said rushing over to Aubrey. "What's—"

"It's Zoey. Her water just broke," Aubrey said a little breathless but with a smile.

"Okay." She smiled and then glanced back at Brett. "Rain check?"

Brett smiled. "Yeah, go." He waved her away. "Have a baby. Take care of our girl," he called after her as she and Aubrey sprinted down the pathway again.

"It's supposed to be a baby shower. No one was expecting actual water," Aubrey said as they ran. Lea chuckled.

When she stepped into the room, she was slightly surprised to see Zoey standing there, calmly commanding the entire room while her friends surrounded her. Elle was on the phone, no doubt to Dylan. Hannah held onto one of Zoey's hands and Scarlett held the other. They were trying to get Zoey to head towards a car, but Zoey was too busy talking to Elle.

"It's in the closet by the front door," Zoey said, a little exasperated.

"He's got it and is going to meet us at the hospital," Elle said.

"Lea's here," Aubrey burst in. "We can leave now."

Lea rushed to Zoey's side and started asking questions. If she'd had any contractions and how far apart they were.

She'd spent an entire year in medical school preparing to help in a childbirth. It wasn't the first baby she'd help bring into the world. There'd been three others at this point.

Still, she knew the best place for this baby to be born was at the hospital, surrounded by medical equipment and other medical personnel. Not to mention the baby's father.

She rode in the back of the car with Zoey as Elle drove them to the hospital, all the while counting off the time between the contractions and checking Zoey's and the baby's vitals.

When they pulled into the parking lot at the hospital, Dylan was waiting outside with his brothers, Owen and Liam, and their father, Leo Costas.

Lea estimated that the baby would be arriving within the hour since the contractions were growing closer and closer together.

Since Zoey and Dylan had requested that she take part in the delivery a few months back, she scrubbed up to assist as they waited for the OBGYN doctor to arrive.

When Zoey's OBGYN arrived a few minutes later, Lea stood aside and watched Dylan support his wife and answered any questions they directed at her.

When Paige Emily Costas was finally born at seventeen after eleven o'clock that evening, Lea was just as exhausted as the mother and child.

"Thank you," Dylan said, giving her a hug.

Lea laughed. "I didn't do anything except stand there watching your wife do all the hard work and the staff do what they do best."

"Just knowing you were here in case anything went sideways helped a lot." He gave her another hug. "Zoey, Paige, and I appreciated it."

Lea smiled over at the new mother, holding the little girl close to her chest. Paige was already enjoying her first meal.

"Congratulations you two," she said before quietly leaving the room.

Since she'd been one of the lucky few to see the baby first, when she walked out, she shared a few pictures she'd taken on her phone of the happy family with everyone who'd been stuck in the waiting area. Then she made her excuses and started heading out. Her mind was so focused on getting back to Brett, maybe catching the end of a movie and enjoying time with him, that she hadn't spotted Dr. Sanjay Rufkin until he blocked her exit.

"You just can't stay away from me, can you?" he joked. Normally, she would have smiled, but over the past year, this was his standard greeting when he ran into her when she was off duty.

"Just heading home." She tried to sidestep him, only to have him block her way again. Her back teeth clenched, and she felt her spine straighten. "Sanjay, it's been a very long day."

"Why is it that you and I have never gone out? I'm off shift now. Why don't we head out and grab a drink?" He leaned on the doorway.

"We've never gone out because I keep turning you down." She moved to pass him again, only this time he put his hand on her shoulder. Instantly, she thought of Aubrey's judo moves and wished more than anything she could flip Sanjay onto his back and walk out the door.

But practicality settled in, and she curbed the urge to even try it. Instead, she glared down at his hand until he dropped it.

"Isn't it past time you changed your mind? It's not like you have a line of men wanting to take you out." He smiled down at her. "Most men don't like smart women. I'm willing to tolerate it."

She arched her brow. "Tolerate?" She held in the curses she wanted to let loose.

Sanjay ran his eyes over her. "Sure. I mean, you do have a nice tight package…" At this, she swiveled around and marched in the opposite direction. She'd have to weave her way through the hospital hallways to exit the building, then walk through a dark parking lot to wait for her Uber driver, but if it meant not having to listen to Sanjay talk about her body, then it was worth it.

"Hey," he called after her and then jogged behind her to catch up. "I was just joking."

She turned on her heels quickly and bolted for the door again, this time making a point to leave him far behind her.

"Well, if you change your mind," he called after her.

When she stepped out into the April night, she was thankful it wasn't raining so she could wait under the lights for her driver, who was less than five minutes away, according to the app.

Rubbing her forehead, she looked down at her phone and sent a text to Brett about heading out to the cabin to see him. When he didn't immediately respond, she wondered if he was asleep and if she should just head home instead.

"I'd love to see you too, but I'm not at the cabin," a deep male voice said near her.

She turned to see Brett leaning against the wall, watching her.

"How did you…"

"I heard you were tied up and thought you'd like a ride." He took his cane and started walking towards her slowly.

"You… drove?" She glanced around.

"I have a difficult time walking, not driving. It's my left leg, remember?" He smiled. "So, do you want a lift?"

"Sure," she said quickly. She pulled out her phone to cancel her ride. "But how about we stop off and grab something to eat? I think I earned a greasy cheeseburger and fries."

Brett smiled. "A woman after my own heart."

CHAPTER 12

He sat across from Lea at one of the only places open at one in the morning and watched her nibble on Whataburger fries as he sipped on a chocolate shake.

She was still dressed in the sexy silver dress that clung to her, and he realized they should be somewhere a little fancier than a fast-food joint. Still, he was thankful he'd switched out of his board shorts and T-shirt from earlier and had pulled on a pair of khaki pants and a button-up shirt.

He'd been waiting for Lea to come back when Aubrey had sent him a text letting him know that the baby had been born and that Lea would probably need a ride home since she'd ridden in the car with Zoey to the hospital.

Something told him that Aubrey was rooting for their relationship. That just made him like his best friends' fiancée even more.

He looked around the brightly lit dining room. They weren't the only ones sitting in the fast-food place, but it was as quiet as if they were. That wouldn't have been the case during the day.

"So, a girl," he said with a sigh and leaned back in the booth as he thought about Zoey and Dylan's new family. "They sure kept it a secret from everyone. I would have thought that they'd have a big gender reveal party and all."

"They wanted to keep it a secret." Lea smiled. "Do you know how hard it was for me to keep that from them and everyone else? I was actually getting bribes."

"You knew?" he asked, shaking his head. "And you didn't tell me?"

She chuckled, the sound of it warming his heart. He couldn't help but smile when she was around him.

Reaching across the table, he took her hand in his. "So, I was thinking…" He lifted her hand up to his lips and brushed them across her knuckles. "Instead of heading back to the cabin, we could head over to your place."

Her instant smile told him that she was up for the idea of spending the night with him. He couldn't explain the feelings rushing through him.

Just then, they glanced over as several loud men walked in and moved up to the counter. The young teenage boy who'd taken their order a few moments earlier looked a little overwhelmed when the men started making trouble and teasing him.

"They're drunk," Lea said with a shake of her head. "That poor kid looks like he's scared to death."

Brett could see the same thing. The kid's face was pale, and his hands shook as he tried to take their orders.

"Isn't there a manager here? Someone older who might know how to handle four large drunk men?" Brett turned slightly in his chair and successfully got the attention of two of the men.

Normally, this wouldn't have been an issue. He was a cop. Well, ex-cop at this point. He would have handled the men and was sure that he could have stopped any fights. But then he moved wrong, and pain shot through his thigh, and he remembered that he wasn't his normal self.

"Lookie what we have here," the man in a red shirt with a long blond beard said, leaving the counter to come to stand next to their table. "A real live Chinese."

Brett tensed, but Lea reached across the table and took his hand in hers and squeezed it gently.

"You speak English?" the other man, who was wearing a dirty white T-shirt and had a long black beard, said loudly. As if any person who didn't speak English was also deaf, or as if shouting at someone in a different language made them understand it.

"It would be best if you just ordered your food and were on your way," Brett said in a low tone. He knew how to handle men like this, he had handled troublemakers for the past few years without raising his heartrate. But now Lea was sitting here, exposed and unprotected. There was no way he was in physical shape to fight off one of the men, let alone four.

"I wasn't talking to you. I was taking to this chink here," the redshirt said with a laugh. "You know why they call them chinks? Cause they're all named by the sounds their silverware makes when you toss 'em down the stairs." The man's eyes turned dark as he looked down at Lea. "What's your name, chink?" he said loudly.

Damn his injuries. He'd go down fighting. He made a move to stand up and fight, but the white shirt pushed him down into the chair. Because of the pain in his leg, he folded back into the chair.

"Tough guy here must think he's a real big man," the white shirt man teased with a laugh.

At this point, the other two men had left the teenager alone and had moved over to stand next to their buddies. Brett hoped that the kid was smart and that he was on the phone with the police.

"I can be," he said calmly, knowing he had to stall for time. A few of the other people in the dining area had rushed from the room, and he was sure at this point that someone had called the police. "I'm a cop, so you'd better move along. You don't want to end up in a jail cell tonight." He watched the men's faces for any change. Normally, that bit of news would have helped his cause, but seeing the sneers and heat in two of the men's eyes, Brett realized he might have just made a huge mistake.

Red shirt laughed. Brett would never forget the man's cackle, as if he'd just told them the best joke in the world.

"Tonight is our lucky night. Got us a foreigner and a cop having…"—white shirt flipped Brett's shake over, sending chocolate shake all over his pants— "a date." All four men laughed loudly.

Brett once again moved to get up, but two of the men held him down.

"There ought to be a law against it. Dating someone from China," the red shirt said with a shake of his head. "We need to send all these gooks back where they came from," red shirt added. "China."

The way the man said the word made it sound like a curse word instead of just another country on the only planet in the solar system that held intelligent life.

At this point, Brett's back teeth and his fists were clenched.

"Aren't you supposed to uphold the law?" the white shirt said, squeezing Brett's shoulder painfully. "You can start by sending this one back where she came from."

Where was his backup? He glanced quickly towards the large dark windows, looking for any sign of red and blue lights.

For a moment, he thought about what might happen if he had to fight off the four men himself. He could envision the scene in his head, him jumping around on his good leg, swinging his fists as the men easily ducked and dodged his blows. Then, after the men saw his weak leg, they'd kick it, he'd end up on the ground and maybe do some permanent damage in the process.

"Oooo weeee, lookie here." One of the other men, the one in a blue T-shirt, yanked Brett's cane out from under the booth. "We got us a cripple too." The man twirled the cane several times, almost hitting Brett in the face.

"A China woman, a cop, and a cripple hobble into Whataburger…" the red shirt said and then laughed at his own lame joke as he took the cane from the blue shirt man.

"Is this your boyfriend?" the white shirt man yelled at Lea. "Boyfriend?" he said again, a little louder, spitting towards her.

"She's an American," Brett barked out. "Leave her alone."

That seemed to stop all four men. "Probably 'cause she got one of them green cards they were handing out in that lottery. You don't belong here…" red shirt yelled, holding the cane inches from Lea's face.

The entire time this was going on, Lea sat silent. Her eyes were glued to Brett's face. Suddenly, Brett realized what she was doing and, after a heartbeat, decided to play along with her until the police showed up. Taking her hand in his, he looked directly into her eyes and willed the four men's jaunts and stabs to fade away in his mind.

Instead of focusing on the hateful words being hurled at them, he focused only on Lea. The beauty of her face, the richness of her dark eyes looking back at him. Her long silky hair that he loved to run his fingers through. Her full perfect lips that he enjoyed kissing.

Ignoring the men pissed them off even more. He didn't move when the end of his cane jabbed into his ribs.

He didn't blink an eye or flinch when the man in the red

shirt started hitting him in the shoulder with it. He heard the cane snap in two, felt the sting of pain in his shoulder as splinters from the cane embedded in his skin. Still, he didn't allow the men the reward of seeing any weakness or pain.

Instead, he sat there, holding onto Lea, willing the police to show up before he lost the last threads of his control.

It seemed to take hours for the blue and red lights to finally appear outside the dark windows. He marveled at the fact that the four men were too busy trying to get a response from him to notice them until it was too late.

Carl and Steven, two of the area's best, and friends of his, rushed in and tackled red shirt and white shirt. The red shirt had been in mid-swing with the broken cane in his hands when Carl took the man down. The white shirt had just laid his hand on Lea's shoulder, a move that would have caused Brett to act if he hadn't seen the lights.

Steven yanked and twisted the man's hand away from Lea, while two more officers, Mary and Rick, grabbed the other two men, who had tried to run for the door.

"Damn," Carl said a few moments later when everything quieted down as he wiped a drop of blood from his nose and looked at them. "You two sure know how to have a fun night."

Two more officers showed up and hauled the three men out, while Steven jerked red shirt's arms and led him out of the room. The man was yelling about who he was related to and that he knew his rights, yelling all about his freedom of speech as he glared back at them, as if they had caused the entire ordeal instead of him.

"Thanks." Brett dropped Lea's hands to shake Carl's.

"No problem." Carl looked down at Lea. "You okay, Dr. Val?"

"Yes, thank you, Carl," Lea said in a calm voice. "Want me to take a look at that?" she asked, motioning towards Carl's hand, which was bloody and raw from his brief fight with the red shirt.

"Naw, I'll get it looked at after I drop these four off at the station. I don't want to spoil your date further," Carl said with a wink. "Try not to let these idiots ruin your night."

"Don't you need us to fill out a report or something?" Lea asked him when Carl started to leave.

"No, we've got this. You two can stop by later and give us your statements. On your own time. Night."

They watched as Carl and the rest of his coworkers and friends stepped outside to deal with the mess.

Brett glanced around, looking for his cane, which was broken in two and lying on the ground.

"Gosh, I thought they were going to kill you." The teenage employee rushed towards them. "I called the cops the second they left me alone. I am never working the night shift again." The kid shook his head. "Are you okay, mister?"

"Yeah." He sighed and glanced around, wondering how he was going to get to his car without his cane.

"Here." A woman's voice sounded directly behind him. He glanced over and saw a middle-aged dark-haired woman holding a metal cane towards him. "You can borrow my mother's cane. When those four men started in on you two, I had to get her out of here and took her to the car to call the police ourselves. Mother saw what they did to you and thought you might need this more than she did. She has a spare," the woman added.

"Thanks." He took the cane from the woman and stood up, instantly feeling pain in his shoulder. He kept his face straight as he held out his hand to Lea. "Shall we?" he asked. He just wanted to get out of there as quickly as he could and knew that she felt the same way.

"Yes," Lea answered softly. He took her hand, and they walked towards the door.

"Hey." The teenager came rushing after them. "You're that hero cop, aren't you? The one that got shot saving that family?" he asked. Brett nodded quickly. "Thank you." The kid smiled. "For standing up to people like them." Brett gave the kid another quick nod and walked towards the doors.

The moment they stepped outside, he could see the four police cruisers, their lights still on, as his friends talked to witnesses, no doubt taking down as much information as they could. He knew the drill. They would write up the report, adding in their personal details since everyone knew him and Lea.

"Hey." This time it was a twenty-something girl and boy who rushed towards them in the parking lot. "I, um..." The girl looked towards the boy. "We recorded that, what happened to you two in there. I sent a copy to the cops so they have it for their records, but I was... we were wondering if you'd allow us to put it online? You know, to raise awareness to this kind of hate."

Brett glanced down at Lea. "It's up to you," he said softly.

Lea sighed and closed her eyes for a moment. He could tell that she was calculating her decision. When she finally opened her eyes, she gave the kids a quick nod.

"Sure," she said softly.

"Thanks," the girl said quickly.

"I'm sorry I didn't help you," the young man said. "I took judo, but... there were four of them."

"You did the right thing," Brett told the kid firmly.

"How did you just sit there? Wow, I wouldn't have had so much self-control." The kid shook his head.

Brett glanced down at Lea and smiled. "Sometimes what is

worth fighting for is worth not fighting." He smiled at her. "Let's go home." He took her hand again and they walked to his car.

He was thankful when Lea took his car keys from him and helped him into the passenger side and then slipped behind the wheel. His shoulder was hurting, and he wasn't sure it was safe for him to drive.

They rode in silence for a few moments, and he kept his eyes trained on her face in the dark car.

"I'm sorry," he said when they were driving over the Pelican Bay bridge.

"For?" she asked, glancing at him.

"For the human race," he said with a burst of laughter.

Lea smiled at him. "That's a lot of guilt you're putting on yourself."

"Yeah, there are a lot of idiots out there," he admitted with a sigh. "Not the kind of ending to the night we wanted."

"I don't know about that." She glanced at him. "I went to a great party, helped bring a new life into the world, had a meal, and watched four jerks being tackled to the ground and arrested." She smiled. "I'm hoping to finish off the night with some really hot and heavy sex with the man strong enough to not fight for me."

His smile doubled, and he felt a burst of energy rush through him. "Sounds like an excellent way to end the night."

She reached over and took his hand and squeezed it lightly. "Yes, it does."

CHAPTER 13

This hadn't been the first time something like this had happened to her. Nor, she figured, would it be the last.

The entire time they'd sat there, listening to the four men spew their hate, her thoughts had been on Brett and how to keep him from fighting them and getting hurt. She knew that if he stood up to fight, there was a possibility that he would get hurt beyond her ability to repair him.

As it was, his recovery was slower than she'd anticipated. She knew that he couldn't withstand any injury to his leg and still heal properly. All it would have taken was one of the four large men kicking or hitting him in the thigh, and he would have been down for the count.

She doubted men like that would stop fighting simply because he'd passed out or fallen to the ground.

So she'd done what she'd been taught to do. Nothing.

Thankfully, there had been enough people around them to call the police, and they had arrived before the men had thought to pull Brett from the booth.

She hated watching the men hit him with his cane. She doubted she would ever forget the sound of the wood breaking on his back as he was hit repeatedly with it.

It had taken all her will to not cry out, to not fight back. But in that moment, she'd vowed to herself to sign up for Aubrey's judo classes the following day.

There was no way she was going to allow herself to feel so helpless again. Not when she had someone worth fighting for.

She parked in her driveway, turned off Brett's car, and looked at her little house for a moment.

"Nice place," Brett said.

He'd helped her move into the place less than a year ago, but she couldn't remember the last time he'd been over there.

"Yeah." She nodded. Her entire body had started to shake, and she knew it was the last of her adrenaline leaving her as her body finally caught up with what had happened.

"Hey." Brett took her hand in his when she reached for the door.

She shook her head, willing the tears not to fall. "Inside," she said, hearing her voice crack slightly. "I think I need some wine."

Brett nodded and followed her slowly inside.

She locked the door and tossed her purse down on the entryway table and took a moment to take in a deep breath.

She smelled the lavender and mint scents of her home and settled herself before walking into the kitchen and pulling out a bottle of her favorite wine. As she poured two glasses, Brett moved over and leaned against the bar top, leaning a hip on one of her bar stools.

"Wow, you've done a lot in here. I like your color choices." He took the glass that she offered him. "Bright and cheery." He took a drink as he looked around.

She glanced around and realized just how much better she

felt since she'd walked through the door. Especially having Brett around.

"To Paige." She held up her glass and tapped his glass before drinking the entire glass in one swallow.

She didn't know who moved first, but after that, they moved as if in unison. They set their glasses on the breakfast bar, and then they were suddenly in each other's arms, their lips fused together as their hands moved quickly to remove each other's clothes.

The moment his skin was under her fingertips, she sighed with relief. It felt as if she was breathing for the first time in hours.

Her fingers shook as she pulled his pants snap loose, and she knew that it had nothing to do with what they'd just gone through in the last hour. Her desires and wishes were completely under the control of her body at this point.

She needed Brett. Needed to feel him over her. In her. Around her.

"Please," she said as he trailed his mouth down her neck while he hiked up the skirt to her dress. "I need to feel you inside me."

A low groan reverberating in his chest made her smile. Then, in one swift move, he hoisted her up, knocking over their glasses as he set her on the countertop.

She laughed with excitement and joy as he ripped her black silk panties from her and tossed them onto the floor. Then his mouth covered her pussy while her fingers dug into his hair. She held onto him while he lapped at her, and when he plunged his tongue into her pussy, it made her come almost instantly.

"My god," he said as he trailed his mouth along her inner thigh. "You taste like nectar."

"Brett." She didn't know what she was going to say, only that she needed more.

When he moved up to wrap his arms around her, she reached for him, but he leaned back slightly.

"I want to have you in a bed, this first time." His eyes searched hers. "I hate that I can't carry you there myself…"

She smiled and pulled him close. "You can do that later." She took his hand and slid off the counter.

He was standing there in nothing more than his shoes and blue boxer briefs, looking sexier than any man she'd ever seen before.

Since his injury, he'd been working more on lifting weights and now he had even more beautiful muscles and a new six-pack to show for all his hard work.

How had she gotten so lucky to be with someone like him? He was beautiful inside and out.

They moved down the hallway and into her bedroom together, slowly. She tried to move over to her bed, but he stopped her and searched for the light switch.

When she opened her mouth to argue, he found the switch and her bedroom was bathed in bright light.

"The lamp is less bright." She walked over to turn on the bedside lamp. He flipped off the main light, and she helped him towards the bed. She knelt beside him when he sat on the edge of her bed and removed his shoes.

"Careful," he said with a chuckle. "I might get used to you waiting on me."

She laughed. "Once that leg is healed, you're on your own again."

He nodded, then gripped her hips and pulled her up onto his body as he lay back on her bed. She was careful around his left leg, but after he started kissing her again, she forgot all about his pain, focusing only on the pleasure he was giving her.

When his finger dipped into her pussy, she cried out, on the brink of coming again. Part of her mind screamed that she needed to move, to give him as much pleasure as he was giving her, so she reached for him.

He was hard and as she rubbed him through the cotton of his boxer briefs, and she enjoyed feeling his hips swaying with her movements.

"Lea, tell me you have some condoms," he practically groaned out.

"Yes." She smiled and reached for the box of condoms on her nightstand. She'd purchased them in hopes that this very scenario would play out.

Taking one, she knelt next to him and helped him slide off his boxers. The doctor in her zoned in on his puckered scar, looking for any signs of infection or damage that might have happened in tonight's events. Seeing none, she leaned over him, opened the foil package, and slowly slid the condom over his length.

When he made a sound, her eyes moved to him.

"Am I hurting you?" she asked.

"God no," he groaned quickly. "You're killing me."

Her hands stilled over him, gripping him slightly tighter. "This?" she asked, sliding up and down him slowly. She smiled when his hips jerked, and he fisted his hands on her bedspread.

"Lea." It was a warning, one she should have headed, but she continued to slide her hand up and down his length as she leaned forward and placed her lips over his six-pack.

She licked her way over the ridges of his muscles, tasted him, working her way up his body until she finally straddled his hips.

His hands moved over her breasts, pinching and teasing her nipples lightly. Then they worked down to her hips and he guided her to slide down, taking all of him deep into her.

She arched back, enjoying the feeling of being complete. Marveling at how wonderful he felt inside her, under her.

She opened her eyes and watched his enjoyment flood his

face for a heartbeat. Then she began to move and lost herself completely in his blue eyes until they fell together.

The dream started differently this time. Instead of a bunch of college kids heckling her for being too smart and too young, there were four large men dressed in red, white, and blue surrounding her. Taunting her, pushing her, telling her to go back to where she came from.

In her dream, all four of them had canes. Instead of using them just on Brett, they lifted them towards her. And, as if in slow motion, powerful arms with thick wooden canes descending on her small form. She knew in that instant that she was going to die. There was no way she would survive such a vicious attack. It was impossible.

"Lea!" Brett was shouting at her, shaking her body.

When her eyes flew open, she had to blink a few times for his worried face to come into focus.

"My god. Are you okay?" Brett asked as he pulled her into his arms.

"I…" She held onto his naked body and closed her eyes. She breathed his scent in and instantly felt steadier. "It was a dream," she said a few times. more to reassure herself as much as him.

"You were screaming like someone was killing you." He held onto her. She felt him stiffen in her arms. "Was it about last night?" He leaned back slightly to run his eyes over her.

That's when she noticed it was daylight out. They must have fallen asleep, holding onto one another.

She instantly wished they would have woken up slowly, wrapped in each other's embrace, and made love again. Instead, the terrible dream had taken that from her.

"I'm okay." She laid her hand on his face, enjoying the stubble that had grown overnight on his otherwise smooth skin. "It was just a dream."

His eyes searched her face, and he must have been able to tell that she didn't want those four men to ruin any more of their time together. He relaxed and moved to pull her closer.

Shifting, she laid her cheek against his chest as he leaned back on her headboard. She felt him tense for a moment, but then he sighed and relaxed.

"I don't suppose you'd be willing to help me move my things out of the cabin this morning?" he asked her.

She smiled. "Since it's my official day off... I'd be happy to. Just as long as we make enough time to stop and have breakfast first." She glanced up at him as she trailed a finger over his chest. "For some reason, I'm famished this morning."

His smile was quick just before he dipped his head down and kissed her.

"We might have a few moments to grab something to eat," he said between kisses. "After a very hot, very long shower."

"Hm," she groaned, running her hands over his shoulders.

She'd never woken up in a man's arms before. Actually, she'd never let a man spend the night at her place or slept with one in a bed before. There were a lot of firsts she planned on doing with Brett. One of those firsts was taking a shower with him.

"A very long... hot..."—she shifted slightly, rubbing her body against his— "shower sounds really good."

He smiled up at her. "Witch." He chuckled as she jumped up from the bed.

She had just turned on the shower, warming it up, when he stepped into the bathroom and made his way towards her. Just then, she happened to get a look at his back in the mirror and gasped.

"What did they do to you?" She moved around him and ran her fingers lightly over his black and purple skin. There were two long shallow cuts along his right shoulder blade. When she looked closer, she saw a few splinters of wood from his cane embedded in his skin.

"It's nothing." He started to move past her, but she stopped him and nudged him until he sat on the counter, facing away from her.

"You have chunks of wood in here from your cane and you're bleeding," she informed him.

"I am?" He glanced back into the mirror and then winced. "It looks worse than it feels."

She grabbed her first aid kit from under the sink and quickly took a couple of pictures of his shoulder for the police file before she started cleaning his back. He sat patiently as she used her tweezers to gently pull the pieces of wood from his skin. He hissed when she cleaned it.

"I'm not going to bandage it, since I'll want to rinse it out in the shower. After, I'll put a bandage on it." She opened the shower door and helped him hobble in. "Sit on the shower bench," she said as she stepped in.

"Yes, doctor," Brett said. He wiggled his eyebrows, making her smile.

"Oh, you want to play?" She moved over to him and picked up her shampoo bottle behind his back. After he sat down on the shower bench, she turned the bottle upside down and dumped a bunch on his head while the water ran over the both of them.

He gripped her hips and kissed her until she melted against him.

When she stepped out of the shower, she was trying to figure out how to convince him to spend the entire day in bed with her. But the sound of her cell phone ringing and the dozen or so messages on her phone had instant worry replacing those thoughts.

Images of something going wrong with baby Paige had her answering Zoey's call.

"What's up? Is Paige, okay?" she answered quickly.

"Yes, we're all fine. How about you?" Zoey asked, and Lea could hear the worry in her tone.

"We're— I'm good," she corrected quickly.

"You don't know, do you?" Zoey asked.

"Know?" Lea glanced over and saw Brett check his phone and frown down at it. Then he turned his screen towards hers, and she saw a grainy image of last night.

"It went national," Zoey said softly. "What the two of you went through last night."

Lea closed her eyes and sat on the edge of her bed with the towel still wrapped around her. All thoughts of sexy fun time with Brett disappeared.

She remembered telling the girl last night that it was okay to share the video. After all, if there was a possibility that it would help someone else out, she was all for it. Besides, she didn't think anyone would be able to tell who they were, since the video was very grainy and taken from outside the Whataburger.

"I... didn't think... We're okay," she reiterated. "Brett has some bruises."

"Bruises?" Zoey jumped in. "Hang on, I'm putting you on speaker phone. We're all here."

"Here?" Lea asked.

"Still at the hospital. We're checking out in a few hours and heading home," Zoey answered. "But the gang is all here."

"Hi," several people called out at the same time.

"Brett's here too," she said, putting her phone on speaker. It wasn't until the other side of the call went quiet that she realized that she had just broadcasted to everyone they knew that they'd just spend the night together.

"Morning," Brett said easily. "As Lea said, I'm okay."

"What the hell," Aiden said. "Tell us the four of them are rotting in a cell."

"Yes, Carl hauled them away and assured me that they'll be

charged for last night's hate crime and attack on an officer, since I clearly told them I was the police, and my official retirement isn't until next month," Brett said. She must have been too busy trying to stay calm last night to hear that bit of information. To be honest, she wasn't quite sure how she'd made it through everything, let alone made it home.

"Good," Aiden said. "So now you're famous again."

Brett sighed and looked at her. "We're going to stop off and get some breakfast… then Lea's going to help me move my stuff back to my place."

"We'll come help," Aiden said. "See you in about an hour. We can get the full story then."

"Sound good," Brett said and then hung up.

"I'm sorry," she said once the line went dead. "I… didn't mean to tell them about us."

"Why not?" Brett frowned over at her. "Whatever this is, I hadn't planned on it being a secret. Not from our friends."

She relaxed. "You didn't?"

He smiled and pulled her close to him. "No. Something this good, I don't want to hide."

CHAPTER 14

*H*e knew his friends were trying to make them feel better about what they'd been through the night before, but he was worried that highlighting the scenario was just pouring salt on Lea's open wound.

Even though she laughed and joked when everyone packed up his stuff in three boxes to take back to his place, he remembered seeing her cry out and shiver as he woke her from the nightmare that morning.

He'd wanted to protect her last night and had failed, having to wait around for people who could. That played heavily on his ego, something he hadn't struggled with for years. He supposed it was because he had never been weak or vulnerable before now.

Whatever the reason, he wasn't enjoying it now. Especially sitting back with his feet up, watching his friends cart out his stuff and load it in his car. After which, no doubt, everyone would end up at his place to listen to the entire story of last night.

Everyone, that was, that didn't have to work that day. An hour later, sure enough, his apartment was crowded with Aubrey, Aiden, Elle, Levi, and Scarlett. Someone had stopped off and grabbed sandwiches and beer. He sat on the sofa, his left leg propped up again, as they conveyed everything that had happened to them.

To be honest, at this point, after having taken more than two dozen calls, he was tired of the story and knew that Lea felt the same way.

Her parents had called her in a frantic state of worry when they'd been driving back to his place, and he'd listened to the two-sided conversation through her car's speakers while she explained that they were both okay.

He felt honored that her parents had been equally as concerned for him as they were for their own daughter. After everyone had left his apartment later that night, he realized that there was one phone call he hadn't gotten that day. The one from his own parents.

What had he expected? After all, the men that had attacked them last night were his dad's kind of people. Right?

Still, seeing as their son was on national television being attacked a little over a month after he'd been shot, he would have hoped that they'd call to see how he was doing.

"You're quiet," Lea said as she helped clean up the dishes and toss the beer and soda cans away.

"Just… thinking," he said with a sigh. "My parents didn't call." He glanced down at his phone.

She stopped clearing the coffee table and set the pile of plates down. She sat next to him and took his hands in hers.

"I know they shouldn't matter to me." He looked down at their joined hands.

"But they do," she said softly and he nodded in agreement.

"So call them yourself. Tell them what happened. Maybe they don't know."

He rolled his eyes. "My mother works at the library and usually hears the gossip before it's on the morning news. My dad…" He looked up into her eyes. "Well, you know."

"Yeah." She sighed. "Call your mother then. Something tells me…" She dropped off and shook her head.

"What?" he asked after a moment.

She sighed heavily and then blurted out, "I've always thought that it was your father keeping her from you."

His eyebrows shot up at her words. "You think…" He shook his head in instant denial. His mother had been distant with him as far back as… He stopped and really thought about it.

In his earliest memories, his mother had been kind, caring. She'd gone out of her way to make him special treats every day for his school lunch. When his parents had fought, she'd sheltered him, comforted him, and assured him that everything was going to be okay.

Then he'd grown up. Gotten tired of her lies. Of the way his father had treated her. He'd grown mad at her for allowing his dad to do that to her, to him, to their family.

He remembered the day his mother's attitude towards him had changed. It had been career day at his school, and Tommy Stephan's father had talked to their class about being a cop for a career. He'd come home claiming he'd wanted to be a cop when he grew up.

"Since the day I decided to become a cop," he said out loud.

"What?" Lea asked, causing him to blink from the memory.

"She changed the day I came home excited that I'd chosen my career as a cop." He closed his eyes.

"She probably felt shame then and now," Lea said after a moment of thought. "Not of your career choice but because she couldn't protect you the way a mother should have." Lea squeezed his hand lightly. "Call her. Even if she acts like she doesn't care, at least she'll know that you're okay."

He nodded and pulled out his cell phone. His mother picked up on the first ring. Her voice was soft as a whisper, just as it had been his entire life. Even when his father was standing over her, yelling at her and threatening her life and his, she'd spoken so softly sometimes he couldn't hear her.

"Hi, Mom, I just, uh, wanted you to know that I'm okay. In case you saw the news today," he said quickly.

"Oh, Brett, how nice of you to call," she said in a cheerful tone. "Yes, I did see that. It's so wonderful of you to check in. Your father and I were just sitting down to dinner. I'm afraid we can't talk right now. Thank you for letting us know. Goodbye."

She hung up before he could say anything else, leaving him to stare down at the phone.

"Well?" Lea asked.

"She… blew me off." He tossed his phone down on the coffee table in disgust.

Once again, Lea took his hands in hers. "Sometimes people locked in relationships can't always… articulate." She sighed. "Was your father there?" she asked after another moment.

"Yes, she said they had just sat down for dinner." He rolled his eyes. "She told me that they couldn't talk right now. Like they don't have time for me."

Lea sighed and then shook her head. "You know, for a cop, you're pretty dense."

"What?" He frowned over at her.

"Your father was there," she said slowly. "Of course, she couldn't talk. She probably couldn't even show that she was worried about you. In college, I had to take an entire course on how to spot abuse in patients."

"Yeah, I had to as a law officer as well."

"Then you must have skipped the class where they explained how the abuser controls their victims by separating them from everyone who cares about them. Sometimes the victims push away those they love to shelter them from their pain or to ensure that they themselves don't become a victim," she said slowly.

He felt his heart sink in his chest, and he had to swallow a lump in his throat.

"You think that my mother pushed me away because she was shielding me from my father?" he asked.

"Who knows your mother's reasons. I'm just saying, you should give her the benefit of the doubt. She loves you, even if she can't show it. Especially around your dad." Lea hugged him.

"Can you stay?" he asked her after they'd finished cleaning up.

"I have the early morning shift at the hospital," she said with a half groan.

"I can wake you up early." He pulled her close to him and kissed her.

"I have a double shift tomorrow. I can stay for a while, but I should go home and get some sleep... after," she said against his neck as he continued to rub his lips against her skin just under her ear. She groaned and then laughed when he tried to walk them back to his bedroom.

His apartment wasn't as big or as nice as her place, but he was proud of his king-sized bed. He'd spent almost an entire month's salary on the pillow top.

"Brett," she said, an hour later, when they lay in each other's arms, cooling off in the warm night air.

"Hm?" he asked, his hands lazily drawing circles on her lower back.

"Don't give up on your mother." She looked down at him.

"Never," he answered with a smile.

"Good." She leaned down and kissed him. "I'd better go."

She rolled away from him and started to get dressed, and his body instantly missed her heat, her softness.

He wanted to reach for her, to pull her back down next to him. But he knew she had commitments.

"Want me to…" He started to roll out of bed.

"Nope, you lay right there." She stopped pulling her shoes on and leaned in and kissed him on the lips. "Go to sleep. I'll text you tomorrow when I have time."

He took her hand and stopped her from walking away. "This." He motioned between them. "I don't want this to just be a once in a while thing." He felt foolish. But there was no other way to explain to her how much this meant to him.

"Good, because I don't do casual." Lea smiled down at him. "We've known each other too long for that."

"Which brings me to my other thought. If something were to go wrong with this." He motioned between them again. "I don't think I could lose you as a friend. No matter what, I want you in my life."

She smiled and nodded, then bent down and kissed him again. "Sleep well."

"Drive safe. Text me when you get home." He watched her walk out.

Less than ten minutes later, he got her text that she was home safe.

He thought he'd fall asleep quickly after that. After all, he'd spent most of last night pleasing her and being pleased by her, then most of the day explaining what had happened with them. He should have been very tired. Instead, he stared up at the ceiling, thinking of her.

His thoughts turned to his mother and, as he drifted off,

memories of how she'd changed from a loving, carrying woman to a cold, distant one played in his dreams.

When he woke, he felt more tired than he had before he fell asleep. Since he had no place to be for the day, he bummed around his apartment. After making dry toast from a loaf of bread that had been in his freezer, the only bit of groceries he had left in his apartment, he showered off. Then he spent an hour doing laundry and surfing the internet. Totally bored just before lunchtime, he grabbed his keys and hobbled out to drive to the library.

He didn't know his mother's schedule, but he knew that she worked most Saturdays. If she wasn't there, he figured he could at least pick up a few good books to fill his time.

Living in a small town, he knew almost everything about everyone. Half the people he grew up with knew everything there was to know about him.

He could hardly remember a time when he hadn't bumped into someone and chatted with them when he went anywhere in town, even when he was just pumping gas.

That was the case today. The moment he stepped out of his car and started up the path to the library, he bumped into three people who stopped him and asked him questions about the other night.

"You're quite the celebrity," a couple of them told him. A few asked how he was doing physically. Some had even heard that he was going to quit the force to work at the camp.

By the time he walked into the library, he was feeling slightly drained. He saw his mother behind the counter and walked up to her.

"Morning," he said as he searched her face, a face he'd known as well as his own. Yet it was as if he was seeing it for the first time. He saw the weariness in eyes that matched his almost perfectly. Weariness and a hint of fear. Normally, he wouldn't have thought anything about her scanning the area when she saw him, but now, after what Lea had said last night, he realized what his mother was doing. She was checking to see if his father was anywhere in sight.

"Morning," she replied softly.

"Do you have a moment?" he asked. "Is there someplace we can talk in private?"

She glanced around again, and he saw her relax slightly. "Sure." She walked around the counter, and he followed her into a private reading room. The walls were glass, but the moment they stepped inside and the door shut, all sound from the outside was cut off.

"Are you okay?" his mother said, watching him move slowly to take a seat at the small conference table that sat in the middle of the room.

"I am." He watched her, then he motioned for her to sit. She glanced out the windows before sitting down across from him, making a point to face the windows.

"Worried Dad will show up?" he asked, trying to hide the sarcasm in his tone.

"N-no," she responded a little too quickly. "Just, I'm at work."

"Right." He nodded. "I won't take up much of your time then." He took a deep breath. "It's been almost a full month since I was shot, and I've only seen you once in all that time."

His mother's eyes finally moved away from the glass wall and focused on her hands instead. All his life he could remember her fidgeting with her fingers. Not once did he think of the movement as anything other than just something she did. Now, however, he saw it for what it was. Fear and nerves.

Reaching across the table, he laid his hands over hers. "Mom?"

Her eyes moved up to his and, for a moment, he believed she

was going to open up to him. But then she jerked her hands away and stood up.

"I… can't." She shook her head and straightened her shoulders. "I need to get back to work." She moved to walk past him, but he took her hand and stopped her.

"Mom? What have I done to earn your contempt and disdain?" He felt his heart breaking a little that he would even have to ask his mother that question. Still, he'd bottled up his feelings for too long. If he could survive being shot, then he could survive hearing the answer.

It was as if his question had opened a portal and the kind-hearted, caring woman he remembered from his youth once more reappeared.

His mother's entire body transformed from a rigid shield to something softer.

Her hand came up and rested on his face. "Oh honey, I've never stopped loving you. I never will. I'm so very proud of who you have become." She smiled weakly and her eyes watered. "It's just…" She glanced towards the doorway. "We can't all be who we want. Some of us don't have that freedom."

"You could." He laid his hand over hers.

He watched as her protective shield slipped on once more. Her spine straightened and her eyes grew more distant. The love he'd seen in her eyes disappeared, replaced by fear.

"No." She removed her hand and dropped it to her side. "I can't."

With this, she turned and walked out of the room. When he made his way through the library, he noticed his mother was not behind the counter when he passed by. He was pretty sure that she was hiding somewhere, waiting for him to leave.

Instead of checking out books, as he had intended, he made his way back outside.

He wasn't even slightly surprised to see his father leaning on his car in the parking lot. Every time he'd visited his mother in the past, somehow his father had always shown up during or after his visits.

He knew that if he didn't play this right, his mother would be the one to pay the price for his little visit. Normally, he could lie and say he'd just been there to check out some books, but this time, he just didn't have it in him. Nor did he have any books.

"Morning," he said, trying to sound cheerful. He stopped by his car, knowing that his father wouldn't move until he was done with whatever he wanted to say to him.

"So, now you're a hero?" His father's tone was snide.

"Nope, just someone who has learned not to take shit from assholes," he said, making sure he had a solid footing on his right leg. Whatever came next, he wanted to be positive he could protect his left leg.

His father stood straight up quickly, coming inches from Brett. Normally, he wouldn't have flinched. After all, they were in public, and he was slightly taller than his old man and in better shape. But now, with his injury, he felt his entire body tense. His father saw the move and a slow smile curved his lips.

"So, you're with the Chinese woman?" his father taunted. So many times in the past, Brett had wanted to punch the man. But he knew the law and practiced extreme patience when it came to his father. There was no way he was going to let the man goad him into doing something stupid.

"She's not from China. Nor is her family. But you know that," he said in a low tone.

"No?" His father's smile grew. "It's so hard to tell them all apart," he said with a dismissive shrug.

"It's the twenty-first-century, Dad. Get with the times. Racism is antiquated. Only the uneducated separate the masses by the color of their skin, their religion, etcetera." He leaned forward slightly and smiled. "Are you that ignorant?"

He saw his father's fists clench as hatred filled his eyes.

"What are you doing here, son?" His father's voice rose.

"Here?" He glanced around as if realizing where he was for the first time. "Oh." He smiled. "Visiting my mother." His father's eyes heated even further. "It's not against the law. Seeing one's mother."

"She doesn't want to see you. Neither of us do," his father barked out.

Brett chuckled. "Yeah, apparently you've trained her well." He narrowed his eyes. "Or scared her enough that she'd turn her only child away." He shrugged. "Either way, she made your wishes perfectly clear." He tried to stay in line, but his father had a way of agitating him. He hated that his mother would pay the price for his short visit, either by a verbal attack or by a physical one. No matter what, one thing had been made clear to him over the years—whatever his father did to her, she would never betray or leave him. Not even for her son.

That thought had his stomach turning.

Brett started to move past his father, but the man took a step to block his move.

"Stay away from us," his father said in a low voice. "We don't agree with your beliefs."

"What? That all people deserve to be on the same planet as you?" he asked. A few people had stopped to watch them at this point.

One thing had been clear his entire childhood—his father hated causing a scene in public. His entire life, his dad had kept his fights to the privacy of their own home.

"Not everyone is created equal," his father replied in a low voice.

Brett smiled. "At least we finally have something we can

agree on. Lea and her family are far superior to you," he said. He easily slipped past him this time and climbed into his car.

As he drove away, he glanced in the rearview mirror. His father stood on the sidewalk, fists clenched and fire in his eyes.

That was the first time Brett felt like he'd won an argument with his father, and it felt so good. Riding on a high, he figured he'd swing by the camp for a celebratory lunch and maybe a dip in the pool.

CHAPTER 15

*L*ea tried to push past everyone's concerns and comments about the viral video of her and Brett ignoring the four racist men. So many of her coworkers urged her to get online and look at some of the comments, but she knew already what most of them would say.

More than half would be encouraging while a few hate-filled comments from trolls and haters would slip through the line of well-wishers. She just didn't have the energy or time to wade through it all.

She was surprised when halfway through her first shift, Carl and Steven showed up at the nurse's station, looking for her.

"Hi." She smiled at the two officers. She'd dealt with enough of the men and women on the police force to know most of them by name. Carl and Steven had been friends with Brett, and she'd hung out with Carl and his wife, Kayla, a few times during one of Brett's many game nights.

"Hi there, Dr. Val." Carl smiled at her. "Got a second to chat?"

"Sure." She motioned for the men to follow her into one of the private consultation rooms. She shut the door and moved over to sit down. One thing she'd learned early on in her career was that when you get a chance to sit down, you take it. Especially if you were working a double shift. "What's up?"

Carl set a folder down in front of her. "Just need your Hancock on the official report from the other night. Two of the men, Robbie Dixon and Larry Ryan, are being charged with aggravated assault and hate crimes. The other two just with hate crimes. Witnesses claim only Robbie and Larry physically assaulted Brett."

"One of the men in blue shirts," Lea started, "the blond one, grabbed Brett's cane, but the red shirt…"

"Robbie," Carl supplied.

"Robbie took it from him before hitting Brett," she finished.

"Right." Carl nodded. "That's what witnesses claim, as well as what the video shows." Carl shook his head and sighed heavily. "I'd like to say this thing doesn't happen often, but lately, well, we're seeing more and more of it." He glanced over at Steven. "This might be a tough one to push through since Robbie's grandfather is a judge."

Lea sighed. She'd heard of Judge Dixon. After all, her mother was a public defender. Robert Dixon Sr. was one of the crookedest judges in the county. According to her mother, anyone of color who stepped in front of the judge usually got the max sentence for whatever crime they were being charged with while those with… fairer skin usually walked free.

There was no doubt that the judge's grandson would skirt the charges. He'd probably done so many times before he stepped foot in Whataburger. After all, men like Robbie didn't just one day wake up and decide to be racist.

"Right," she said with a sigh. "I have pictures of what they did to Brett." She pulled out her phone and sent them to Carl's phone. "Is it even worth pressing charges?"

Carl nodded. "Yes, this will be his fourth time being charged this year alone. This will help." He waved his phone before putting it back into his pocket.

"Four?" She balked. "He's done this to three other people?"

Carl glanced over at Steven. "This year."

She laid her head in her hands and had to take several deep breaths before she looked up. "How many times has he gotten away with it?"

Carl sat down across from her. He reached out and took her hand, a move she knew that he only felt comfortable with because he knew her personally.

"Lea, I'm going to be honest with you. Mainly because, well, Brett is our brother and..."—Carl smiled quickly— "Kayla really likes you. When she found out that the two of you were on a date, she kicked my butt for not telling her that you two were an item."

Lea smiled at the mention of his wife. "We... weren't really yet."

"Now?" Carl asked, then shook his head. "Never mind. I'll get to the gossip later." His smile faded. "The last couple of people who filed charges against Dixon ended up receiving death threats."

Lea tensed and looked down at the paper in front of her.

"I won't lie to you and say that there isn't a chance he will walk away free in the end, or that he won't come after you in any way, but I will promise you this. We protect one of our own and... you are one of ours," Carl said.

Steven nodded quickly in agreement. "That SOB needs to be locked up before he kills someone."

"He crossed the line this time by hitting an officer. Even one on medical leave. Before now, he was just verbally abusive. The moment he hit Brett was the moment we finally got him. He won't walk away so easily this time. Not without a good fight," Carl added.

Lea smiled and, after taking a deep breath, she signed the report and slid it back to Carl. "Thank you," she said softly.

"Just doing our job." Carl tucked the paper back into the folder.

"Has Brett signed it yet?" she asked.

"We're heading out to the camp now to meet with him," Carl said.

"And have lunch," Steven added. "Nothing beats one of Chef Isaacs's meals."

Lea smiled and showed the two men out. For the rest of her shift, she thought about what they'd told her. Normally, her mother would have been hired to defend men like Robbie and Larry. She couldn't imagine having a job where she had to save someone so evil from rotting in a prison cell.

Her mother was a stronger person than she was. Which reminded her that it was past time she took some time out to have dinner with her family.

Maybe she'd invite Brett along. After all, her parents loved him like a son. Actually, they treated Aiden, Brett, and Elle like their children, along with a handful of Raya's friends. It was one of the reasons she loved her parents so much, their ability to embrace others and bring them into the fold of family.

By the time she dragged herself into her bed almost twenty-four hours later, she was too exhausted to even think.

Brett had texted her that he'd signed the report and that he was missing her. He'd suggested that they meet up for breakfast at the camp and a quick swim the following morning.

Since it was the first time that she'd fallen asleep alone since the Whataburger incident, she had a difficult time drifting off. After almost an hour of trying to fall asleep while images of Robbie and Larry taunted her, she turned on the television. That ended up being a huge mistake, as the story was playing on every news channel.

She flipped channels until cartoons flooded her screen. She finally settled back and watched one of her favorite childhood shows.

When she woke, she grabbed her bag with her swimsuit and some scrubs, then headed out to the camp to meet with Brett.

She'd never really been nervous around Brett before except for a few times, but this morning she was overly so.

Walking from the parking lot to the main building, she reminded herself that they were friends first and that she'd known him since before she was ten.

Still, when she saw him sitting at a large table with the rest of the normal gang, she felt her heart flutter. The chair next to him was the only empty seat, and it was obvious that he'd saved her a spot.

Setting her bag down, she greeted everyone cheerfully, trying desperately to hide her nerves. She was thankful that the conversation at the table didn't seem to pause too long for her arrival and everyone continued talking about the day's itinerary. Over the past two years, she'd sat through more makeshift meetings than she could count. So she ordered her breakfast and ate quietly while everyone droned on or debated who was going to take over Zoey's and Dylan's tasks while they were out on maternity leave.

She must have stopped listening at one point because the entire table grew quiet, and she looked up to see everyone looking at her.

"Sorry." She set her half-empty tea mug down. "I must have dozed off for a moment," she said, getting a few chuckles.

"We were asking when you were going to clear Brett here for work?" Elle asked.

"My medical leave is up next week, and my retirement officially kicks in the following day," Brett added. "So until both take place and Lea signs off on me, I'm spending my days enjoying—" He cleared his throat. "I mean, surveying the property for security risks," he finished in an official-sounding tone. A couple of people chuckled again.

"If he sits behind a desk, he can go to work tomorrow," Lea said, knowing full well what Brett would think of that.

"Hey, let's not be too hasty," Brett said, holding up his hands, causing her to smile. "I'd at least like to be able to stand up without the aid of a cane first."

"I think two weeks is soon enough," she relented with a smile.

She watched Brett relax slightly.

"I'll send you over everything I have for this place as far as security goes so you can take a look at it," Aiden said.

"Oh." Elle snapped her fingers, getting everyone's attention. "That reminds me." She dug in her large bag and came out with a box. "There, now it's official." She slid the box in front of Brett.

Brett slowly opened the lid and pulled out one of the standard camp shirts with his name on the front. When he turned it around, he smiled at the bold "River Camps Security" on the back.

"There are business cards." Elle motioned to the box. Brett pulled out a smaller box and took out one of the shiny blue business cards, looked at it for a moment, then handed her one.

She had a few of her own and knew that there were some in each cabin. No doubt when Brett officially started, his cards would be added.

"There, now it's official," Elle said with a smile before standing up. "On that note, I have a class to fill in for." She turned and left.

Everyone else at the table took their cue from her and left shortly after, leaving Lea alone with Brett.

Once again, her nerves of being around him surfaced, and

she started fidgeting with his business card. His eyes tracked her movement, and he had a slight frown on his face.

"Problem?" she asked, setting the card down.

"No, it's just... I spoke to my mother yesterday." He leaned back.

"How did that go?" she asked, already seeing the answer in his eyes.

"As expected. Mom skirted my questions. Dad threatened me and tried to get me to fight him." He sighed. "If I didn't know the law, I would have taken him up on the offer and punched him." He glanced around as if looking for something else to hit.

She laid her hand over his and waited until he looked over at her.

"I'm sorry," she said softly. "I know it's not perfect timing, but my family has invited you to dinner tomorrow night," she said with a half-smile. "They wanted to thank you for... well, everything."

"I didn't do anything." He looked down at their joined hands.

"That's the whole thing, though, isn't it," she said with a smile.

He shrugged and sighed as he glanced around. "I'm not really in the mood for a swim."

"Okay." She tilted her head to look at him. "Then how about we do something different?"

His eyebrows shot up. "Like what?"

A wicked grin spread on her lips, and she rubbed her hands together as a worried look crossed his eyes.

Forty minutes later, Lea was beginning to think that her idea of taking Brett to the gym and letting him box his anger away was questionable. The man was a drone. She'd never seen anyone pummel the punching bag as many times and as hard as he did. Beads of sweat rolled down his arms, his back, and his forehead as he concentrated on his moves.

She was impressed at his balance, standing on his right leg while he threw the punches over and over again.

He'd shown her how to throw a punch, and she'd tried her hardest, but after a while, she'd settled on watching him instead. The show made her realize just what an impressive specimen of a man he was. Full-on Captain America physique.

The fact that she could still remember him as a slightly chubby ten-year-old had her smiling as he continued to pummel the bag.

"Someone's in a mood," Aubrey said, coming up beside her.

Lea sighed. "He ran into his parents the other day."

Aubrey nodded. "Yeah, just a phone call with my dad makes me want to do the same." She motioned to Brett. "How's he holding up?"

Lea knew what Aubrey was asking. Not about Brett's leg or injury from the cane, but about his mental state.

She took a moment to assess his mood earlier. "He's holding up. I think things will look better for him once he officially starts working at the camp." She turned slightly towards Aubrey. "How are the wedding plans coming along?"

Aubrey smiled. "Busy and wonderful. Still, I can't believe all of us original Wildflowers will be married by this time next year."

"Original?" Lea asked.

Aubrey rolled her eyes. "Yes, some people, such as yourself, have earned honorary memberships to the exclusive club." She smiled. "Welcome aboard." She patted Lea's hand. "With that, I'm off to my judo class."

"Oh." Lea stopped her. "I, um, wanted to sign up for that." She glanced towards Brett, who was still slamming his fist into the punching bag.

"I have another one this afternoon, at two," Aubrey said. "You're welcome to join in the fun."

"Thanks," Lea said as Aubrey made her way out of the gym.

When Lea turned back to Brett, he was standing there, watching her.

"Everything okay?" she asked, moving over to him.

"Yeah," he said with a sigh. "I think I'm ready for that swim now."

She walked over and took his gloved hands in her own. "Sometimes it's good to get all that frustration out."

"Thanks. I guess I needed the outlet." He pulled her in close for a hug.

"You're all sweaty." She tried to back out, only to be held closer as he chuckled and kissed the top of her head.

"And now you are too." He laughed. "You're good for me."

She could have imagined he'd said those words; it was nothing more than a whisper. She held onto him, not caring about anything except how he made her feel.

A while later, as she floated in the pool, looking up at the robin's-egg-blue sky, she wondered if life could get any better.

She had the perfect job, the perfect home, a wonderful family that loved her, and now she had a boyfriend that made her toes curl.

Brett's hands circled her waist and pulled her under the water. She laughed the moment they surfaced.

"You're just lucky I'm too hungry to fight back," she said, holding onto him. Just then she heard his stomach growl loudly. She was pretty sure the water rippled from the sound. "Sounds like you are too." She laughed at him.

"I could eat." He pulled them towards the stairs of the pool.

They sat at the pool bar and ordered lunch, chicken salad for her and a grilled chicken sandwich for Brett.

When he ordered a beer, she wanted to stop him, but then she realized that he'd mentioned that he'd stopped taking his medicine last week. If she wasn't on call for the camp, she would have sipped on a margarita herself.

It was easy to forget in such a beautiful setting that she was actually working. The occasional emergency shook her out of her relaxation pretty quickly.

Such was the case the moment after they had ordered their lunch. Her phone started ringing and a few moments later she was sprinting towards the medical cabin. Thankfully, it was only a twisted wrist instead of a broken one. After dressing the cuts and giving the guest a sling and some pain pills, she returned to Brett and their lunch.

"It's a good thing you ordered a salad and not something hot," Brett said.

"I learned that lesson a long time ago. Never expect a normal meal when you're on duty." She shrugged.

"Working here must be a million times better than the hospital," Brett said once they started eating.

"It does have its perks." She glanced around. "Good view, food, and people."

He frowned over at her. "Aren't the people at the hospital good to you?"

"Oh, sure, it's just..." She bit her lip and realized that she didn't want to go into the details with Brett about avoiding Sanjay all the time. In the past few months, he'd become quite... bothersome. "It's nothing."

"There's something you're not telling me." The look Brett was giving her was one that she knew all too well. She wasn't going to be able to avoid telling him. The determination in his eyes told her that he wouldn't stop until he had the entire story from her.

Words flowed from her lips as she told him all about how, after Sanjay's divorce, he'd started giving her extra attention.

How he was starting to become more aggressive and corner her, even though she'd made her feelings clear.

"Is he at the stalker level?" Brett asked.

"No, nowhere near, just… creepy coworker who doesn't get the hint level."

"I know you can handle yourself, but if you want, I can have a chat with him. Or look into him if you need," Brett offered.

"No, you're right. So far, I've been handling him fine by myself. If he starts to cross the line, I can talk to my superiors."

"Next time you're working, I can swing in and make some sort of public display." He wiggled his eyebrows and she chuckled. "You know, so he gets the hint that you're taken."

"Regardless of what Sanjay thinks, I'd like you to visit me at work," she answered with a smile.

"So, dinner at your folks' place tomorrow night?" he asked.

"Yeah, if you're up to it." She felt nervous waiting for his answer. She could tell that earlier, he'd been so preoccupied with his own thoughts that he hadn't really registered the invite.

"I'd love to. What can I bring?" he asked, and she relaxed.

"Nothing. Dad's making his famous grilled fish. He wanted me to ask you if you'd be up for a fishing trip tomorrow morning, but as your doctor—"

"Yes," he broke in. "Tell him yes. I always love going out on the boat with your dad."

She frowned over at him. "Are you sure you're up for it?" She looked down at his leg, which he'd been rubbing absently.

"Lea, it's been almost two months, and I'm starting to go stir crazy. Being out on the water fishing with one of the only men I've looked up to my entire life would be choice. Even if I have to sit the entire time, I could sure use the reprieve."

She smiled. "Then I'll tell my dad to pick you up at five." Brett groaned at the early hour, and she laughed. "You asked for it."

CHAPTER 16

Sitting on the speeding fishing boat with the salty warm air hitting his face, Brett figured the trip was worth the lack of extra morning sleep he would have gotten.

Not to mention that talking to Ken Val was nothing short of entertaining. The man was funny and witty enough to be a stand-up comedian. Lea's mother, Katie, on the other hand, was all business and very lawyer-like.

By the time they had caught enough red snapper for dinner, Brett had laughed more than he had in years.

They'd spotted a pod of dolphins, and a few hammerhead sharks had tried to snatch the fish off their lines. It had been a long time since he'd had a such a relaxing day.

Ken was easy to talk to and asked about Brett's future plans without seeming like a nosy father trying to butt in.

Maybe it was because he'd known the man most of his life, but either way, he explained how he'd been hired on by the camp as head of security. Since he wasn't sure about his physical abilities, he figured it was the best choice, at least for the time being.

Ken talked about Raya and Lea as if he was proud of them no matter what path they took in life. As if they were equally loved in his eyes, even though Raya hadn't finished college and dressed up as a princess while Lea quite literally saved people's lives every single day.

Not that he had anything against Raya's job. Hell, he had a friend who'd worked at Disney for a few years to pay for college. In Orlando, it seemed like the best option for most college-age students. If they could get the job.

He'd been lucky enough himself to go from the local community college after getting his associate's degree straight into police training. He'd never had to worry about paying the bills after he'd gotten a scholarship for his first two years of college.

He'd known that Lea had rushed away at a very early age to Harvard. He also knew that she'd worked her butt off her entire life to get there. Even now, she was juggling two jobs to save up for her own medical practice.

What other twenty-seven-year-old could say the same? Those four men the other night probably drank their way through high school and barely passed their classes. Yet something deep inside them said that they were superior to her because of the color of her skin and which continent her ancestors had come from.

It ate at him to know that his father felt the same way. He could still remember the first time he was ashamed of his father's views.

He'd been in the library and had overheard an older kid talking about how they'd learned in history class how the Germans had tried to wipe out an entire race of people.

It had taken him a moment to understand, as he'd grown up hearing how proud his father was to be German and how honored he was that his grandfather had fought in the war and killed all those evil Jews. How the man and his wife had escaped prosecution for the good they had done and had fled to the States so they wouldn't end up like the rest of the men he'd fought beside.

He'd grown up thinking that his father had been telling him the truth. That the Jews had indeed been evil somehow. That his great-grandfather and great-grandmother had been lucky that they'd escaped.

He'd spent a week learning about what had really happened, and it had made his stomach twist in knots.

He'd never looked at his father or his ancestors the same after that. When it had come time to learn about World War II in class, he'd hung onto every word, fearful that he'd see his great-grandfather's pictures in the history book or in the black-and-white movies they'd watched in class.

He'd never told anyone about his heritage or just where his father's ancestors had come from. Somehow, even though the men he was related to didn't feel shame for their actions, Brett had.

When the boat's motor cut off, Brett cleared his mind and realized they were already back at the Val family's private dock. Their massive white three-story home sat on the back of Pelican Bay and had killer sunset views. There was a two-story dock that not only held their boat up out of the water but had a sundeck and a viewing area. There was also a wide seawall that kept the high bay waters out of the plush perfectly manicured yard during a storm.

A large rectangle swimming pool, complete with a hot tub and waterfalls, sat close to the house and its wraparound back porch.

Tall picture windows, which he knew would be boarded up if a hurricane rolled through, overlooked the water. The main floor of the home was a living and entertainment space. There was a detached five-car garage, complete with a spot for her parents' stylish motor home. He'd only been upstairs once in all these years, to visit Lea when she'd been sick and drop off some of her homework. Her room had been on the second floor and had a view overlooking the water. He knew that her mother had a home office on the top floor, along with the main bedroom, since Lea had told him many years ago that her parents lived on the top floor.

He helped Ken clean, winch, and hoist the boat back up onto the lift, securing it with the lines the way Ken showed him. Then they cleaned the fish in the sink and cutting area on the dock, placed them in a cooler, and hauled them up to the house. He had left his new cane at his place, so it was slow going.

He was trying to be more independent and had figured that he didn't need it any longer. Now, however, he was seriously wishing he had something to steady himself.

He was surprised to see Lea sipping drinks by the pool with her mother when they passed by.

"Don't mind us, boys, we've just gotten off work and are taking a break," Lea's mother said, tipping her glass towards them. "Beers are in the fridge."

Katie Val could easily pass as Lea and Raya's sister. The woman didn't look a day over thirty, with the exception of a few gray hairs around her temples. The woman was a knockout, just like Lea.

"I'll get this started. Why don't you get off that leg?" Ken said as they set the cooler by the outdoor kitchen area.

"Sure." Brett nodded and then headed back towards the pool. He stopped by Lea's chair and sat down next to her. "Hey."

She handed him her drink and he took a sip. Cold sweet liquid soothed his thirst and aches.

"This is good. What is it?" he asked, handing her the drink back.

"It's a famous Val sunset," Katie answered. "I'll go make you one if you want?"

"Thanks," he said and moved over to take the seat next to Lea. "So, how was work?" he asked her.

She sighed. "Good. Thankfully, Sanjay wasn't on shift. Which meant I had a great day." She smiled. "You? It looks like you caught some fish."

"Enough for dinner," he agreed. "I'd forgotten that your dad goes out on the boat all day. Thankfully, he packed lunch for the both of us."

"Dad doesn't do anything halfway," Lea replied with a smile.

"I could help..." He started to get up when he noticed Ken carrying a large tray out to the grill area.

"Don't you dare," Lea said in a low voice. "The way he views it, now that you're here, you're a guest."

He sat back and took the drink from Katie when she handed it to him. Then she disappeared to help her husband.

"How about a dip?" Lea asked after he took a drink.

He set his plastic glass down and followed her slowly to the edge of the pool.

"I remember a few pool parties here when we were younger," he said, sliding into the cool water.

"A few. Not as many as most, but I did have some normal childhood moments," she said with a smile.

While they played around in the water, her parents grilled and cooked dinner. When the table on the back porch was set and the food ready, they dried off, wrapped a few beach towels around themselves, and headed up to eat.

Sitting under the shade of the porch eating grilled fish and vegetables all while having a stimulating conversation, Brett realized just how lacking his family life had been.

Every single meal he'd spent with his mother and father in his youth had been in silence or listening to his father complain about one thing or another. Usually his mother's cooking or meal choice if he wasn't gripping about politics.

Normally, the television would be blaring some news station while his father talked about his latest conspiracy theory of how the system was rigged against him.

He had never once imagined, growing up, that families could be so much fun. The four of them sat around the table for hours, talking about a wide range of topics from politics to the latest movies playing in the theaters.

At one point, the dishes were cleared away and fresh watermelon appeared. More drinks were poured, and everyone moved down the yard for another dip in the pool.

He couldn't remember having a more relaxing day in his life. He watched the sunset while floating in the pool next to Lea.

"Thanks," he said, glancing over at her.

"For?" She smiled back at him.

Reaching across the water, he pulled her floaty towards his and took her hand. "For today."

She chuckled. "Thank my mother. It was her idea."

"Thanks, Mrs. Val, for today," he called out to her mother, who was lighting the firepit.

"You're welcome," her mother called back with a chuckle.

"I think she needed today as much as you did. She's got a couple of big cases coming up," Lea said.

"Tell me she's not defending the guys from the other night." He half groaned it.

"No." Lea shook his head. "She's made a point to request that she remains off the roster if they need a public defender. Besides, it's a conflict of interest, so I don't think they'd ask her."

"Good." He glanced over at her mother and wondered how anyone could defend people they knew were guilty. "How does she do it?" he asked after a moment. Shifting off the float, he stood in the water next to Lea so that he was closer to her.

"How does she defend people like them? I mean, when I arrest them, I can easily keep my feelings in check, since I usually arrive there after most of the damage is done. Still, a few times I've had to put my emotions aside when someone's been abused. But the other night… It was the first time I've been on the receiving end of things."

"Being vulnerable for the first time opens your eyes to a lot of things," Lea agreed as she slid off her float.

He helped her down into the water and ran his hands over her hips, nudging her closer.

"Nothing like this has happened to you before, right?" he asked, suddenly realizing the possibility that this was something she dealt with on a regular basis. After all, she'd remained so calm through it all and had only broken down after she'd fallen asleep.

"Not like that, no. But I'd be lying if I said I hadn't felt the sting of racism before now."

He sighed heavily and glanced at her parents. "Them?"

"Everyone in my family has at one point." She nodded. "The other night was by far the worst of it. Normally, it's little stabs. My mother and I are told often how we belong in a nail salon instead of an operating room or a courtroom. My father…" She glanced over his shoulder at her parents. "No one believes he owns his business. They think he's just an employee. I think Raya is the only one in our family that gets perks for being who she is. She is only one of half a dozen women who tried out for the Mulan role."

"I would suspect that most people don't understand what it's like to be on the receiving end of hate." He let his body brush up against hers.

Her arms wrapped around his shoulders.

"You'd be surprised. I wasn't the only one who got bullied in school. At Harvard, there were other kids, not as young as I was, but all of us were taunted for being smart. It was as if being smart at a young age was an opening to some for instant disdain." She shook her head.

"Was it that bad?"

"No, I kept my head down and ignored most of it."

"Is that how you were able to remain so calm the other night?"

She smiled. "It was easy when all I had to do was focus on you." Her eyes met his.

He smiled and then pulled her in for a soft kiss.

Suddenly a huge splash of water fell over them when her father executed an expert cannonball right near them.

Laughing, he released his hold on Lea. "Your father's wishes are very clear," he said before her dad surfaced from the water.

"He's harmless," Lea said quite loudly after her father's head resurfaced.

"Who me?" Ken said with a smile. "Remember, my little sea turtle, I'm a shark." He laughed watching Ken swim, hands pointed like a dorsal fin above his head, after a very giggly Lea.

CHAPTER 17

It took Lea a few days to stop daydreaming about the wonderful time she'd had at her parents' place with Brett. Each time she had a moment alone, she fantasized about spending more free time with him like that. Or, better yet, how it would be if they were married and had a home and children of their own.

After two days of silence from Brett, she sent him a text message and asked how he was doing. Since he wasn't at the camp any longer, bumping into him each day wasn't possible as it had been.

She could have gone over to his place to check up on him, but she didn't want to come across as desperate.

It had almost been an hour since she'd shot off the text message, and she was beginning to worry that he was avoiding her.

She was sitting in the medical cabin at the camp, bored out of her mind. She'd just finished wrapping up a guest's sprained ankle and was staring down at her phone, willing it to chime with his message when the screen door opened and the bell above it sounded.

"I'm bored and missing you," Brett said as he walked in.

She smiled instantly. "You went radio silent on me," she said after he gave her a kiss.

"I didn't mean to." He frowned. "I think I left my phone at the gym the other day, or someone stole it." He shrugged and held up a new phone. "It took them a whole day to get me a new one." He shook his head and tucked it back in his pocket. "Plus, I was so sore after the workout, I slept most of yesterday away."

She frowned. "You shouldn't push yourself so much."

He shrugged. "What else is there to do?" He moved over and sat down on the edge of her desk. "I've looked over Aiden's security plan for this place more than a dozen times. I've even reevaluated the entire thing twice." He sighed. "I've read more than a dozen books." He rolled his eyes. "I was hoping you'd be around here today to keep me company." He took her hand in his. "When do you get off work?"

"Eight," she said while her heart skipped a few beats. Thoughts of spending the night with him again played in her head, making her body go weak.

"Want some company tonight?" he asked, brushing his hand softly over hers. Using just one finger, he traced the inside of her wrist, up to her elbow. If she had been standing, her legs would have folded.

How was it possible that the man made her weak all over? Just a simple touch from him and she went into full swoon mode.

Thoughts of locking the door to the cabin ran through her mind.

"I have some free time now," she said with a smile.

His eyes moved towards the open door.

"Tell me that locks," he practically growled out.

Instead of answering, she walked over, shut the heavy inner door, and flipped the lock, then turned the Doctor is In sign to the side that read the Doctor is Out before walking back over to him.

She stepped between his legs as he pulled her close and started to kiss her.

She melted against him, her hands running over his shoulders, his arms, and chest. Everywhere she could touch him, she marveled at his strength.

"God, I've missed you," he said against her lips.

"Hm," she responded as he started to pull her camp shirt up, exposing her belly. When his fingertips touched her skin, a sense of urgency spiked in her.

"Brett." Just saying his name had the desire doubling. This was Brett. Her Brett, she said over and over in her mind as he peeled her clothes off her slowly.

When all their clothing lay on the floor, he lifted her to the edge of the desk and stepped between her hips.

"Look at me," he said softly. "I love watching your eyes go soft when I enter you."

She did as he asked and marveled at the feeling of him filling her. Arching towards him, she held onto him as he began to move.

As with before, she felt like it was impossible to get close enough to him. Like even the slightest barrier separating them was too much. She wanted speed. Needed it this time.

She'd worked up being with him in her mind over the past week and had dreamed of the moment so many times that all she needed was to feel him inside her in order for her to burst into shards.

Her nails dug into his shoulders as he kissed her, swallowing her cry as her entire body convulsed around him just as he followed her.

"That was…" Brett said into her hair.

"Needed," she finished for him.

He chuckled. "I was going to say fast and unexpected. I just came here to see about the possibility of having lunch and dinner with you."

"Lunch, dinner." She leaned back and smiled at him. "Breakfast."

He smiled back at her, then kissed her. "I'm game. Just as long as there is some exercise between all those meals." He wiggled his eyebrows, making her laugh.

"Oh, you know it," she said as he handed her the shorts he'd pulled from her moments before.

"You know, I may need more visits to my doctor from here on out," he said, pulling on his own board shorts. "Do you do house calls?"

She laughed and slapped his shoulder playfully when he handed her back her shirt.

She pulled it over her head just as her cell phone rang. She saw her mother's face on the screen and frowned as she answered it.

"Hey, Mom, what's up?" she asked, slipping on her shoes.

"Hey, sweetie, I thought you'd want to hear it from me first, but both Robbie Dixon and Larry Ryan have made bail," her mother said in a worried tone.

Lea's heart sank into her gut, making her feel slightly nauseated. She'd known this was going to happen. She had figured the men would get out days ago.

"Thanks for letting me know." She glanced over to where Brett stood, fully dressed again with a worried look in his eyes.

"I was going to let Brett know, but Dad says that he left his cell phone on the boat the other day."

Lea's eyes shot up. "He did?" She smiled. "I'll make sure to tell him that."

"Well, if he wants it back, it's at our place," her mother added. "I've got to get back to court. I just… Be careful okay. With their history, I wouldn't put it past them to do something stupid."

"I will," she agreed. "See you later."

"Your mom?" Brett asked.

"Your phone is at my parents' place. You left it on the boat," she said with a smile.

He rolled his eyes. "Well, now I've got two, I guess." He chuckled.

"Also, Robbie Dixon and Larry Ryan are out on bail."

"Yeah, I'd heard that earlier. It's one of the reasons I came over here." His eyes avoided hers. "I… um, will be keeping an eye out for them."

She thought about it for a moment then smiled. "Babysitting me?"

"Guarding," he countered. "And besides, I like the excuse to hang out with you more."

"I'll allow it," she said with a smile.

His smile brightened. "Good, then how about we head down to the pool for some lunch? I'm starving."

She laughed. "When aren't you starving?"

He wrapped his arms around her. "Hey, this time I worked up an appetite."

They walked hand in hand down the pathway to the pool dining area. She noticed his limp was growing less obvious and figured he'd been working on that as well as his muscles, which had easily doubled since his accident. Apparently, the way he staved off boredom was to work out.

"One of the best perks about working here has to be the food," he said after they'd ordered.

"Hey, what about your coworkers?" she teased.

He shrugged and smiled. "I guess working with Aiden will be fun."

She rolled her eyes and stuck her tongue out at him, causing him to laugh loudly.

So much had changed between the two of them, yet this was one steady fact—Brett still made her laugh. He'd always had that ability. Even when she'd been the butt of his jokes, she'd found him funny, smart, kind, and, as much as she'd like to deny it, hot. All those years ago, even when she'd had a crush on Aiden, her eyes had always found Brett.

Something she would never admit to him. Ever.

After they were done eating, she had a call to check up on a guest who had diabetes and hadn't been feeling well that morning. Brett rode along with her on one of the camp's golf carts. She drove on the pathway, making her way to one of the farthest cabins, and chatted with Brett about the campgrounds and guests.

She could tell he was trying to get a handle on what his job would entail. She listened to him talk there and on the way back from the couple's cabin about changes he would be making, and she had to admit, he had some really great ideas.

She was counting down the minutes until she could clock off and head home with Brett. Being with him filled part of her that she didn't know had been empty before.

When they parked the golf cart and started walking back to her medical cabin, they noticed Zoey and Dylan heading down the pathway towards the main building with baby Paige in a stroller.

They made their way over to the new family and, after chatting for a few moments, followed them up to the main building instead of heading back to the medical cabin.

"We're actually here for the party," Zoey told them when they reached the main building. "It's Paige's first official outing."

"And, of course, it had to be a dinner here," Dylan added with a smile.

"Of course," Lea replied.

Most nights dinner at the camp was an ordinary event. But on Fridays and Saturdays, that changed. The normal plain dining room turned into various wonderlands, fulfilling whatever fantasy the Wildflowers had cooked up for that weekend.

During major holidays, parties usually spread out over a few weeks so that all guests could enjoy the seasons.

Tonight's theme was April Showers. Lea had been curious about what that entailed and had stopped by the dining hall to help Hannah and a few others decorate the room with flowers of all colors and sizes. She wasn't joking about the size thing. Hanging over the main dance area was a pink rose with petals easily the size of a grand piano.

The five of them entered the room through a waterfall of blue streamers.

"Wow," Zoey said, "the room looks amazing. I don't know how Hannah does it. Each time she comes up with a new theme, she outdoes decorations of the last one."

It really did look amazing. Since she'd seen it last, there were more flowers, electric Tiki torches on the outskirts of the room, and what looked like white puffy clouds with blue sparkly raindrops hanging from each light.

"How does she do that?" Zoey asked, looking up at the clouds.

"She's a fairy," Lea answered under her breath.

"She certainly looks like one." Dylan nodded towards Hannah as she made her way gracefully across the room towards them. Sure enough, the woman was dressed in a soft blue chiffon dress with a wide tulle skirt that looked just like a summer cloud. It appeared as if Hannah was floating on air instead of walking.

"Wow." Zoey shook her head. "Just…" She moved around her friend and assessed the dress further. "Wow."

"Thanks," Hannah said with a smile, then she immediately frowned. "You're late. You were supposed to come early. I had a surprise for you and Paige." She turned her eyes towards Dylan. "I told you to get them here half an hour ago."

Dylan winced. "Sorry, Paige had other ideas."

"She made a mess in the first outfit we put her in," Zoey said.

Hannah waved her hands and then took the stroller and started making her way back out of the room.

"Hey, where are you going with my daughter." Zoey laughed and kept up.

"To change. You two simply can't be seen dressed like this." Hannah stopped and glanced back at Lea. "There's something for you too if you're going to stick around."

Lea glanced at Brett. He shrugged and said, "I could have a couple of drinks and some food, if you're game."

Smiling, Lea followed her friend back to Zoey's office, where an entire rack of dresses matching Hannah's hung.

Less than half an hour later, she walked back into the dining room in a long strapless dress made from dark blue tulle that would have normally looked ridiculous on her. But there had been a hairdresser, and her long black hair was now tied up in several intricate twirls with glass beads in it. Along with the makeup Hannah had helped her apply, she looked like a princess.

While she'd been getting transformed, so had Zoey and Paige. Zoey wore a soft peach dress that almost matched Hannah's and Lea's perfectly. Little Paige had on a smaller version of Zoey's dress in a matching peach color.

Mother and daughter looked so cute, she couldn't pass up Lea snapping a couple of pictures before heading out.

She couldn't remember ever going from feeling dull and plain to beautiful so quickly before.

The moment Brett spied her, she felt even more beautiful than she had. Seeing the way that he responded to how she looked had her instantly smiling.

He was sitting at the bar, sipping a beer when she walked over to him.

"Wow, just… wow." His eyes ran up and down her. "You're making me feel seriously underdressed now."

She laughed. "You've got your boardshorts on. Perfect attire for a spring rain shower." She motioned to the clouds above them.

He set his beer down and reached for her, but then he yanked his hands back. "I'm not sure I should touch—"

He stopped talking when she plastered herself against him and kissed him.

"I feel like a princess," she said with a smile. "No wonder Raya likes her job so much. She gets to feel like this every day at work."

Brett smiled and wrapped his hands around her waist. "This color suits you," he said, his eyes running over her face. "Did they even do your hair and makeup?"

"Yes."

He shook his head. "Hannah has thought of everything."

"Not everything. I'm the one who found my prince charming." She kissed him again.

CHAPTER 18

Brett's last official day on the force was an emotional one for him. Not that he'd show it to any of his friends. His father had taught him at an early age that real men didn't cry.

Still, when he packed up all his things from his locker and walked out to find a large cake in the breakroom, with everyone packed in the small space, he had a very difficult time holding it in.

He was surprised to see Lea, Elle, and Aiden there as well. It filled his heart to know that his friends had come out to show their support. Yet neither of his parents could be bothered. Actually, since he'd seen his parents at the library, he hadn't talked to either of them.

He knew that he should give his mother another chance. Lea had been working on him to open his eyes about how his mother was a victim of an abusive relationship. But the sting he felt from her abandonment clouded his judgment. After all, phones did work both ways. Surely his mother could have found some time to call him over the years without his father finding out. Right?

"You look worried." Aiden slapped him on the shoulder.

"Worried?" He shook his head. "Scared shitless is more like it. I've just officially quit the only job I've ever had to go off and…"

"Babysit a summer camp?" Aiden supplied.

Brett laughed nervously.

"Trust me, when I started working at the camp, I felt the same way. Well, except at that point I didn't have a job." He tilted his head. "Okay, basically, I was desperate for work back then."

"Now look at you," Elle said with a smile. "Overseeing the construction of one of the largest subdivisions in the area. Not to mention still adding new cabins for us at the camp."

Aiden smiled and wrapped his arms around both Elle and Brett. "That's what friends do."

"Did I tell you their latest wild scheme?" Aiden asked.

"No." He wrapped his arm around Lea, who remained by his side, quietly listening. "What?"

Elle rolled her eyes. "It's not going to be that difficult of a job. I mean, it has to be far easier than building cabins."

"What?" Lea asked.

"Tents," Aiden chimed in.

"Glamping tents," Elle said with an excited tone. "All our boy here has to do is—"

"Electric, plumbing, and foundation," Aiden broke in.

"Yes, but you don't have to do the walls, the roof, and all the other stuff inside." Elle stabbed Aiden in the ribs.

"That's a great idea," Lea said. "My parents go to a place in Tennessee each year and go glamping.

"Oh?" Elle took Lea's arm and dragged her towards the cake, all the while drilling Lea about the place her parents went.

"Tents shouldn't have floors and full-sized king beds." Aiden shook his head.

"I don't know about that. It sounds pretty cool. Besides, I'll bet it will easily double the camp's occupancy at half the cost," Brett said.

"Yeah," Aiden nodded. "It's a smart move. There's no doubt about it. It just means I'll have to hire a few more contractors to get the work done." Aiden glanced over to where Elle and Lea were laughing together. "So, you and Lea? Everyone saw that coming from miles away."

"They did?" he asked, a little surprised.

Aiden chuckled. "Yeah, everyone except you." Aiden slapped him on the back again. "The way she is around you..." Aiden shook his head.

Brett frowned. "She had that crush on you back in school. I was sure..."

"Me?" Aiden laughed. "Maybe for like two seconds. But ever since that day you rescued her from Tim Crawford, she's followed your every move. Tim was an ass."

"Still is. He's been in and out of here"—Brett motioned to the police station—"more times than I can keep count."

"Right. Half of the kids we went to school with have, I'd wager."

Brett sighed and glanced around. He was going to miss being here. Knowing all the juicy details of the town. Feeling like he was doing something good, keeping people safe.

"Hey." Aiden laid a hand on his shoulder. "Trust me when I say, you'll have your hands so full at the camp that you won't have time to miss things around here."

"Right," Brett said absently.

He enjoyed getting a chance to say his goodbyes to a few of the crew, but he knew that it wasn't really goodbye. After all, he lived less than ten minutes from the station. It wasn't as if he was moving across the country.

An hour after he'd walked into the station to gather his things, he left with a box full of his items, some leftover cake, and his last paycheck.

In the past few weeks, he'd spent a lot of nights over at Lea's place. So much so that he had a bag of clothes and things there at this point.

Each time he thought to return to his apartment, she would text him that she'd see him at home, and he'd head to her place. She'd even given him a key, and he had returned the favor.

She had a bottle of her shampoo at his place as well as a drawer or two of clothes, mainly scrubs, since his place was ten minutes closer to the hospital than hers was.

On nights where she had an early morning shift the following day, they would head over to his place instead of hers.

He'd gone with her to look at the space she was purchasing for her clinic. It was far bigger than he'd imagined. She talked about how Aiden was going to build out five exam rooms, the waiting area, two offices, and the reception areas, as well as restrooms.

The building was in a newer part of town, close to Lea's house and a few new shops, including a big new grocery store that was due to open in less than a year.

With each new passing day, his body grew stronger again. He still struggled with his left leg, but he was building up the rest of him to compensate for the slight weakness.

Still, walking or standing on it for too long caused him a lot of pain in the evenings. There was no chance of him jogging or running anytime soon.

Thankfully, he had the hot tub at the camp or at Lea's clubhouse to soak the soreness away.

Almost a week after his official retirement from the force,

Lea finally signed off on him to start working at the camp. In order to prove his abilities, she'd taken him on an all-day hiking trip. He hadn't known why she'd wanted to go on the trip at first. In the end, it had been a good thing that he'd had a good leg day and hadn't complained once during the entire hike. When they had finally gotten home that evening, sometime after dark, she'd informed him that she'd signed off on him to start work that next day.

Of course, that evening he'd lain in bed, desperately wishing for a day of rest after that hike, but he was so excited to start work again that he pushed through his pain.

At least he'd no longer need to chase kids half his age through soft hot sand. Now he could look forward to easy days lounging around the pool or walking the grounds of the camp, watching over older people. Not to mention getting to spend more time with Lea and his friends.

"Are you excited for today?" Lea asked him the moment he opened his eyes.

He gathered her in his arms and kissed her before answering. "Very."

To his surprise, she rolled him over and sat on top of him, looking down as her long hair fell around her face.

"Looks like Aubrey's taught you a few new judo moves," he joked, letting his hands run over her hips and butt.

Lea smiled down at him, then leaned forward and placed her hands firmly on his chest.

"You have no idea," she purred, and he felt his entire body come alive in that instant.

Each time he touched her, it was as if it was the first. Discovering all the nuances of her body, finding what she liked and disliked, was like exploring a whole new world.

Whenever they were together, he wanted to spend as much time exploring her as possible. But they were both due at work in less than an hour, so he'd have to settle for enjoying her quickly.

That took him to a whole new level of excitement. The faster they moved, the more he demanded from her, and the more she demanded from him.

When they lay breathless on the bed, their arms and legs tangled in each other's, he realized that he could easily spend a lifetime doing what they had just done.

"Wow," Lea said against his chest.

He smiled. "I agree with that diagnosis."

Then she shifted and let out a soft curse. "We're going to be late." She shoved him off her, and the next fifteen minutes were spent quickly getting showered and dressed.

He had to admit, putting on a pair of khaki shorts and a camp T-shirt was a lot easier than a uniform with a gun belt that easily weighted fifty pounds.

For his first day on the job, he had been asked to join in the early morning meeting in the employee's dining room. Since he'd attended many of the breakfast meetings, he'd figured he knew what was in store.

What he hadn't planned on was every employee of the camp crowding into the room to welcome him.

He stood by a small podium while Elle introduced him and talked briefly about a few of the changes that he and the rest of the team had agreed on.

"Good morning, everyone. As most of you have heard, we have a new head of security." There were several cheers and claps. "Today is Brett Jewell's first official day." More cheers. This time Elle had to hold up her hands to get everyone to quiet down. "This means a few changes." A couple of groans could be heard throughout the room. "Good ones," Elle added. "New digital security locks will be installed on all employee areas so that guests can't wander into an off-limits area. And all employees will now have employee badges and key cards." Elle held up a photo badge on a lanyard. "This is to help distinguish employees from guests and allow employees into restricted areas." Brett already noticed a few employees wearing their new badges. "Brett will also send weekly security updates to your employee email and post them on the back-end website, so make sure you check for any further changes." Elle glanced over at him. "Do you want to say anything?"

He quickly shook his head no.

"Okay." Elle turned back to the room. "Since I have you all here, I wanted to let you know that we've decided to move forward with the glamping program." There were several cheers, and Elle waited until they died down.

"So, welcome aboard," Aiden said, nudging him.

"Thanks." He smiled back at his friend.

"Let's just hope you don't get too bored," Aiden added under his breath.

Within the first hour, Brett had more than a dozen calls. The new security system was having issues letting employees into the restricted areas. He'd wanted to hold off flipping the switch on the new system until he'd had a chance to test it out, but Elle and the other Wildflowers had wanted the system operational on his first day, so Aiden had moved forward with turning it on.

After the tenth call, he'd walked into his small office and shut the system down. That unlocked all the digital locks and allowed everyone to come and go as they needed.

He spent the rest of his time up until lunch trying to reset the entire system and testing it out on a few locks himself. By the time he took a break for lunch, he believed he had it all figured out and was once again ready to turn the system back on.

"So, are you done locking everyone out today?" Aubrey said, standing next to him in the lunch line. "When Brett's around, security is so tight, no one can get into anything." She laughed at her joke.

He rolled his eyes. "You should be a comedian," he said dryly.

"There he is, our man Brett. Keeping the camp safe from everyone, even the ones who work here," someone else jeered.

By the time Lea found him sitting with the rest of his friends, he'd heard more than a dozen jokes, all as lame as the one before.

"Don't mind them," Lea said quietly. "You're the new guy. They always find something to hold over the new employees' heads. Even though they've known you forever, maybe especially since they know you. I think that they're just jealous."

"Of?" He laughed.

"That you have the ultimate power. To decide who works and who gets to stand around." She smiled as she took a bite of her salad.

He knew she was joking, just like the rest of them, only Lea's words made him smile brighter. Then he looked down at her plate and the small salad she always ate.

"Don't you eat anything besides salads?" he asked her. "How do you expect to keep up your energy?" She narrowed her eyes and then reached over to take a few of his French fries. "That'll help," he said, dumping another handful of them onto her plate. "A little," he said with a smile.

"So, outside of the little glitch, how is your first day?" Lea asked between fries.

"Honestly, it's nothing like I imagined and yet everything I envisioned it would be." He took the last bite of his lunch.

"Good? Bad?" Lea asked, her eyes scanning his face.

Reaching over, he took her hand in his and squeezed softly. "Good. All good."

"That's... good," she said and seemed to relax.

It appeared as though she'd been really nervous that he

wouldn't like the job. He couldn't describe how wonderful that made him feel.

So far, he hadn't worked up the guts to tell Lea how much he enjoyed being with her, spending his nights with her wrapped around him. Waking up to her rushing around and getting ready for work.

Each day that he went to therapy, she was sending him encouraging text messages or just asking how it went.

He was quickly becoming addicted to her presence. At this point, he couldn't imagine a day without being near her.

Here it was, almost three months since he'd been shot. His skin had healed within the first week, and the scar was now just a thick white line on his thigh. According to the latest X-ray, his bone was almost completely healed as well. It was the muscle and nerve damage that he still struggled with. The soreness kept him from walking too far or standing too long.

Physical therapy helped, as did the classes at the camp that Lea convinced him to sign up for. He'd never taken yoga before, but after the last two weeks in Elle's class, his leg and body felt better than they had in years.

"So, when is your last day at the hospital?" he asked her, changing the subject.

She bit her bottom lip and sort of cringed before answering. "I'm thinking of putting in my resignation next week."

"When will you be able to open the doors to PPMC?"

She pushed her salad plate aside, and he noted there was still a little more than half her salad left, but she'd eaten all the fries he'd given her.

"Not for a few months. I'll need the free time in my schedule to oversee the construction and order supplies. Not to mention hiring staff." She pulled out her phone and looked down at the list he'd helped her create.

Placing his hand over hers, he waited until he had her full attention. "There's plenty of time. No need to stress."

Just then her phone went off in her hands. She glanced at the message.

"Sorry, I have a call." She stood up suddenly.

"I should get back to it too," he agreed.

He followed her out as they dropped off their dirty dishes.

The second part of his first day went a lot smoother than the first. Now that all the locks were working smoothly, he spent his time walking around and readjusting some of the security cameras, making sure the angles showed the areas that needed it the most. Some of them had been turned completely away from key areas.

By the end of his first day, he was not only more excited about the job than he had been before, but he was positive it was the best move he could have made for himself and for his future with Lea.

CHAPTER 19

*L*ea could tell that Brett was enjoying working at the camp. Each day that she worked there with him, she could see his transformation from strict cop to relaxed camp security guard.

She worried that he was overtaxing his leg and often said so. She feared she was nagging him too much, but each night as they laid together in bed, she watched him rub his sore muscles.

She tried to convince him to go in and have either Andrea or Kara give him massages, but each time she brought it up, he acted strangely.

The closer her friendship with Kara got, the more she came to understand why. Kara was a flirt. Of course, the woman had made it very clear to Lea that she thought they were a cute couple, but maybe Brett was concerned that Lea would be the jealous type.

She wasn't. Not really. But at this point, she didn't mind Brett not knowing that. Besides, he was doting on her as all new boyfriends should. Or at least as she'd always dreamed they would.

They spent most nights together, except for when she worked a double shift. She'd been trying to work more hours leading up to her quitting.

Her stomach hurt each time she thought of not having that reliable paycheck each month. But she knew that if she did things right, she'd be making far more soon enough. Besides, her work at the camp was steady and something she didn't plan on giving up. No matter what. Even if she had to cut back her hours or have guests shuttled to her new location, she was going to make a point to continue helping Elle and the rest of her friends out.

Even Sanjay had backed off from his flirting after Brett had showed up to have lunch with her one day. Brett had let it slip out that they were living together, even though, technically, he still had his apartment and stayed there at least twice a week.

It was nice not having to contend with sneaking through the halls of the hospital in fear of running into Sanjay any longer, which had grown old.

In the last hour of her double shift, she'd dealt with a drowning victim, a male in his late sixties who hadn't made it, and a pedestrian who had been involved in a hit and run. He was now recovering from a broken pelvis, two broken legs, and a concussion. He also had road burns over a third of his body.

She was so exhausted when she walked out of the hospital that she didn't register what she was seeing at first.

Her car was parked in the back parking lot, which was reserved for medical staff and doctors. Each doctor had their own parking spot, marked by a white sign with their name on it. This was to make it easy for them to get into the hospital quickly for emergencies when they were on call. The last thing a doctor wanted to do was search for a parking spot when they were trying to save lives.

The sun wasn't fully up yet, and in the early morning fog,

she had to blink a few times to make sure her eyes were working properly.

She'd purchased the Tesla Model Y almost a year ago and loved the car, not only because she didn't have to buy gas but because it was fast, sporty, and sexy as hell. She'd decided on the car after she'd driven Dylan's Tesla a few times.

Now, however, her white paint was covered with bright red words so full of hate, her eyes teared up.

Die gook rat. Go back where you came from. Gook rodent rat. All were completed with several spelling mistakes and scribbled boldly all over her white paint.

"Oh my god!" someone exclaimed behind her, causing her to jump and scream. "Dr. Val, it's me, Robin." One of the nurses she'd worked side by side with for the past few hours rushed up to her and wrapped her arms around her. "Are you okay?"

"I..." She blinked a couple of times and took several deep breaths. "I'm fine."

"That's your car?" Robin said, giving Lea a look that told her that she already knew the answer.

"Yes," Lea said softly.

"I'll call the police." Robin took out her phone.

Lea walked over and opened her car. She took a few seconds to appreciate that at least they hadn't smashed any windows or lit the thing on fire. She slid into her seat and tapped the screen. Within seconds she had sent the footage to Tesla and watched on the screen as two men approached her car.

She could easily tell that it was Robbie Dixon and Larry Ryan, complete with face masks that didn't hide their faces very well. The men rushed drunkenly around her car and spray-painted the terrible words. Then, for good measure, they pissed on her driver's door and kicked it a couple of times, causing a dent that she hadn't even known was there until she'd looked closer.

While Robin was on the phone with the police, she called Brett and told him what had happened.

Shortly after, two officers that she'd seen before arrived. Brett parked his car behind hers and rushed out to wrap his arms around her.

"Are you okay?" he asked. Just having his arms around her made her feel steadier.

"I am now," she said into his chest.

"Come on, I'll take you home. Rick and Mary can wait for the tow truck," he said over her shoulder.

She glanced back at her car, knowing that her insurance would pay to have it returned to its former glory. But at this point, everything was tainted. Just like how her fear and anxiety spiked every time she stepped into a Whataburger now.

When she got her car back, would she ever be able to drive it again without seeing those hateful red words on the sides?

They rode back across Pelican Bay in silence. She closed her eyes, not wanting to let the foggy morning drag her down any further. Tears stung her eyes as he parked in her driveway.

"Why don't you put in your resignation a little early?" Brett asked. "So you can stick closer in town."

Her first instinct was to shake her head and tell Brett that she needed the extra money and hours, but then she realized it wasn't true. She'd saved up far more than she would need to open her place. Especially since she planned on continuing working at the camp while she waited to open the doors to her clinic.

She wasn't scheduled to work at the camp that day, but since she didn't want to be left alone, she turned to Brett and said. "Do you have time for me to shower? I'd like to go with you to work today."

He opened his mouth, then shut it quickly and nodded.

"Sure. I'll let Elle know what happened and that we'll be

there a little late." He pulled out his phone as he followed her inside.

She stood under the hot water and let everything from her double shift rinse off with the water. Her muscles relaxed as the water flowed over her.

Since it wasn't a workday for her, she figured she'd bring her swimsuit and lie by the pool. Maybe she'd even see if Kara or Andrea could fit her in for a massage.

The moment they parked in the camp's parking lot, she was surrounded by friends and engulfed in hugs from people she knew cared as much about her as her family did.

Family. She'd have to call her parents. Her sister. Tell them what had happened and warn them about the men who were hell-bent on hurting her.

First, though, she needed her friends.

"Are you okay?" Aubrey asked.

"Yes." She wiped a tear from her cheek. "It was just my car."

"Just?" Hannah said, squeezing Lea's hand. "A Tesla isn't just a car," she said with a weak smile.

"No, but it was just the paint and a few scratches. It should be fixed soon enough. I'm having a rental..." She started but shook her head when her throat closed up.

"Come on. What we need are chocolate donuts and mimosas by the pool." Elle took Lea's hand, then stopped and looked at Brett. "We've got her. You can go on."

Brett's eyes met hers and Lea nodded.

"Thanks," she mouthed as she was pulled in a different direction.

She followed her friends to the pool deck and took a seat at one of the empty tables. At this time of the morning, there were only a handful of guests sitting around the pool.

Elle took charge and ordered a round of mimosas while Hannah ordered a platter of donuts and muffins.

The mimosa helped curb the rest of her nerves, and she relaxed in the shade while her friends chatted about work and how quickly Paige was growing.

Her friends talked about everything else to keep her mind from what had just happened, and it worked.

She sat around the pool, eating and drinking sugary treats and laughing at stories Scarlett told about her and Levi.

Brett's and Levi's senses of humor were a lot alike. Then again, Levi had only been a grade below them and had followed Aiden and Brett around in school.

It wasn't until the third round of mimosas were ordered that Aubrey asked what had happened.

While Lea explained how she'd walked out and found the hate message written on her car, she avoided everyone's eyes. For as long as she'd been friends with the ladies, not once had they talked about racism.

"I'm so sorry that happened to you," Elle said, taking her hand. "Just know that we are here. If you want to increase your hours here to cut back your hours there, we're all for it. We know you're about to put in your resignation so you can start focusing on your own place. Whatever you decide, we're here for you."

Several others of her friends nodded in agreement.

"Thanks," she said, feeling her heart swell with love and friendship.

"But today is not about decisions or work," Aubrey chimed in with a smile. "If all has gone well, Andrea has shifted her schedule and has a whole hour carved out just for you. You're going to spend the entire day relaxing by the pool, getting a massage, and spending it with..." She nodded over her head, and they all watched as Zoey strolled towards them.

"Someone else who needs a day off," Elle added.

"Okay, I'm here wearing a swimsuit." Zoey stopped by the

table, "Do you know how hard it was to find a suit to squeeze my out-of-shape ass into?" She sat down when her sister Scarlett nudged her into the chair and handed her a glass of orange juice. "What's all this?" Zoey asked.

"You are taking your very first mommy's day off. And since Lea needs a day as well, the two of you will be keeping each other company," Scarlett said cheerfully.

"I..." Zoey started to get up, but the look from her friends had her sitting back down.

Aubrey nudged Lea under the table and then motioned towards Zoey.

"Uh, right." Lea thought quickly. "After the morning I just had, I could sure use some company."

"What?" Zoey turned to her and ran her eyes over Lea's face. "Did something happen?"

For the next half hour, Lea explained what had happened again, while the rest of the friends headed off to work.

Whatever they had planned, it was nice not having to spend the entire day alone.

Less than an hour later, Kara and Andrea stopped by and gathered both women for their dual massages.

The drinks were making Lea feel nice and relaxed, and Zoey seemed to have a lot to chat about. She filled her in on everything Paige, how the baby was holding her head up and smiling and laughing.

Lea thought about someday having her own children. She'd always known she'd wanted kids. Much later in life. After she'd become a very successful doctor.

Which she supposed she was at this point. Well, not successful, but... once she had her practice, she figured that was as close as she wanted to get.

Every time she closed her eyes and tried to relax, blood-red letters with a hateful message flashed behind her eyes. So she kept her eyes open as Kara massaged the rest of the tension away.

By the time they stepped back out to the pool area, the morning fog had burned off and the sun was beating down, warming everything up.

After a soothing dip in the pool, they found some lounge chairs and sat back to relax.

"It's going to be a hot one," Zoey said, shifting to get comfortable on the lounge chair.

"Yeah, it's official, summer is here," Lea said with a sigh.

"Okay, I can't stand it. I know Scarlett warned me not to call, but I just have to check in on Paige," Zoey said, pulling out her cell phone.

Lea chuckled. "I won't tell." She waved her hand and headed to the bar to get them some water. All that sugar was wreaking havoc on her system.

Stepping up to the bar, she spotted Damion Wells heading her way.

"Morning." The man smiled at her and leaned against the bar. "I just ran into Brett, and he told me what happened. How are you holding up?"

She took a sip of her water and shrugged. Damion wasn't the only other non-white person that worked at the camp—there were a handful of others—but Damion was the only one she'd known since school.

"This helps." She motioned to the pool area. "Zoey and I have been keeping each other company."

"That's good," Damion said with a sigh. "Brett says that he'll know the moment they catch the guys. I'm sure you have nothing to worry about here."

It was strange. Up until that moment, she hadn't worried that Robbie Dixon and Larry Ryan would come to the camp to find her.

"Hey." Damion's hand gripped her arm. "Oh, shit, I didn't mean to freak you out."

"You…" She took another sip of her water. "You didn't," she lied quickly. "I think I've just had a little too much sugar."

"Well, you could always come out on the water with me. I'm about to take a group out on the sailboat," he offered.

She glanced over at Zoey, who was still talking on the phone, and knew that her friend wouldn't want to be that far away from her daughter.

"I…" Just then Zoey hung up and made her way towards them.

"Lea, would it be okay if I skipped out? Paige is hungry and I didn't pump enough milk to be gone this long," Zoey asked.

"Sure, I was just thinking of going out on Damion's next sail," she said, already feeling more at ease. She loved going out on the sailboat and figured the fresh salty air would do her wonders.

"Are you sure?" Zoey asked, taking the water Lea offered.

"Yes, go on. I hope this morning helped," she said, hugging Zoey.

"It did." She sighed. "More than anyone will ever know. I hope you're okay. Remember, you always have us fighting for you."

Lea nodded. After Zoey shuffled off down the pathway, she turned back to Damion. "It looks like your timing is perfect."

He smiled at her. "It's a lunch sail, so you don't need to worry about a thing. Everything's packed and ready. We're boarding in"—he glanced down at his watch—"ten minutes. We'd better hurry."

She rushed to gather her bag and things and then followed Damion down the pathway towards the boathouse. He helped her onto the deck of the sailboat, and she sat with the rest of the guests and sent a quick text message to Brett, telling him where she'd be.

His reply was simple. "Have fun. See you for dinner."

Damion went through his safety speech, but since she'd been out on the boat with him more than two dozen times, she pulled out her phone and sent a text message to her parents, filling them in on what had happened. She knew her mother was probably in court and her dad, since he was now officially retired, was probably out on his boat for the day. She didn't expect a reply back from either until later that evening.

They took off out of the small dock area on the bay side of the camp, and she let the wind blow her hair as she put the entire ordeal behind her. Or at least tried to.

It was hard to put it all aside when she wanted justice. What she wanted more than anything was to never worry about men like Robbie Dixon and Larry Ryan again. To live her life, helping others and being with Brett, without being looked at as if she was lesser than someone else because her ancestors had come from a different part of the world than theirs.

It wasn't as if she'd had a choice in the matter. Just like they hadn't chosen where their family had come from.

The sailboat turned and started heading out to the see-through emerald water of the Gulf. Someone spotted dolphins, and Damion did his best to slow the boat so that the group could take pictures.

Since most of the other people on the boat were couples, she sat next to Damion and chatted with him while they made their way to a small island, where they planned on having their picnic lunch.

She sat on the small sandy beach, watching the boats go by, and ate her turkey sandwich, wondering just what Brett was doing at the moment.

She knew how she felt towards him but wasn't sure if he

knew it. After all, they hadn't talked about it or about their future together.

She knew that there was more to their relationship than just the physical. They had been friends long before anything else. She wondered whether, if anything happened between them, their relationship could ever go back to the way that it was.

Her parents had made a point to tell her how much they liked and respected Brett. They said how happy the two of them looked together and reminded her of how nice it had been watching the pair of them grow beyond just friends. His mother had claimed that she'd known for ages that she'd had a thing for Brett and was positive he'd had his eye on her as well.

It seemed as if every single one of their friends was rooting for them as well. Everyone except for his parents.

She was positive that Brett's father was pulling all the strings in his parents' relationship. Lea had been around his mother plenty of times during her youth. After all, she had spent more time in the library than anyone else in town.

Clara Jewel had never been anything but kind and helpful to Lea her entire life. She'd never spoken an unkind word and every time her husband called Lea or someone else a derogatory name, Clara had an almost embarrassed look.

Still, the woman had stuck by her husband's side, which either meant she was okay with the way her husband acted or she was too afraid of the man to say anything. Lea believed it was the latter, especially since the woman acted like a timid little mouse. Lea wondered how she would behave if someone tried to treat her like that.

Most women didn't go into a relationship believing they were going to be abused. But since she'd been raised under the guidance of a loving and caring relationship, she didn't have any insights into what made women stay other than what the psychology books said on the subject.

"You're deep in thought." Damion broke into her daydreaming.

Smiling, she tucked her knees up to her chin and sighed. "It's a perfect day." She glanced around.

"It is." He sat in the sand next to her. "Looks like everyone's having fun." He motioned to the three other couples. Everyone was done eating and now they were all splashing in the water.

"Yeah." She chuckled when one of the men picked up his wife and tossed her into the water. She came up laughing and pushing her wet hair out of her eyes.

"Have you heard from Brett yet?" he asked.

She glanced down at her phone and shook her head. "Not yet. I'm sure they'll catch them soon."

Damion shook his head. "Those two are a special kind of stupid. Everyone knows the Teslas have like a dozen cameras."

"I for one am thankful they didn't know. Out of the many ways they could have gotten back at me"—she swallowed the terrible feeling in her stomach—"this was by far the best possible outcome."

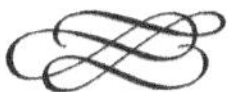

CHAPTER 20

In the end, it took them almost a full week to catch both Robbie Dixon and Larry Ryan. Larry had high-tailed it out of town when he'd seen the video and his face on the evening news. They'd caught him in Louisiana, where he'd had a few more warrants out for his arrest.

Robbie, on the other hand, hadn't been too hard to find. But he had been harder to arrest because, the moment his father and grandfather saw the news report, they had marched down and filed an injunction against Lea.

The man claimed that his grandson was being harassed by Lea and her family and that he was acting out due to fear. He actually tried to have the warrant voided.

In the end, the case was taken in front of a different judge, and Robbie was forced to show up to defend himself. He was quickly arrested when the judge sided with Lea and her mother, as there was overwhelming evidence that refuted his claims.

Now both men sat in a jail cell, waiting for their trial dates. Bail had been denied this time, thankfully.

That didn't stop Brett from worrying about Lea. After all,

there had been four of them there that night. The other two men had kept a low profile after their initial arrest.

Brett knew more than anyone how vindictive criminals could be towards their accusers. What hadn't been in all those books and lessons about helping people who had been abused was the fact that most of them willingly went back to their abusers. Once they did, the outcome was usually worse than the initial event.

The entire gang was sitting around a campfire when they heard the news that Robbie was finally in jail. He watched Lea change the moment she heard the news. She'd been jumping at shadows since her car had been vandalized.

For the remainder of the evening, she'd relaxed, laughed, and joked with everyone like before that night in Whataburger. It tore him up that she had to go through this. After all, that was the number one reason he'd become a cop in the first place. To protect people like her.

Even though he was thoroughly enjoying his new position, part of him still yearned for the old days. There were times when he wished more than anything that his body would allow him to return to his old job. But then he'd spend too much time standing or step wrong and almost double over with pain and he knew it wasn't possible.

The next day, he and Lea had the day off. It was one of the first times their schedules had lined up since he'd started working at the camp. He had a few ideas of what they should do with their time but wanted to run them by Lea.

The first thing they decided to do was to head into town for breakfast at Sunset Café. He desperately wanted one of their double-chocolate-chip waffles.

"There's just something soothing about an early morning sugar rush," he said after his first bite of the chocolaty goodness.

"Yes," Lea agreed, taking a bite of her plain waffle with fruit on it.

"There's not enough chocolate on that," he said, motioning to her waffle.

"I like fresh fruit," she said with a smile. "And Cool Whip."

"You know, every now and then you can cut loose." He held up a forkful of chocolate waffle for her.

She willingly took the bite and smiled. "It's good. Not as good as mine." She held up a bite of hers for him.

He had to admit, both tastes were good. "Good, but you can't beat double chocolate."

"So, Ken tells me that you're almost ready to move over to twice a month instead of once a week," Lea said.

Ken was his physical therapist. He was seeing the man once a week at this point. Shortly after he'd been shot, he'd been going to him twice a week.

"Yes, I've finally graduated," he joked. "I'm hoping to be able to start jogging in a few weeks."

She winced. "I'd give it a little longer. I've seen your X-rays. Your bones need a little longer to heal."

"You're the doc," he said cheerfully, and shoveled another bite into his mouth.

Just then, the bell above the door chimed, and he glanced over to see his parents walk into the café.

In one moment, thoughts of having a good day disappeared. Especially after he saw his father's eyes zone in on him and Lea. With the heat that filled his gaze, he knew what was about to happen before his father even took a step towards them.

"Brace yourself," he said quickly.

Lea glanced over her shoulder and tensed as his parents made their way towards them. Correction. As his father marched towards them and his mother followed behind like a lost sheep following its shepherd.

"Morning, Mom, Dad," Brett said, trying to sound cheerful.

"You've got some nerve," his father said, starting in immediately. "Embarrassing us like this."

"I'm not sure what I've done now," he said casually as he gripped his fork and set it down next to his plate. The other half of his waffle, he knew, would go untouched. After this, he doubted he'd have the stomach to enjoy one more bite.

"This." His father waved at the pair of them.

"I assure you, us eating waffles is not even close to the most embarrassing thing I've done." He tried to joke, knowing that it would only further his father's wrath.

At this, his father's voice went from a medium volume to a loud rumble, gaining the attention of everyone in the café almost immediately.

"You know what you're doing. You're tearing this family apart by being with this..." his father started.

"Careful," Brett interrupted with a low growl. "Let me make myself extremely clear. You had better choose your next words very carefully."

His father's eyes narrowed.

"William, let's just..." His mother tried to take his father's arm as she desperately looked around the café with an embarrassed look on her face.

His father jerked his arm free and turned back to him. Since he'd stepped into the café, his father's face had grown even redder. His voice lowered a degree but was still loud enough for everyone in the café to hear his next words clearly.

"You chose your side, son." The fact that the last word came out as almost a curse wasn't anything new to Brett. "You side with scum, trash, lowlifes like her." His father's hand waved frantically towards Lea.

At this point, he didn't know if his dad just misjudged how close he was to Lea or if he had intended to knock the fork out of Lea's hands. Either way, the moment his father's hand connected with Lea's, Brett was out of his seat facing the man, his temper slipping from his control.

He was nose to nose now with his father. They were the same height, but his father had twenty pounds of fat on him, and Brett had spent the months since his injury honing his new muscles.

"I won't warn you again," Brett said in a low tone. He watched his father's face grow even redder.

"Everyone knows you're nothing but a nigger gook lover," his father spat out.

Brett's fist connected with his father's chin before he had a moment to gather his thoughts.

"And everyone knows you're an obsolete racist asshole who takes pleasure in controlling and beating his wife for fun." He watched his father smile as he wiped a trickle of blood from his lip. At this point, most of the people in the café had gasped and were either watching the show or rushing for the door.

Lea stood by his side, holding onto his arm. With her by his side, he was back under control. He hated himself for letting his old man goad him like that. He knew that if it came down to it, he could be charged with assault.

"Everyone knows what you are," his father spat out. "Gook..."

Brett's fist rose again. But at that moment, something strange happened. Instead of finishing his sentence, his father gripped his left arm. His face twisted and then drooped as his eyes rolled to the back of his head. Then he dropped to the floor so quickly, all Brett could do was watch.

"Call an ambulance," Lea shouted, then shoved past him and started rolling his father onto his back.

He stood in complete shock as Lea started CPR on his father

while his mother screamed hysterically for someone to save her husband.

Part of him wanted to pull Lea away from there. To let fate and all the years of pent-up anger and hate consume the old man. To watch karma take what was due.

The rational part of his mind had him pulling out his cell phone and calling it in. He stood by as Lea continued to relentlessly work on his father.

Each time she did a chest compression, her knees would lift off the ground. Once he'd made the call, he knelt by his father's head and helped by taking over the breathing portion for her. With each breath that filled his father's lungs, he knew that if the old man made it through this, he would never again want to see him.

As far as he was concerned, his father was dead to him. He'd made his choices in life. William R Jewel Jr. no longer mattered.

Shortly before the ambulance arrived, Lea bent down to check for a heartbeat and breath and glanced up at him and gave him a weak smile.

"He's got a heartbeat and is breathing on his own now." She touched his arm before continuing to monitor his father's vitals. He leaned back and glanced around the café.

It seemed as if every single eye was on him. Did they blame him for this? After all, he'd just punched the man. His father.

He glanced down and, for the first time, saw what everyone else did. Even though the man was his height and heavier than him, he was old and frail. His parents hadn't been young when they'd had him. His father was pushing seventy and was massively out of shape. And because of his temper and control issues, he hadn't lived an easy life.

Then his eyes moved over to his mother. She was pretty much the same with the exception of her weight. If anything, his mother was too skinny. You could see every bone and blood vessel in her hands. Her cheekbones stuck out, making her appear even frailer.

Most people had always thought that his parents were his grandparents instead. Looking down at his father, he saw the trickle of blood by his lip and a wave of guilt washed over him.

He'd allowed the man to goad him. Had he come into the café that morning to cause problems? To see how far he could push his son, who was no longer working for the law.

When the ambulance arrived, he stood back as Lea directed them and helped them load his father into the back.

When they drove away, carrying both of his parents, he remained silent as Lea took his hand in hers.

Then he noticed Carl and Steven standing just outside the café. His heart skipped as he dropped Lea's hand and walked over to his old coworkers.

"Morning," he said to the pair of them.

"Brett." Carl nodded.

"I suppose you heard what happened," he said with a sigh. Carl gave him another nod. He glanced back at Lea. "I'll come in myself."

"Why?" Carl asked, causing Brett to turn back towards him.

"I struck my father. In public."

"From what we've heard, your father struck Lea first. Knocked her fork right out of her hands. He shouted racial slurs loud enough that several customers felt uncomfortable around him and left the building." Steven motioned to a small crowd of people who had gathered in the parking lot. Families of all different races were gathered around, watching to see what happened next.

"I..." He felt his throat close up. Then Lea was there, taking his hand.

"I don't want to press charges," she told Steve and Carl.

Both men nodded and turned to him.

"We'll get a few more witness statements and write this up, so you can head on over to the hospital if you want," Carl said.

"No." Brett shook his head. He glanced down at Lea, who was watching him. "I think we're going to skip the hospital." He took her hand as he took a deep breath. "He wouldn't want us there anyway."

Carl nodded and touched his shoulder. "We've got this."

"Thanks," he said quickly. He pulled Lea towards the car, then stopped and rushed back into the café and tossed some bills down on his table. Seeing the half-finished waffles on both of their plates, he felt his heart sink.

He'd spoiled everything. Well, his father had. Why had he egged the man on? He should have stopped the argument before it had started. He should have…

He stepped outside and saw Lea standing by his car, smiling back at him.

When he walked over to her, an older black woman approached them.

"That was amazing," the woman said to Lea. "Even though that man was spewing racist hate at you, you still saved his life." The woman shook her head. "I don't know if I'd have the power to do something like that."

Lea smiled at the woman. "I'm a doctor. I've saved worse," she said softly.

"Bless you," the woman said ironically. "You're a stronger woman than I will ever be." The woman chuckled as she walked away, but then she stopped and glanced back at Brett. "You'd do well to hold onto that one," she added with a smile.

Brett took Lea's hand and called back, "I intend to."

CHAPTER 21

*L*ea didn't know where Brett was driving to. She didn't mind that he had opted out of going to the hospital to check in on his father.

When she'd helped put him in the ambulance, his vitals had been good enough. Far from perfect, but good for someone who she would wager had just had a major heart attack.

She knew that the first few hours after were vital to the man's recovery and health. But, after that display, she knew that Brett wanted to be as far away from his family as he could get.

This is why she didn't argue when they hit the highway and headed south. The car weaved around, and then he exited the main road and turned down more narrow windy ones that butted up against the shores of the Gulf. She leaned back and enjoyed the view of the Emerald Coast out her window.

Almost two hours later, he pulled to a stop in Apalachicola, a small town along the Gulf. He parked in front of an old building that appeared to have been a saloon back in the old days. Now, however, there was a massive wood sign that hung from the second-story balcony that read Up to No Good Tavern. On the sign, a mermaid sat in a martini glass, having a drink.

"How about some lunch?" Brett said, speaking for the first time in almost two hours.

"I could eat."

She knew that he'd needed the silence. If he'd wanted to talk, he understood that she was there for him.

They were seated up on the outdoor balcony, overlooking the small town. Brett ordered a beer, and she ordered a glass of wine.

"Does it ever get to you?" he asked her once their drinks were delivered.

"What?" she asked after a sip of her wine.

"Helping people like him?"

She shrugged and answered honestly, "Sometimes."

"Do you ever think that if you do nothing, there will be one less racist asshole in the world?" he said, looking down in his beer.

"No. Mostly what I think of is that if I don't help them, then I'm just like them."

"How so?" He frowned over at her.

She set her wine glass down and took a deep breath. "If I did nothing and they died, then I'm no better than them spewing their hate at me and anyone else they despise." He tilted his head at her. She thought of it in a different light. "When you were on the force, if you had seen a man beating his wife but then the wife pulled out a gun and shot and killed her husband, would you have arrested her?"

"Yes," he answered quickly.

"It's the same thing. My job as a doctor is to save people. No matter what they believe," Lea explained.

Her words seemed to sink in. He sipped his beer in silence until their food was delivered.

"I'd like to think he hasn't ruined double-chocolate waffles for me," he said when his burger was delivered.

"I'm hoping the same about my car," she admitted. "I'm thinking of having it painted a different color. I'm afraid that every time I look at it, I'll still see those red letters."

He reached over and took her hand in his. "Then paint it cherry red. I've always wanted a cherry red car," he said with a smile.

She laughed. "You are not taking over my Tesla. Get one of your own."

"I might," he said with a chuckle. "I've driven Dylan and Zoey's a few times."

She smiled and wanted more than anything to keep the conversation light, but then he sighed and glanced off over the street.

"I should call my mother," he said softly. "See how my dad is."

"Want me to call the hospital?" she offered.

He looked at her and for a moment she could tell that he was debating. "No, I'll call after we're done eating. I don't want that man to spoil another meal of ours on our day off."

She nodded and finished her salad, along with the handful of curly fries he placed on her plate.

"This isn't such a bad little town," Brett said as they were walking out of the restaurant. "I've been here a few times and have always enjoyed it."

"I've only been here once before. Well, I drove through it at least."

"Oh?" He stopped. "How about we see some sites, do a little shopping, before I make that call then?"

She knew he was stalling, but it was up to him, so she tagged along. At one of the little boutique stores, she found a sign like the one she had at the camp that read The Doctor is In on one side and The Doctor is Out on the other and purchased it for her new office.

She found a couple more things that she just couldn't live without, and then they found a small brewery and sat down for a cold beer along the water's edge. While they sat there, he pulled out his phone and called his mother.

She wasn't surprised when he had to leave a message. If her father was in the ICU, visitors were asked to turn off their cell phones.

"Want me to call and check on him?" she asked.

Brett sighed and then nodded. "Thanks."

She called and spoke with Karen, who told her that Brett's father had already been moved to recovery.

"When the man was brought in, he was yelling and cussing up a storm. He wouldn't let Dr. Rufkin work on him. Yelled at the top of his lungs that he wasn't going to put his life in no foreigner's hands."

"What happened?" she asked Karen.

Karen sighed. "Dr. Rufkin mentioned that if it hadn't been for you, he wouldn't be here. That he'd heard that you had brought him back from the dead and that he should be thankful. I've never seen the doctor go off on anyone like that before."

She smiled and realized that maybe, just maybe, she'd misjudged Sanjay.

"How is he now?" she asked.

"Still cursing every non-white nurse that walks into his room." Karen chuckled. "I'm half tempted to only send in the ones he doesn't want." Karen sighed. "But unfortunately, that's not who we are."

"No," she agreed. "Please keep me posted if anything changes."

"Will do," Karen agreed and hung up.

"So?" Brett asked after she tucked her phone back into her purse.

"Your dad is in recovery. Sounds like he'll be back on his feet in no time," she relayed.

He leaned back and glanced out at the water. "How about a walk?"

"Sure," she said. She finished the last of her beer.

After putting the items she'd purchased into his car, they strolled hand in hand towards the edge of town and out onto a long fishing pier that overlooked the Apalachicola Bay. Leaning on the pier, they watched the small fishing boats come and go.

A few minutes of silence passed by before he turned towards her.

"What would you think of me moving into your place full time?" he asked.

She was a little taken aback by the question. Not that she didn't think it was a great idea. Actually, she'd been wondering how to convince him to move in with her. It was just that she hadn't thought he'd wanted to make that big of a move yet. He'd seemed pretty happy with staying at his place two nights a week.

"I'd love it," she blurted out, afraid that if she didn't answer right away, he'd change his mind.

His eyebrows shot up as he pulled her into his arms. "Love?" he asked, his voice going low.

She felt her entire body melt against his. Swallowing, she nodded.

He smiled. "I'd *love* to as well." He emphasized the four-letter word that sounded so good to her ears and her heart. "Do you know what else I love?" he asked. She held her breath as she shook her head slightly. There was a long pause before he finally finished. "Chocolate cake."

She couldn't help the laughter or stop herself from playfully punching him in the shoulder.

Then he pulled her closer, tight up against him, and kissed her so deeply that she wondered how she could be expected to walk after.

"I love you," Brett said when he pulled back slightly from the kiss. "Just so we're clear." He smiled down at her.

Her smile was instant. "I love you too," she said, knowing that, with everything she was, she meant it. Down to her core, she couldn't imagine being with anyone else. Brett had spoiled her. Ruined all other men. He was the one. Without a doubt.

They walked hand in hand back through town. They found a small bakery and sat down to some coffee and chocolate cake.

They had spent only a few hours in the small town before heading back up the Gulf shoreline towards home. Their home.

She didn't ask when he'd move his things into her place. Didn't even ask what the next step in the process was. What she did was a marvel at the fact that he'd said he loved her.

They talked about her business as they drove back to Pelican Point. She had signed the last of the paperwork and was not only the unit's owner but an official business owner in the town. She had her business license and all the legal paperwork had been dealt with, thanks to her mother.

Tomorrow, she was officially going to put in her resignation at the hospital. She was so nervous that she was dreading going to sleep.

"Ready for tomorrow?" he asked as he drove into town.

"No," she admitted. "How did you get through it? Quitting a job that you loved?"

He shrugged and glanced at her. "It was easy. I focused on what was ahead. Knowing that I had you. The camp." He smiled. "I had to admit to myself that it was the best move. I've probably only walked about two miles today and my leg is killing me." He rubbed his thigh. "There's no way I could ever spend an entire day standing, let alone chase someone." He shook his head. "Besides, I like my new job. You'll still have the camp."

"Yes," she agreed. "But I won't get to cut people open," she said with a shrug.

He laughed. "That would be something I wouldn't miss."

"Squeamish?"

"Not really. But anytime I had to help someone not bleed was a bad day in my book."

"You really loved your job?"

"I did," he agreed. "At least at first. If I'm being honest with myself, it's sort of a relief that I've moved on."

He turned into the neighborhood and slowed down. "If it's okay with you, I'll move the rest of my things in this weekend on my day off."

"Will you need help?" she asked.

"I can ask Aiden to help." He parked in her driveway next to her rental and shut off his car. "I'm not sure what to do with my sofa and other furniture."

"Well, since I like your sofa and chair better than mine, how about you move it in here and find something to do with mine?"

"Really?" he asked, turning towards her.

"Sure." She nodded. "I think your bed is better than mine. But we can put mine in the guest room. I haven't gotten a chance to put a bed in there yet and we might decide to swap them out later."

"Okay, you're being really cool about all this." He took her hand.

She laughed. "I want you here, and I'm smart enough to know that that includes having your stuff move in as well."

"Okay, yeah." He smiled. "So, it's settled." He pulled her across the console and kissed her.

Just then his cell phone rang. Rolling his eyes, he pulled out his phone and groaned. "It's my mother."

"Take it. I'm going to head in and shower. I have an early morning tomorrow and I have to write my resignation letter still," she added with a slight groan.

"I'll be in shortly," he said and then answered his phone.

Lea stepped into her house, shut the door, and leaned against it. Her eyes moved around her living room as she thought of how much her place had changed in the past few weeks. It wasn't as if Brett hadn't been living there already. Sure, most of the things in the place were hers, but there were some of his items. A pair of his shoes by the front door. A raincoat or umbrella in her hall closet. His shaving kit and other items in the bathroom, not to mention some clothes in her closet. And he had a whole drawer of things in her dresser.

Now, as she looked around, she imagined the rest of his things in the space. His soft leather sofa and chair replacing her stuffy white set. She'd purchased the items solely on looks and hadn't realized just how uncomfortable they were until she'd tried to snuggle down one rainy night to watch a movie.

Her dining room sat empty, as she hadn't wanted to spend money on a dining set until after she'd saved up enough to open her clinic.

He had a perfect oak table and chair set that would fill the space. It was manly yet practical, like him, and she loved it.

Sure, she'd have to make some compromises. That was the case in any great relationship. Her parents hadn't always agreed on what to put in their home, but they had always made concessions when needed.

She headed into her bathroom, tossed off her clothes, and stepped under the hot spray. She replayed that morning's events in her head. She'd tried not to let his father's words affect her.

Really, she had. But she was human after all. She wondered what she'd ever done to Brett's father to make him believe she was less than worthy to be with his son. What anyone had ever done to make him believe such hateful things.

As far as she knew, William Jewel had been born and raised in the area. He'd attended the same school they had gone to and had gone into the military at an early age and served side by side with men and women of all nationalities.

Brett had told her of his father telling stories of his youth, of how he'd been. Then she and her family had moved into town and… well, even though Brett didn't say it directly, his father had grown bitter.

To her knowledge, her parents had never had a run-in with Brett's father before. Her parents had known to avoid the man since it was all over town that he was how he was.

She wondered what sort of event had turned him into the bitter man that he now was.

A few moments after she'd stepped into the shower, hot hands wrapped around her naked body. Moaning, she relaxed back into Brett's chest and felt just what he did to her.

"You make things better," she said softly.

His hands moved to her hips, and he slowly turned her around until she faced him. His eyes searched hers.

"You've been crying," he said softly. "God, I'm such a fool. I didn't think how today would have affected you."

She shook her head and wrapped her arms around his shoulders. "I'm not crying for myself," she admitted.

"No?"

"No," she said with a smile. "It hurts me to know that you have had to deal with far worse growing up."

He rested his forehead on hers. "Whatever happens, I will never let him get between us again."

She nodded and felt her heartbeat kick violently several times in her chest.

"Tell me again," she said with her eyes closed.

His fingers brushed under her chin, raising her face until she was looking deep into his eyes. Then he finally said, "I love you." He brushed his lips against hers. "Now and forever."

CHAPTER 22

About the only thing keeping Brett's feet on the ground the following morning was the pain in his left thigh. He practically glided into the employee's dining room. Of course, his friends noticed right away.

"Someone's in a good mood," Aubrey said with a smile.

"For good reason. I'm moving in with the woman I love this weekend," he said quickly.

"So, does Lea know?" Levi said, getting a nudge in the ribs from Scarlett. Brett chuckled.

"Haven't you been living with her for a few weeks now?" Scarlett asked.

"Yes, but this weekend it will be official," he answered with a smile.

"Congrats," Liam said, holding up his orange juice.

"Thanks." He laughed and tapped his glass to the other glasses that had been held up.

"We heard what happened yesterday. How is your dad?" Hannah asked

"Is he okay?" Elle asked.

"He's recovering," he said with a shrug. "I don't know the details. I haven't visited him." The table was silent. "He knocked a fork out of Lea's hand."

Several people gasped. "Is she okay?"

"She's fine. But my dad, being the kind of man he is, didn't stop at calling her all the terrible things he could think of."

"So you punched him?" Aiden asked. When everyone looked at Aiden, he shrugged. "Carl texted me and told me to check up on you."

"Yeah, I punched him. Then he yelled some more and had a heart attack." He looked down into his plate of scrambled eggs and wheat toast. "The only good thing that has come out of this is that my mother called me last night. For the first time, she talked as if she was free. If for only a little while."

Aubrey reached over and took his hand. "How's Lea taking all this?"

"She saved his life. Seconds after he called her a ..." He shook his head. "She knelt on the floor and breathed life back into him. She didn't even bat an eye at helping the man who had just terrorized her." He hadn't realized he'd been babbling. When he stopped talking to take a deep breath, he realized it. "She's freaking amazing."

"Yes, she is," several people agreed.

"I told her I love her." He closed his eyes. "I could have done it better. I didn't even get her flowers." He shook his head.

"Oh." Hannah clapped her hands. "I've got a crazy idea."

Several people groaned.

"What?" he asked.

"When Hannah gets an idea, it usually means we're going to have some extra work to do," Aubrey said.

"Oh, hush." Hannah waved her hand towards her friends. "It's not going to be too extravagant. Some rose petals, candlelight, maybe a band, and a picnic on the beach..." She was now writing things down in the big black binder that she always carried around.

"What do…" he started to ask, but Hannah looked up at him.

"No, do nothing." She stopped him. "I'll take care of everything. When is her next evening off?"

He thought about it. "She's officially quitting the hospital today. She gets off shift around six."

"Perfect." Hannah rubbed her hands together. "She's been moping around for days leading up to her quitting. This is going to lift her spirits." She smiled. "I'll text her and tell her that we need her help tonight. I'll have her meet us on the beach around seven for a sunset dinner. I'll get her to change into a sundress." Hannah said all this while typing on her phone. "And done." She set it down. Then her eyes narrowed at him. "Do you have a cream-colored jacket, a white button-up shirt? Some nice khakis?" He thought about it but before he could answer, Hannah had picked up her phone again. "I'll have it delivered here so you can change."

He glanced around at the smiling faces. "Hannah is a miracle worker when it comes to romantic dinners," Scarlett added.

"What about flowers?" he asked.

"If you want, you can swing by the florist in town at lunch and pick something out for Lea yourself. If not, I'll have her favorite flowers delivered." Hannah looked down at her phone again.

"You know her favorite flowers?" he asked, wondering if he even knew this.

Hannah chuckled and ignored him as she typed.

"Why do I feel like she has a better handle on my love life than I do?" he asked the table.

"Welcome to the club," Levi said, earning himself another stab in the ribs from both Scarlett and Aubrey.

An hour after Brett got off work, he stood on the private

white-sand beach in khakis, a white button-up shirt, and a cream-colored cotton jacket. Beside him, there was a table, complete with a crisp white tablecloth. More lilacs than he'd ever seen adorned the table and flowed over the sides. Two places were set for when their food arrived, and a bottle of champagne was chilling in a stand next to the table.

The setting reminded him of a classic proposal spot, which had him sweating profusely.

It wasn't as if he couldn't see him and Lea living happily ever after. Hell, at this point, she was the only woman he could see himself with. But…

They'd only been official for four months. Wasn't that too early?

Okay, sure, they'd known each other all their lives. He probably knew more about Lea than he did any other woman.

Was she thinking about marriage? They weren't even officially living together yet. Officially.

By the time Lea walked down the pathway, he had removed the jacket and rolled up the sleeves of the shirt.

"Wow," Lea said, taking in the entire scene. "This is… like a scene from *The Bachelor*." She stopped next to him and then gasped. "Oh my god." She turned to him. "You're not going to propose, are you?"

The sick look on her face had him laughing. "No, but I think Hannah might have gone a little overboard." He motioned to the table. "I mentioned that I hadn't bought you flowers when I told you that I loved you and"—he waves his hands to the display—"this happened."

Lea began to laugh and didn't stop until she was doubled over. "That's Hannah for you."

"Don't get me wrong. This is… amazing. I could have never pulled something like this off if I had a month to put it together." He pulled out the chair for her to sit. When she sat down, the chair sank slightly in the sand. He moved over and sat across from her.

"She is pretty amazing," Lea said as he poured them each a glass of champagne. "So," she said after they both had a glass, "this is all so you can tell me that you love me again?" she asked with a smile.

"Yeah." He held up his glass. "So, it's official. We love each other."

She tapped her glass to his. "Officially." She took a sip.

Suddenly Dean appeared with two plates of food.

"What did you two do to earn such a cool dinner?" Dean asked.

"We're in love," Lea said with a chuckle.

"Cool," Dean said before disappearing.

"He's just jealous," Brett said, causing Lea to laugh some more. "So, today? How'd it go?"

Her smile slipped just a little. "I handed in my resignation to Laura."

"And?" he asked as he dug into his steak.

"And she was happy for me. Even told me that if I needed I could come back and work any shifts I wanted." Lea relaxed back in the chair. "I don't know why I was so afraid. I work with some great people." She leaned forward slightly. "I had a talk with Sanjay today. I told him that I had heard what he'd done, that he'd stuck up for me. I guess I'd judged the guy wrong." She shook her head. "He's been pretty cool lately."

"That's good," Brett said and waited for a heartbeat. "Did you see my dad?"

She took up her glass and took a slow sip. "I thought it was best to avoid him."

He nodded. "That's for the best, I suppose."

"I hear he's doing well. If he makes some changes in his diet and health, not to mention controlling his temper, he'll have a full recovery," Lea added.

He looked down at his steak. "Guess I'll have to be wise to the fact that it's in my family history now," he said with a slight groan.

She reached across the table and took his hand. "I don't think it's mostly his diet. I think the hate he's been holding onto had a lot to do with it."

He nodded. "In case I haven't said it, I'm really sorry."

"Don't you dare." She set her glass down with a slight bang. "Don't you apologize for anything that man has said or done. You are not your father."

"No," he agreed, "I'm not."

"Good, now…" She leaned on the table and smiled at him. "Tell me that you love me again."

He laughed, then snapped his fingers. "I have…" He took the bundle of flowers that he'd sat on the other chair. He'd picked them out on his lunch break. It had been so long since he'd walked into the florist that he'd been completely lost about what to get Lea.

"Lilies." Lea gasped. "My favorite." She buried her face into the soft white and pink petals.

"Yeah, thanks to Hannah, I know that now," he said with a shrug.

"Okay." She set the flowers down. "Since we have the time and the romantic spot, what do you say to getting to know more about each other?"

"I'm game. What did you have in mind?"

"What's your favorite flower?" she asked him.

He laughed. "I'm not sure. Those are nice." He pointed with his fork to the bundle he'd gotten her.

"Not fair. Pick something else out. These are my favorite," she joked.

"Roses are cool." he said with a shrug. "I like the smell of honeysuckles."

"Okay." She nodded and tilted her head. "Favorite sport?"

"To watch or play?"

"Watch."

"Soccer," he answered quickly.

"Mine too," she said with a smile.

"Nope, not fair, pick another one," he joked as he threw her words back at him.

She laughed. "Okay, European football."

It was his turn to laugh.

While they ate, they went down the entire list of favorites. Colors, food, movies, music, and even travel spots.

He enjoyed getting to know more about her and telling her about him. He was discovering more about her than he'd ever known about anyone.

By the time their desserts arrived, he had laughed more than he had on any other date in his life. Lea was like an old friend that he was lucky enough to be attracted to physically and love for the person she was. She was the best of everything in life.

As the evening progressed, he realized just how easy it was to see their future together. By the time they walked down the beach to watch the sun sink below the crystal-clear waters of the Gulf, the thought of marrying her didn't seem so crazy anymore. Actually, it was the most natural thought in the world. She had always been there. Even if he hadn't known it.

But one thing was clear—he was not going to let Hannah pick the time or place that he proposed to the woman he was going to spend the rest of his life with.

"I get my car back tomorrow," Lea said after they started to drive back home.

"It's done?" he asked, glancing at her. "That was fast."

"My dad knew a guy," she said with a shrug.

"What color did you have it painted?"

She smiled. "Cherry red." She quickly held up her hand. "But that does not mean…" Her words dropped off when he turned the corner out of the campground's driveway. "What the…" She gasped.

He jerked the wheel and skidded around a massive carcass.

"What is that?" Lea asked when the car came to a stop.

"A pig." He put the car into park.

"Pigs aren't that big." She glanced behind them.

"Wild boars are," he said quickly. "I'll go move it out of the road. I'd hate for someone to hit it or swerve and cause an accident."

Putting on his hazards, he turned to Lea. "Stay in the car."

She nodded and he got out of the car and got a tire iron out of his trunk so he could shove the thing out of the road without touching it with his hands.

The massive thing probably weighed more than two hundred pounds. At first, he tried to shove it, but when it didn't budge, he figured he'd flip it over and roll it off the road.

That seemed to work at first. The moment the boar flipped, he noticed the perfect gunshot wound in the boar's head area and froze. Glancing around, he felt the familiar prickle at the back of his neck.

The moment he moved to rush back to the car, he saw a figure in black step up to the open door of his car. He watched in horror as the man slid in behind the wheel of the still-running car and took off with a squeal of his tires. He had heard Lea scream briefly just before the door slammed shut.

He screamed and ran as fast as his leg would take him, chasing the fading taillights. When his left leg folded under him, he pounded the pavement with his fists.

He'd left his cell phone sitting in the middle of the console. He couldn't even call for help.

Thinking, he turned back around and rushed as fast as he could back to the camp, cursing the entire way at his leg. At his ignorance of the situation. What had he done? He'd put her in harm's way.

Why? Who?

All of those questions flooded his mind as he ran for help. It took longer than it would have had his leg been back to its normal health.

When he rushed into the main lobby area, he was covered in sweat and even angrier at himself for falling for the trick.

"My God, what's happened?" Julie gasped from behind the counter.

"Police, someone's taken Lea," he managed to get out before he passed out cold.

When he woke, he was still on the floor of the entryway, surrounded by his friends. A glass of water was shoved in front of him. He drank it like a man who had just crossed the desert.

"Lea," he said when he could speak.

"We've called the police," Aiden said quickly. "What happened?"

"There was a dead boar in the road. I got out to move it to the side, and someone jumped in the car and took off with her," he said quickly.

"Your car?" Aiden said, pulling out his phone.

"Yes." He nodded.

He listened while Aiden relayed the information, most likely to Carl.

"They're putting an alert out," Aiden said.

"Are you okay?" Aubrey asked. He was rubbing his leg, which was hurting almost as bad as when he'd been shot.

"I'll survive." He stood up with the help of Aiden. "Got your keys?" he asked his friend.

"I'll drive," Aiden said.

"We'll all go out and look," Aubrey said. "You were heading home? To the right?" she asked.

"Yes, but that won't stop them from turning or going a different direction," he said as they made their way back to the parking lot. He was thankful that Aiden took his arm and threw it over his shoulder so that he could take most of Brett's weight.

"Could it be Robbie or Larry?" Aiden asked once they were in his truck quickly heading back down the long driveway of the camp.

"Last I heard they were both still locked up. That wouldn't stop either of them from coordinating it or stop their buddies Dale and Billy from taking their revenge. Everyone knew that we worked here." He silently cursed himself again for falling for the ruse.

"We'll get her back," Aiden said several times, almost as if he was chanting it in order to make it true. "Is your phone still in the car?"

"Yes," he gasped and reached for Aiden's phone.

"Find-my-phone app," they both said at the same time.

"Where is it?" he asked, frantically looking on the screen.

"The second screen," Aiden replied.

He couldn't count the times he'd forgotten or lost his cell phone. Enough times that Aiden had installed the app on his phone to help him find it.

Within seconds, he saw the little blue dot that was his phone traveling down the highway towards Panama City.

"I need my gun," he said more to himself as he relayed the direction to Aiden. "Swing by my place."

"No, you need to call Carl and let him know where we're going," Aiden corrected.

"When I find the bastard that took her..." he started.

"We're going to let Carl and the police handle it," Aiden said firmly. "But just in case, we'll stop off and get your gun."

CHAPTER 23

The moment the dark shadow jumped into the car, she knew it wasn't Brett, and she screamed.

She'd been so occupied with watching the man jump behind the wheel that she hadn't seen the gun until it was too late.

She didn't even have a second to try and remember anything Aubrey had taught her in judo class that could help her out of this situation. She fought and tried to scratch her attacker, only to see stars as everything faded into darkness when he hit her with the butt of a gun on the side of her head.

She woke quickly when the car came to a screeching halt. Her head snapped forward and, before she could recover, arms grabbed her and pulled her out of the car. Instantly, she fought and screamed in hopes that someone would come to her aid.

She was shoved, pushed, and even hit a few times.

"Get the bitch inside," someone growled. "Quickly."

She was pushed again. When she screamed at the top of her lungs, a meaty hand covered her mouth, blocking the sound from traveling.

She kicked out and used her elbows as Aubrey had taught

her. Nothing could have prepared her for two large men manhandling her and finally lifting her and carting her through the darkness.

"We're just going to teach you a little lesson on who you shouldn't mess with," one of them said the moment they carried her through a doorway.

The hand over her mouth shifted slightly, and she bit down hard and didn't let go until the man screamed in pain and she felt a trickle of blood ooze into her mouth. She wanted to gag, to spit it and the skin she was cutting loose out of her mouth. Instead, she clenched down even harder.

Then her legs were dropped, and a fist connected to the side of her temple. She released her bite as stars exploded behind her eyes. Everything spun so quickly, she felt her stomach lurch. Her body went limp, even though she didn't completely lose consciousness.

She drifted just on the verge of awareness as they carried her down a hallway and up a set of stairs, and finally dumped her unceremoniously onto a hard floor.

"Tie the bitch up," one of the men said.

She knew that if they managed to tie her up that she would never leave this place alive. It was the raw desire to live that once more had her kicking, screaming, and fighting away the hands that reached for her.

The room was too dark for her to see who her attackers were. Besides, the multiple knocks to her head had her seeing double. Triple even. Everything shimmered as if she was wearing glasses that had been shattered into millions of pieces. The pain in her head was so great, each time she moved, she felt nauseous.

Then she remembered something Aubrey had told her. Abductors didn't like bodily fluids. If you could, you should pee yourself. Throw up. Spit. Aubrey had taught her to use more than just your muscle.

She jerked her head around and instantly felt the steak dinner and wine that she'd just shared with Brett begin to come back up. She made a point to try and aim and when the hands that had been grabbing her jerked away, she continued to let her stomach revolt.

"The bitch is doing that on purpose," one of the men screamed.

"Just get her hands. You can shower off after we have her hog-tied," the other man said.

She stilled. Suddenly she knew exactly who was in the room. Her blood grew cold, and she knew that she wasn't going to make it through the night.

After she'd emptied her stomach, she fought off the sticky hands that wrapped around her wrists again. No matter what she tried, this time they easily wrapped a rope around her and yanked her arms tightly behind her back. Her ankles were next, and they were jerked up behind her body in a bent fashion until her hands and legs were tied together. They had indeed hog-tied her.

Then an oily rag was shoved in her mouth. She tried to fight it off, but the man gripped her jaw and squeezed until she cried out in pain. Then he shoved it all the way inside her mouth.

"That should keep the gook quiet until we come back," Robbie Dixon said with a chuckle.

If she hadn't just lost the entire contents of her stomach, the oily rag would have made her throw up again.

She was kicked a few times in her stomach and back and then, thankfully, the room grew quiet. She lay there, trying to catch her breath, but with each inhale came sharp pain. She'd seen enough patients come in with broken ribs to understand that one or two of her ribs were broken, and maybe several more were bruised.

Regulating her breathing, she tried to think of anything that could help her escape. If she didn't, she knew there was no chance of seeing Brett or her parents again.

What would they do? How could they go on without her? Would Brett blame himself? It wasn't his fault. There was no way he could have seen what was coming.

After all, the last they knew, both Robbie and Larry were in jail. If it was Larry with Robbie. The man didn't sound familiar, but she would know Robbie's voice even if she'd been blindfolded. It had been the one constant thing in her nightmares since that first night. That slow southern drawl with his slight speech impediment. The way he rolled his R's was so unique that there was no mistake it was Robbie.

Her eyes teared up as she glanced around the dark room. Since her hands and feet were hog-tied behind her, all she could do was twist her head to try and see her surroundings.

She wondered vaguely if her purse and cell phone were still in Brett's car. Could he find her that way? Was Robbie even now moving the car? She heard the crunch of tires over gravel and figured they were leaving her there. Where was she? It appeared to be an abandoned building. Maybe under construction?

The floor was cement. Most of the high-rise or multistory homes along the water were made of cement to withstand hurricane winds.

Then she noticed a large piece of plastic hanging over a wall. She felt the warm breeze of the summer night, smelled the salt and the water from the Gulf.

She couldn't hear anything beyond the soft sway of the plastic and the crickets outside.

She thought of trying to push the oily rag out of her mouth, but each time she tried to use her tongue or teeth, she gagged at the taste.

Closing her eyes, she wished for someone to save her. Someone to come. She wished that Brett was there. That her parents wouldn't have to be told that she'd been murdered. Wished that Robbie and his accomplice would be found, tried, and found guilty of their crimes.

Clues. Her mind snapped. The only thing she could do now was leave clues.

Her fingers were sticky with blood. She didn't know if it was hers or if it was from the man she'd bitten. Either way, she rolled over and began using her fingers to write what she could, twisting herself over the dusty cement floor until her fingers were dry and raw from the coarse cement.

Still, she was pretty sure she had written Robbie's name out on the dusty floor.

When she'd used up all her energy, she basically passed out from lack of strength and from the fear of what was going to come next.

* * *

"The car has stopped again," he told Aiden.

"Where?" his friend asked.

"Pier Park." He zoomed the screen in. "In the back parking lot."

"Why take her someplace there's bound to be a ton of people around this time of night?" Aiden said. "I still think we should check out the first place they stopped. They could have unloaded Lea there and be dumping your car in a public spot."

"I agree," Brett said. "I'm going to have Carl check out Pier Park. Let's head to the place they first stopped."

"Send him the address of the first stop," Aiden suggested.

Brett shot off a text message with both locations and then called Carl.

"We're going to check out the first place. Have you got someone close to Pier Park?" he asked.

"Yeah, we're about one minute out," Carl answered, and Brett could hear the sirens through the phone. "I'll let you know. Pulling into the parking lot now."

"Keep an eye out. The car stopped almost two minutes ago. They could be on foot or in another car at this point," he suggested before hanging up.

"It says we're less than a minute out," he told Aiden, who stepped on the pedal and sped down the narrow dirt road. "Slow down," Brett suggested. "If someone's here, we don't want to spook them into doing something to Lea."

"Right." Aiden slowed the truck down. The narrow dirt lane appeared to have just been carved out of the thick brush.

"There." Brett pointed to a massive structure. "Turn off your lights and stop here. There's still a truck there."

"What now?" Aiden asked.

"Now, I go in." Brett took out his gun. "You stay in the truck. Call Carl if I'm not back in ten minutes. Move the truck over there." He pointed just beyond some trees. "Turn it around in case we have to get out of here in a hurry."

"Brett." Aiden laid a hand on his arm.

"Yeah?" he asked after a moment.

"Be careful man," Aiden added. "I know I can't talk you out of going. If it was Aubrey, I'd be right there. Have been there."

"Right," Brett said. He slid out of the truck quietly.

He made his way towards the large structure and only when he was a few feet away realized that it was a four-story home under construction. Its thick cement structure was no more than just a skeleton at this point. There were no doors, windows, or walls for that matter.

The first floor was wide open and looked like it was all garage space. The home had obviously been designed for a flood zone. There was a narrow set of construction stairs on the back of the place leading to the second story.

He checked the newer model truck that was parked there but knew better than to try the door handle in case there was an alarm. Instead, he started up the stairs, trying to prepare himself for whatever lay ahead.

He cursed himself and wished for a flashlight when he stepped onto the second floor. As with the first level, the entire space was wide open. No inner walls, windows, or doors. Only large sheets of plastic hung down to keep the rain out.

It was too dark to see clearly, but he knew instantly that there was no one on this floor. When he heard a footstep and a sound on the next level, he started up the stairs once more. Halfway up the stairs, he could hear deep breathing. He jumped when a cell phone went off.

Brett listened and held his breath.

"Damn it, Dad, you scared the shit out of me," Robbie said as he answered the call. He listened as Robbie listened to whatever his father was telling him. Was his dad in on this? "What do you mean the cops are there? How?" He practically yelled it. "Okay, yeah." Another pause. "What do I do now?" He was silent again. "Shit, yeah, okay, just get here quickly. We've got to teach this bitch a lesson," Robbie said. He hung up, and Brett felt his blood boil.

Moving slowly again, he glanced around the corner and saw Robbie sitting on a crate, smoking a cigarette as he looked down at his cell phone.

He looked around quickly for any sign of Lea. But as with each floor before, this one was wide open, a massive empty space. With the light from Robbie's cell phone, Brett could easily see that the room was empty.

Glancing up the stairs, he wondered if Lea was on the top floor. Deciding to take care of Robbie after he'd found Lea, he quietly slipped past Robbie and made his way up the stairs.

Again, it was too dark to see clearly, but one entire wall of plastic had come loose, allowing the moonlight inside just enough that he could see the small mound lying on the floor.

Rushing over to her, he saw the blood around her, clearly saw the name 'Robbie' in it, and then felt for a pulse with shaky hands. Her arms and legs were tied behind her back and there was blood coming from her nose and mouth, and a large gash on her cheek and forehead. One of her fingers was twisted at an odd angle and bleeding. The summer dress she'd worn to dinner was torn, exposing her white bra, which was now covered in cement dust and blood. There was a dirty rag shoved in her mouth, and he slowly removed it, hoping she wouldn't wake up and scream.

He didn't want Robbie to know that he was there. Not yet, at any rate.

Taking out his pocketknife, he cut the bungee cords that held her hands and feet. She stirred slightly when she was free, so he put his mouth up to her ear and whispered.

"I'm here, it's Brett. Don't make a sound. I'm going to get you out of here," he said softly.

She didn't stir until he shifted her to pick her up.

Then she moaned softly, and he stilled.

"Shh," he said. "Honey, just hang on," he whispered.

He heard Robbie laugh at something downstairs and relaxed.

"I'm going to get you out of here," he said to Lea again.

"Brett?" she asked.

"Shh, Robbie's still downstairs," he said right next to her ear.

"My ribs," she said under her breath. "They're broken."

"Okay, I've got you." He shifted her as easily as he could and started quickly walking towards the stairs, ignoring the pain in his leg. Lea held onto him, her head resting on his shoulder, her breathing erratic.

He knew she was trying to stay conscious and as quiet as possible.

His current plan was to get Lea out of the building before coming back in to deal with Robbie and his father. But when his foot hit the last step on the third floor, he realized that the light from Robbie's phone was gone.

The entire floor was now in shadows. Shit.

Shifting Lea, he slid his gun out from his shoulder holster. He didn't know if Lea was strong enough to stand, so he shifted her weight so that he could hold his weapon. He felt Lea tense and knew that she understood something was wrong.

By his internal clock, his ten minutes were up, and Aiden should have called Carl already.

In a flash, he thought about all of the things that could go wrong in the next few seconds, how many different ways he could lose Lea, and he knew that whatever happened next, he would fight until his dying breath to save the woman he loved.

CHAPTER 24

*L*ea was on the verge of passing out. She felt Brett tense and instantly knew something was off. The little hairs on her arms and neck stood up, and she knew something was about to happen.

Brett held his gun in one hand and her in the other. She wanted to tell him to put her down, to run and save himself, but she didn't want to break the silence. Instead, she tapped his shoulder and started sliding down his body until her bare feet touched the cement floor. Only then did she realize that she must have lost her shoes at some point.

Brett took her hand and slowly started moving in the darkness. A two-by-four flew at them out of nowhere, and he used his body to shield the blow. The force of the hit caused Brett to drop the gun, which went scattering over the floor with a dull sound. Then he shoved them both back towards the stairs until they fell together. He landed on top of her, and she cried out as she felt a few more ribs crack.

"Run. Aiden's outside," Brett said into her ear before he

jerked up and threw himself at the dark figure standing over them.

She would have run. Really. But she wasn't dumb. She knew there were two of them and there was no way Brett was going to fend the men off in the shape he was in.

All it would take was one of them kicking or hitting his bad leg and Brett would be helpless. Instead, she crouched down on her hands and knees and felt around in the dark for Brett's gun.

She heard the men struggling, saw the two dark shadows rolling around on the floor, and when her fingers touched the cold metal of the gun, a wave of relief washed over her.

But then she glanced up and saw Robbie standing over Brett, holding his gun. She didn't know who shot first. The blinding blast from both guns made her scream, as did the power of the gun going off in her hand.

Then Robbie was falling forward as if in slow motion. His body landed with a thud on the cement floor, a sound she would never be able to get out of her memories.

Scrambling forward, she pushed Robbie's body off Brett's and started feeling around for the bullet wound she knew was there. After all, she'd shot Robbie from more than five feet away, and Robbie had been standing directly over Brett. There was no possible way that he'd missed.

"Lea, I'm okay," Brett said, taking her hands in his.

"No, you're not. You're in shock. I have to stop the bleeding." She sounded hysterical even to her own ears.

"Lea." Brett pulled her into his arms. "He missed me. I'm fine."

She shook her head as tears rolled down her cheeks. "No, you're not."

"Come on," Brett started to say. Just then they heard the distinct sounds of rushing footsteps, and Brett took the gun from her hands.

A beam of light hit them. "Don't shoot. It's me, Aiden," Aiden said quickly.

Brett sighed and set the gun down. "'Bout time you showed up," he said with a sigh.

"Jesus, is he... dead?" Aiden asked.

Lea glanced over to where Aiden's flashlight beam illuminated Robbie's body. The man was staring up at the ceiling with glossy eyes. A single red hole in his chest directly where his heart was slowly oozed blood. A dark puddle pooled under the man's body.

"Yeah," Brett said and quickly stood up. She noticed that he winced when he put weight on his left leg, but then he bent down and easily picked her up in his arms.

She gasped and held onto her sides.

"She's got some broken ribs, cuts, and a busted finger," he told Aiden. "Tell me you called this in before rushing in here."

"I'm not stupid," Aiden said as he moved closer to him. "Carl says he bumped into Rob Dixon Sr. in the parking lot where they found your car. The man was bleeding from an apparent bite on his hand. The man had other fresh cuts and bruises so instead of questioning things, he detained him. I guess I'll give him a call and tell him... what?"

"I bit him," Lea said softly. Her voice sounded like it was floating with the rest of her. "On his hand and wrist." She motioned to her own hand. "And threw up all over him," she added as she felt her entire body relax. "Sorry, I'm going to..." She closed her eyes as everything went black.

She woke in the back of an ambulance with an oxygen mask over her mouth and nose. Her first instinct was to push it away, but her education kicked in before she could move, and she took a couple of shallow breaths instead and looked around.

"Brett?" she asked the young EMT that sat next to her.

"Your man?" the woman asked. Lea nodded quickly and then groaned with the pain it caused her. "He's talking to the cops."

"Can he come with?" she asked.

"I'll make sure he gets a ride with us," the EMT assured her.

Lea closed her eyes and relaxed back. She felt the quick prick as an IV was carefully shoved into her veins, and then the warmth of the saline solution flowing into her along with whatever medicine she'd been given. Her world went a little wonky, and she smiled as the morphine removed every trace of her pain.

Moments or hours later, she couldn't tell, Brett appeared above her, his perfect features floating in front of her eyes.

"I love you," she said, her voice muffled by the drugs and the oxygen mask.

"She's probably a little loopy," the EMT said.

"I love you too," Brett said, ignoring the other woman. "I'm right here. I won't leave your side."

She nodded and then closed her eyes once more. The next time they opened, it was her parents standing over her. Worried looks flooded their eyes.

"There you are," her mother said as she wiped a tear from her cheek.

Lea felt her hand being held but knew that the drugs were still coursing through her since everything was still numb.

"How are you feeling, honey?" her father asked.

"Drugged," she said and only then realized that the oxygen mask had been replaced with a nasal cannula. "Brett?" she asked again.

"He's here, just in the next room getting checked out," her mother said.

Worry flashed quickly. "Is he okay?" She tried to sit up, but a stab of pain had her lying back down.

"Easy," her father said. "You've got three broken ribs and a few bruised ones."

"He's fine," her mother assured her. "The doctor is just checking him out because he has a black eye and hit his head pretty hard during the scuffle."

She relaxed back. "Robbie? His father?"

Her parents looked between themselves. "Robbie Dixon Jr. is dead. Rob Dixon Sr. is in custody and is being charged with kidnapping and attempted murder," her father finally said firmly.

She sighed. "I shot him. He was going to shoot Brett. I killed Robbie."

"He missed. The bullet came within six inches of Brett's head," her mother said. "Or so they estimated. It put a hole in the cement where he'd been lying."

Lea felt a shiver race through her. She'd come so close to losing the man she loved. All for what? Because he dared to love someone different than him. She closed her eyes. She no longer wanted to talk to her parents. No longer wanted to talk to anyone. Instead, she slept. She slept for so long, that when she woke, the room was engulfed in bright light.

"There she is. Here's our hero now," Aubrey said as she appeared in front of Lea. "The whole gang is here." Aubrey motioned to the room.

Sure enough, there were more than a dozen people shoved into Lea's private hospital room, a room Lea had been in more times than she knew. Not that she could tell which room it was, since they all looked alike, but she was sure she was on the second floor of her hospital. The one she'd worked on for the past few years.

No doubt doctors and nurses she'd worked side by side with were now taking care of her just like they did everyone else that came in through their doors.

"Hi," she said finally. Her eyes scanned the many faces she knew, looking for Brett. She was sort of relieved when she didn't spot him amongst the crowd. "What time is it?" she asked.

"Just past two in the afternoon," Scarlett answered. "We tried not to wake you. We were just dropping off these."

Lea noticed more than a dozen floral arrangements crowding every surface of the room. There were brightly colored balloons as well.

"Thank you." She shifted and hit the button on the side of the bed. Everyone was silent as she slowly sat up.

"How are you feeling?" Elle finally asked.

She assessed herself before answering. "The morphine is doing its job."

"Brett is just outside talking to the cops. Do you want me to go get him?" Aubrey asked.

"No," she said, sounding a little too eager. "I… I'm a little tired."

"Okay." Aubrey glanced at the rest of the people in the room. "We'll leave you to rest." Aubrey walked over and took Lea's unbandaged hand and squeezed it gently. "If you need anything, we're just a phone call away."

"Thanks," she said, closing her eyes. This time, however, she didn't fall asleep. Instead, she waited until she heard everyone leave the room before opening them again. Only she had misjudged. She wasn't alone. Brett stood over her, looking down at her. She noticed a large white bandage over his left eye and forehead. A dark bruise filled his left cheek and chin. His lip was twice the size it normally was and split directly in the middle. Still, he looked too good to be true.

She took a moment to wonder if she looked as bad, but then figured it was better to block that thought out of her mind completely.

"Hey," he said softly.

Her heart broke a little at knowing what she had to do next. He had almost died because of her. Without her knowing, tears rolled down her cheeks.

"Hey." Brett moved closer and sat gently on the side of her bed. "I'm okay. You're okay. We're alive." He took her hand.

She shook her head from side to side. "No, you don't understand." She closed her eyes. "This is all my fault."

"How so?" His tone turned a little sharp.

"If you hadn't been with me. If I'd never overstepped…"

"I thought you were smarter than this." Brett's sharp tone cut into her statement.

Her eyes flew open and locked with his.

"It's because of me. Of what I am. All of this," she said, trying to get him to understand.

"No, it's because of three racist asshats who believe they're above the law." He stood up suddenly, then turned towards the window. "Judge Robert Dixon was arrested a few moments ago. He and his son had arranged to have Robbie released. It was the judge's new house that the two men took you to, to kill you. There'd been an ongoing investigation into the judge's past racist behavior. The moment he arranged for his grandson's release, well, let's just say his career ended."

"Did he know?" she asked, feeling her stomach roll.

"We're not sure. He's playing his cards close to his chest. Claiming that his son and grandson went off on their own. But Rob Sr., his son, is claiming it was all the judge's idea." He shrugged and turned back towards her. "You didn't do anything wrong. This"—he waved his hand, and she noticed a few bandages on his right fist—"none of it is in any way your fault. There are bad people in this world. You are not one of them." He moved over to her again.

"I almost lost you." It came out as a cry. Her chest hurt and no matter how much morphine was flowing through her veins, she doubted the pressure would ever be released.

"And I almost lost you," he said softly, sitting beside her again. He took up her hand, and she felt him lift it to his lips and brush a soft kiss across her knuckles. "Make no mistake, no one in their right mind thinks that this was in any way your fault."

She opened her eyes and met his before nodding slightly. "I was going to break it off with you."

"When?" he asked, frowning. "Before?"

"No, because of what happened." She sighed. "If we've just been through hell and we haven't even officially moved in with one another, what more does our relationship have in store?"

He smiled. "Whatever it is, we'll conquer it together. Like we took out Robbie. That is, if you're game?"

She smiled and nodded. "I think I'd like to recover from this first."

"Me too," he said with a chuckle. "Are you hungry?" he asked her suddenly.

She thought back to the last meal she'd eaten and how that had ended up.

"I'd like a shower first, if possible." She looked down at her crisp hospital gown.

"I'll ask and arrange for some Jell-o or whatever they'll give you." He stood up and walked over to the door.

"Brett?" she said, getting his attention.

"Yeah?" he asked, looking back at her.

"I'm glad you found me," she said finally, swallowing the lump in her throat.

"I'm just glad I lost my cell phone so much that Aiden has the find-me app installed and connected to my number." He smiled.

"Is that how you found me?" she asked, suddenly realizing she didn't know how he'd shown up in the cement building in the first place. She hadn't even questioned it at the time. She must have really been in shock.

"Yeah." He smiled and then stepped outside.

When he returned, she was slowly making her way towards the bathroom, moving like a turtle, afraid that with each step she would crack into a million pieces.

"Here, let me help you," he said, taking hold of her IV pole and wheeling it behind her.

When she stepped into the bathroom, she motioned for him to leave so she could shower and clean off.

"Oh, here." He disappeared and brought back a bag. "Your mother thought you'd want some things." He set the bag down inside the bathroom. "Food is ordered and should be here in about ten. Yell if you need help," he said before shutting the door.

The moment she was alone, she leaned on the sink and let the tears flow. Her vision was too blurry to see what she looked like, nor did she care. She was alive. Brett was alive. Nothing else mattered.

Still, her world had shifted. She'd lost a part of her innocence. The belief that all humans had some trace of good in them.

Was Brett's father the same as the three Dixon men? Would he have held her down, kicked her, tied her up like an animal, and treated her as if she was less of a human being?

Hadn't his words done just that moments before she'd jumped in to save his life?

Could she and Brett ever expect to live a happy life if his father continued to fight against them? Was it worth it?

Her parents had come from different families. Her father's parents had been poor. They'd both worked at a market and had raised their two sons in the same household as three other families, just so they could all afford the roof over their head. Her mother's parents had come from wealth. They'd sent their daughter and son to the finest Ivy League schools.

The fact that they were both from Southeast Asia had just been a coincidence. According to her parents, they would have loved one another no matter what nationality their ancestors were. When they had met and fallen in love, neither family had any problems with their relationship.

As she stepped under the warm water, she thought about her and Brett's future. What would happen if they married and had kids?

She'd never once thought about her children being harassed because of their heritage. Never expected it, even though she'd been slightly harassed all her life.

She'd never once expected anything like this though. How could she hope to raise children in a world that was so cruel towards them?

"You okay in there?" Brett's voice was right outside the shower. "You're taking a long time."

"I'm... okay," she replied. "Just..." What? She hadn't even showered her hair or washed the dried blood and dirt off from her skin at this point. Instead, she'd just sat there and wallowed in her own self-pity.

Then the shower curtain was shoved aside, and Brett stood there, looking at her.

"Need some help?" he asked. His eyes ran over her body. Instead of desire in his gaze, she saw concern and anger.

Instead of waiting for her to answer, he picked up the wash-cloth and poured a generous helping of soap into it and began gently washing away the dirt and grime.

"You'll get your shirt wet," she complained.

As a reply, he stepped back and tossed off the shirt and his jeans before stepping into the shower naked with her.

"This… is highly irregular," she said, leaning against the walls. "The shower is far too small for the both of us."

"We'll only be in here long enough to get the grime off of us." He began to work on cleaning her skin again.

It was then that she noticed that he hadn't showered since last night's events either. Taking up another washcloth, she poured shampoo into it and began scrubbing his skin clean.

They worked in silence for a few moments until he finally put some shampoo into her hair and started carefully scrubbing her hair clean.

"You have a large bump here," he said softly. "I'll work around it. Does it hurt?"

"Everything is dull still."

Then she leaned back and enjoyed the way his hands ran through her long tresses, massaging her scalp, gently washing the bubbles away.

"I think we're clean," he said, breaking into her foggy mind.

"Thanks." She opened her eyes and met his. The look in his eyes had shifted. Now they were full of desire. Full of love.

He pulled her close as the water fell over them, washing away the rest of the soap suds. They held one another like time had stopped. Like the whole world had stopped and nothing but that moment mattered.

$\mathcal{L}$ea was in the hospital for a few days. The entire time, Brett stuck by her side as much as he could, only leaving the room when her parents or her friends were visiting and he knew she was well looked after.

He'd walked down the hallway and stood outside his father's room several times, unsure of what he wanted to say to the man. Wondering if he'd have enough guts to cut both his parents out of his life completely or not.

The last time, his mother had surprised him by opening the door. When she'd seen him, she'd stepped outside and shut the door to the room.

"Your father is resting," she said softly.

"I'm not here to see him," he assured her. Her response was a slight smile.

"How about we go down and get some coffee?" she asked.

He followed her in silence down to the hospital cafeteria. Then he sat across from her and ignored the black coffee she'd gotten for him.

"Why do you stay?" he'd asked her.

At first, he didn't think she was going to answer, but then she sighed and set her coffee aside.

"I was in love. Your father was a better choice than staying in the house I'd been raised in. You never knew your grandparents but let's just say I was thankful the day they were killed in the plane crash." He remembered hearing stories of how her parents had died shortly after his birth. "Your father, well, he used to not be so bad. But then he lost his business because Mr. Val moved his business into the area."

"What?" Brett shook his head. "What business? Dad has worked as an electrician for years."

"Yes, but before that, he owned a small electric store and was the sole electrician supplying lighting fixtures to the area. Your father blames Mr. Val for moving into the area. He claims that he took all your dad's business and your father had to start working small jobs." She sighed. "In truth, your dad closed his business close to a year prior to the Val's moving here. If he showed up to find that the job was for someone of…"

"Color?" he said dryly.

His mother nodded. "He'd leave without doing the job. It took a toll on his business. The word got around town about his reputation and, well, he had to find another job."

"Why stay through all that?" he asked.

His mother's eyes moved to his. "You," she said simply. Then she smiled. "You were worth every moment of pain that man put me through."

"And now?" he asked, shaking his head. "Why stay now? I've been out of the house for years."

His mother's eyes moved down to her fingers.

"Fear. I'm not proud of it, but I know what the man will do if…"

Brett reached across and took his mother's frail hand in his.

"Nothing. He can't do anything to you now."

His mother shook her head. "Not to me." She glanced up at him.

"Me? He threatened to harm me if you, what? Didn't fall in line?" he asked, appalled.

His mother nodded. "Even when you wore a badge, he threatened you. He would say, 'Cops get shot all the time.' or 'Cops die in the line of duty every day..'" She sighed and wiped a tear that rolled down her cheek.

"That son of a…" He glanced up at the ceiling, wishing the worst on the man lying in the hospital bed. "And now?" he asked.

"Now?" She sighed. "He's going to be paralyzed on his left side," she said as if that answered his question.

"So?" Brett threw out.

"So, now he needs me. Things will be different." His mother smiled slightly.

"No, they won't. The only difference is that you'll have to wipe his ass every day." Brett shook his head.

"He's the only thing I have. I can't just… leave." She shook her head as more tears rolled down her cheeks.

"Yes, you can. You have me. You have Lea and her family," he said, but she shook her head.

"I can't," she said softly. He remembered all his training and knew that he couldn't force her to make the next move. The only thing he could do was be there for her when she was ready.

"When you're ready, we're here for you," he told her. "Until then, that man is no longer welcome in my or Lea's life." He stood up suddenly. Then he stopped. "I'm going to marry her, and if you have a problem with it…"

"I don't." His mother smiled up at him. "I've always admired how hard that girl works. She's smart, funny, and…" She looked back down at her hands. "She's a better person than your father will ever be."

He was slightly taken aback by her words, but then he nodded.

"Good, then maybe you'll be invited to the wedding," he said. "I've got to get back up to her."

"I hope…" his mother started. "Tell her I hope she gets better soon." He nodded and left his mother to sit all alone.

When the day came for Lea to be released so she could rest and recover at home, he took her back to her place. He was thankful to see that all his things had already been moved into her house.

Her old furniture had disappeared, and his sofa and chair were arranged nicely in her living room, no doubt thanks to all of their friends.

After carrying her inside, he set Lea softly on the sofa and then covered her with a blanket.

"Wow, you moved everything over here already?" she said, looking around. "It all looks so good together."

"Not me," he admitted. "Aiden asked for my keys. I suspect it was the whole team that did this." He sat next to her. "How about a movie while I order us some food for delivery?"

"Sounds good." She sighed. "I'm so ready to relax and eat some unhealthy food." She lifted her feet to the sofa and tucked the blanket closer around her.

Just then the doorbell rang, causing them both to groan.

"Stay put," he said, getting up.

"I don't care who it is, I'm not moving for hours," she said with a smile.

When he opened the door, Aiden and Aubrey strolled past him. "Hey," Aiden said, handing him a case of beer. "Better put that on ice."

"Hey," he said, frowning after his friends. Before he could shut the door, Zoey and Dylan's car pulled up behind Aiden's truck. He waited as they ran through the light rain to step up on the porch.

"Hey," he said, motioning for them to come in.

"Hey," Dylan said with a smile.

"Where's the kid?" he asked them.

"At grandma Kimberly's for the night." Dylan lowered his voice. "Don't mention it too loud. Zoey's already having anxiety over it."

"Cool." He almost shut the door, only to see Scarlett and Levi's car pull up behind Dylan's.

For the next five minutes, he watched as every single one of their friends piled into their living room.

Lea was now surrounded by her friends and had been handed a plate full of fried chicken, mashed potatoes and gravy, and one of the largest biscuits he'd ever seen.

People kept coming in, so he left the front door open and moved to sit next to Lea with his plate of food.

"I didn't think this many people would fit in here," Lea said between bites.

He chuckled. "Me either. You know, I think we could easily build a covered patio off the back of the house, you know, to barbeque out on and entertain."

"That's a great idea," Lea said with a smile. "Talk to Aiden about helping out."

"I'll do that. Later," he agreed.

It did his heart good making plans with her for their future. At least she'd stopped hinting and talking about moving away from him.

The fact that she believed that any of what had happened was her fault had him growing even angrier. Not at her, but at the Dixons.

For the next two hours, he chatted with everyone he knew

from the campground. Some employees came and went quickly, while others lingered longer.

Shortly before dark, Elle, Hannah, and Scarlett helped clean up the mess and did all the dishes while he talked to Levi and Aiden on the back porch.

Lea was lying on the sofa, watching a movie and trying desperately not to fall asleep.

"So." Aiden glanced around the large backyard. "You want a covered patio?" he asked. "Lea mentioned it."

Brett smiled. "We're thinking about it."

"Does that mean the two of you are going to make things final like the rest of us are?" Levi asked.

Brett smiled. "We're thinking about it."

"Oh?" Aiden said, sounding surprised.

"Not that I've mentioned it to Lea, but…" He shrugged. "You don't go through something like that without reevaluating your relationship."

"The two of you have known each other forever," Levi said.

"Kind of like you and Scar," Aiden added.

"Yeah," Levi said with a smile.

"Did you hear anything more about the Dixons?" Aiden asked.

Brett's smile fell away.

"No. Last we heard, the judge is denying everything his son is saying. The son even tried to deny that he'd known what his son had planned, but when the pair of them were caught on a security camera parking Senior's truck in the parking lot where they would stash my car, he finally admitted that they had planned to kidnap her. They'd followed Lea to the camp and waited for us to drive away. They drove around town with the damn boar in the bed of their truck for hours. They figured I, being the good cop I was, would stop and try to move it from the road." He took another sip of his beer to get rid of the sour taste in his mouth at the thought of it. "Junior jumped in my car and knocked Lea out while Senior waited at the judge's new place. They carried Lea upstairs together, and she took a chunk out of Senior's hand,"

"Way to go," Levi said with a smile.

"Yeah, thanks to the self-defense moves she learned from Aubrey. Anyway, they knocked her out, kicked her, and Senior went to dump my car at the pier and retrieve his."

"What was their plan? To kill her?" Aiden asked.

"Not clear. She said they mentioned teaching her a lesson. But in my mind, two grown men don't go to such lengths to kidnap a woman without that being a possibility." He set his empty beer can down.

"Right," Aiden said with a sigh. "It's a lucky thing you left your phone in the car. Lea mentioned that she hadn't enabled the find-my-phone app on her phone."

"It is now," Brett said dryly.

"Same for all of ours," Aiden added. "I think we all enabled it after that night."

"Yup." Levi nodded. "Who would have thought." He shook his head. "You got lucky."

"Yeah." He nodded and turned to look back in the house at Lea, fast asleep on his sofa.

"She's tired. You both probably are. We'll get out of your hair," Aiden said, shaking his hand.

"Thanks. I don't know if I said it before, but… thanks," Brett said and then let his best friend pull him in for a hug.

"Any time," Aiden said.

After quietly walking the rest of the group out, he locked the door and then moved over to look down at Lea.

She was still covered in bruises all over her body and her forehead. She complained that her ribs hurt every time she laughed or sneezed. He thought about picking her up and carrying her into their bedroom, but instead, he lay down beside her on the sofa and pulled her into his arms. He hit the mute button on the remote and fell asleep right there with his arms tightly around her.

When he woke, sunlight was blinding him, and Lea was nowhere to be found.

When he walked into their room, he could hear the shower shut off.

"There you are," he said, stepping into the bathroom. "Why are you up so early?" he asked, wondering if it was early. He hadn't even looked at the time yet.

"I thought we'd head in and see how Aiden is doing at the clinic. He mentioned they had some of the walls in already."

"Okay, if you feel up to it."

"I do. Just as long as we move slow." She smiled and then leaned up on her toes to kiss him.

"I can do slow." He wrapped his arms around her and brushed his lips across hers. "Or fast. Whatever you want."

She smiled. "Well, I might want some fast..." She brushed her lips across his. "Before we do the slow."

He backed her up until her knees hit the side of the bed, then he smiled when her towel fell to the floor.

"This will never get old," he said as he dipped his head and ran his mouth over her skin. "Tell me if I hurt you," he said before lifting her and laying her gently on the bed.

A little over an hour later, they walked hand in hand into her new clinic. She was correct. Aiden and his men had pretty much completed all the interior walls. They walked through what would be the reception area down a hallway past several smaller examining rooms and back into a larger office area.

"This one is mine," Lea said with a smile.

"Nice," he said, looking around. "It appears as if the workers are done for the day."

"I sent Aiden a text telling him we were coming," Lea said.

"Oh?" He glanced over at her and realized that she looked a little sick. "Is everything okay? You look…"

"I'm okay," she said quickly and then shook her head. "I, um, wanted this to be… I don't know how…" She took a deep breath and shook her head. "I almost lost you," she blurted out.

He walked over and wrapped his arms around her. "We got lucky," he agreed.

"When I was tied up and alone, I wished for several things," she said, meeting his eyes.

"Okay," he said with a smile, figuring she'd continue talking when she was ready.

"I wished that my parents would never have to be told that I'd been murdered by some backwoods…" She shook her head again. "I digress. I wished that I would be able to see you again." She cupped his face. "I wished that you'd move in with me, that we'd live together."

He smiled. "Done and done." He chuckled and got a smile from her as well.

"And…" She paused for a heartbeat. "I wished that we'd have a full happy life together."

"Sounds good to me," he agreed.

"As husband and wife," she added.

"Okay," he said smoothly.

She narrowed her eyes at him. "You…" She shook her head. "I'm asking you…"

"I know what you're asking." He pulled her closer. "You beat me to it though since you're so impatient." He joked. "I had an entire dinner planned for us." He tilted his head as if he were thinking. "Maybe on a private beach somewhere, surrounded by flowers…" She slapped him on the shoulder and laughed. "Okay, how about this." He glanced around, then stood back and got down on one knee, his bare knee landing in a pile of sawdust.

Taking her hand in his, he asked. "Lea Val, love of my life, will you do me the honor of marrying me?"

She chuckled. "Is that all you've got?"

His smile fell away slightly. "I've already proven to you that I'd risk my own life to save you once. I can promise you that for the rest of our lives together, I will continue to do so. You're the smartest woman I know, the kindest and"—he wiggled his eyebrows—"the sexiest. I want to spend the rest of my life making you laugh, making you groan with pleasure." She chuckled. "Making your every wish come true. Marry me?"

"Yes." She smiled down at him.

He stood back up and kissed her slowly.

"I don't think I'll ever be able to work in this office without seeing you kneeling in a pile of sawdust," she joked.

He laughed. "Good. Then it's one of the happiest places I know." He kissed her again. "Is this everything you ever wished for?" he asked, glancing around the room.

She looked into his eyes. "Yes," she said. "Everything and more."

Missy's Moment

Breaking Travis

Roping Ryan

Wild Bride

Corey's Catch

Tessa's Turn

Saving Trace

Christmas Holly

The Grayton Series

Last Resort

Someday Beach

Rip Current

In Too Deep

Swept Away

High Tide

Sunset Dreams

Lucky Series

Unlucky In Love

Sweet Resolve

Best of Luck

A Little Luck

Christmas Wish

Silver Cove Series

Silver Lining

French Kiss

Happy Accident

Hidden Charm

A Silver Cove Christmas

Sweet Surrender

Second Chances

Entangled Series – Paranormal Romance

The Awakening

The Beckoning

The Ascension

The Presence

The Calling

The Chosen

Haven, Montana Series

Closer to You

Never Let Go

Holding On

Coming Home

The Hard Way

Pride Oregon Series

A Dash of Love

My Kind of Love

Season of Love

Tis the Season

Dare to Love

Where I Belong

Because of Love

A Thing Called Love

First Comes Love

Someone to Love

Wildflowers Series

Summer Nights

Summer Heat

Summer Secrets

Summer Fling

Summer's End

Summer's Wish

Distracted Series

Wake Me

Tame Me

Stand Alone Books

Twisted Rock

Hope Harbor

Raven Falls

For a complete list of books:

http://JillSanders.com

Jill Sanders is a New York Times, USA Today, and international best-selling author of Sweet Contemporary Romance, Romantic Suspense, Western Romance, and Paranormal Romance novels. With over 75 books in eleven series, translations into several different languages, and audiobooks there's plenty to choose from. Look for Jill's bestselling stories wherever romance books are sold or visit her at jillsanders.com

Jill comes from a large family with six siblings, including an identical twin. She was raised in the Pacific Northwest and later relocated to Colorado for college and a successful IT career before discovering her talent for writing sweet and sexy page-turners. After Colorado, she decided to move south, living in Texas and now making her home along the Emerald Coast of Florida. You will find that the settings of several of her series are inspired by her time spent living in these areas. She has two sons and off-set the testosterone in her house by adopting three furry little ladies that provide her company while she's locked in her writing cave. She enjoys heading to the beach, hiking, swimming, wine-tasting, and pickleball with her husband, and of course writing. If you have read any of her books, you may also notice that there is a love of food, especially sweets! She has been blamed for a few added pounds by her assistant, editor, and fans... donuts or pie anyone?

facebook.com/JillSandersBooks

twitter.com/JillMSanders

amazon.com/Jill-Sanders/e/B009M2NFD6?tag=jillmcom-20

bookbub.com/authors/jill-sanders